OTHER BOOKS BY BILL MYERS

NOVELS

The God Hater
Blood of Heaven
Threshold
Fire of Heaven
Eli
The Face of God
When the Last Leaf Falls
Soul Tracker
The Presence
The Seeing
The Wager
The Voice
Angel of Wrath

CHILDREN'S SERIES

McGee and Me!
My Life as . . .
Bloodhounds, Inc.
The Imager Chronicles
The Elijah Project
TJ and the Time Stumblers
Secret Agent Dingledorf and His Trusty Dog, SPLAT

PICTURE BOOKS

Baseball for Breakfast
The Bug Parables

TEEN SERIES

Forbidden Doors
The Dark Side of the Supernatural

For a further list of Bill's work, as well as sample chapters, see
www.BillMyers.com.

PRAISE FOR BILL MYERS'S
The God Hater

"When one of the most creative minds I know gets the best idea he's ever had and turns it into a novel, it's fasten-your-seat-belt time. This one will be talked about for a long time."

—Jerry B. Jenkins, *New York Times*
bestselling author of the Left Behind series

"A most fascinating story! Full of heart, suspense, and intelligence, *The God Hater* engagingly illustrates the futility of man-made beliefs as well as the world's desperate need for a God who offers hope, guidance, and help."

—Tim LaHaye, *New York Times*
bestselling author of the Left Behind series

"Bill has written another heart-wrenching, mind-gripping novel that delivers on so many levels. Like the Gospel, *The God Hater* is more than just a great read. I highly recommend it!"

—Doug Fields, teaching pastor of Saddleback Community
Church and bestselling author of *Refuel* and *Fresh Start*

"An original masterpiece. *The God Hater* reopens our eyes to God's absolute justice and His unfathomable love."

—Dr. Kevin Leman, bestselling author of
Have a New Kid by Friday

"If you enjoy white-knuckle, page-turning suspense with a brilliant blend of cutting-edge apologetics, *The God Hater* will grab you for a long, long time."

—Beverly Lewis, *New York Times* bestselling author

"Once again, Myers takes us into imaginative and intriguing depths, making us feel, think, and ponder all at the same time. Relevant and entertaining, *The God Hater* is not to be missed."

—James Scott Bell, bestselling author of *Deceived* and *Try Fear*

THE
JUDAS
GOSPEL

BILL MYERS

HOWARD BOOKS
A DIVISION OF SIMON & SCHUSTER, INC.

NEW YORK   NASHVILLE   LONDON   TORONTO   SYDNEY

Howard Books
A Division of Simon & Schuster, Inc.
1230 Avenue of the Americas
New York, NY 10020

First Howard Books trade paperback edition June 2011

HOWARD and colophon are trademarks of Simon & Schuster, Inc.

For information about special discounts for bulk purchases, please contact Simon & Schuster Special Sales at 1-866-506-1949 or business@simonandschuster.com.

The Simon & Schuster Speakers Bureau can bring authors to your live event. For more information or to book an event, contact the Simon & Schuster Speakers Bureau at 1-866-248-3049 or visit our website at www.simonspeakers.com.

Designed by Jaime Putorti

Manufactured in the United States of America

10   9   8   7   6   5   4   3   2   1

Library of Congress Cataloging-in-Publication Data
Myers, Bill.
    The Judas gospel / Bill Myers.
        p.   cm.
    1. Judas Iscariot—Fiction.   2. Bible. N.T.—History of Biblical events—Fiction.
I. Title.
    PS3563.Y36J83 2011
    813'.54—dc22   2010042107

ISBN 978-1-4391-5354-3
ISBN 978-1-4516-1787-0 (ebook)

For Peggy Patrick Medberry . . .

A woman of faith with the great gift of asking, "Why not?"

In the beginning the church was a fellowship of men and women centered on the living Christ. Then the church moved to Greece, where it became a philosophy. Then it moved to Rome, where it became an institution. Next, it moved to Europe, where it became a culture. And, finally, it moved to America, where it became an enterprise.

—RICHARD HALVERSON
FORMER CHAPLAIN OF THE U.S. SENATE

Suppose one of you has a hundred sheep and loses one of them. Does he not leave the ninety-nine in the open country and go after the lost sheep until he finds it?

—JESUS CHRIST
NIV

ACKNOWLEDGMENTS

———

ANTHONY CAMPOLO FOR the world-hunger content in chapter 2, which, although not a direct quote, is definitely vintage Campolo; Skye Jethani's observations on Van Gogh from his book *The Divine Commodity*; Lee Stanley for the racquetball games and sound counsel; Angela Hunt and Peggy Patrick Medberry for their insights; Oliver Nitz for the research; Larry LaFata, Lee Hough, Holly Halverson; Brenda for her rock-solid love and consistency; wonderful Nicole for her great mind and unquenchable passions; and wondrous Mackenzie for her love and indefatigable joy.

PART ONE

PROLOGUE

———

CHANCES ARE you hate me. Believer or nonbeliever, if you've heard the story, you despise me. And believer or nonbeliever, that makes you a hypocrite. All of you. Believers, because you refuse to embrace the very forgiveness He pleaded for others, even those who tortured Him to death. And nonbelievers, because you pretend to hate the traitor of someone you hate.

"But I don't hate Him," you say.

Really? Pretending you don't hate someone who says all your attempts at being good are worthless? Pretending you don't hate someone who claims to be the only way to God? Pretending you don't hate someone who wants to rule your life? Who are you kidding? You're not fooling anyone, least of all Him.

But hate Him or worship Him, one thing you can say, *He's* no hypocrite. He stuck to the truth all the way through His execution. And He still holds to it today. (Old habits die hard.) Truth is His currency . . . and His Achilles' heel. That's why I knew He'd allow me into His presence. If my question was asked in truth, He'd respond in truth.

Now I'm sure there are some who will debate how I had access to Him—those of you who love to argue about gnats while swallowing camels. And why not? After all, debating about dancing angels and pinheads is far easier than breaking a sweat by actually obeying. Or, as the Accuser recently confided in me, "Spending time arguing theology is the perfect way to ensure a burning world continues to burn."

In any case, my eternal state is not up for discussion. Though I will say I have displayed more remorse and repentance over my sin than most of you ever have over your own. And as to whether I'm actually in hell, I guess that depends upon your definition of the place.

But I digress.

When I came before Him, I was forced to my knees. Not by any cosmic bullying, but by the sheer weight of His glory. Yet when He spoke, His voice was kind and full of compassion.

"Hello, my friend. It's been a long time."

My eyes immediately dropped to the ground and my chest swelled with emotion. So much time had passed and He still had that power over me. Angry at His hold, I took a ragged breath and then another before blurting out like a petulant child, "You . . . never gave me a chance!"

I was answered by silence. He waited until I found the courage, or foolishness, to raise my head. When I did, the love in His eyes burned through me and I had to look back down. Still, He continued to wait.

I took another breath. Finally, angrily swiping at my eyes, I tried again. "If we . . . if we would have handled Your mission my way"—I swallowed and continued—"the world would not be in the mess it's in today."

"Your way?"

I nodded, refusing to look up. "You could have ruled the world."

"I am ruling the world."

I shook my head. "Not souls. But nations, governments. Every earthly power imaginable could have been Yours."

"Kingdoms come and go. Souls are eternal."

"Tell that to the tortured and murdered who scream Your name as an oath every day." I waited for His wrath to flare up, to consume me. But I felt nothing. I heard no rebuke. Only more silence. He knew I wasn't finished. I took another breath and continued, "If You would have used Your powers my way, *everyone* would have followed You."

I heard Him chuckle softly. "And you would have made Me a star."

"The likes of which the world had never seen."

"I did all right."

"You could have done better."

He waited again, making sure I had nothing more to say. This time I had the good sense to remain silent.

Finally He spoke. "What do you propose, My friend?"

I hesitated.

"Please. Go ahead."

Still staring at the ground, I answered: "Rumor has it You're preparing another prophet—though her background is questionable."

"Moses was a murderer. David an adulterer." I felt His eyes searching me. "I've always had a soft spot for the broken."

I nodded and took another swipe at my tears.

"What would you like?"

Another breath and I answered: "Let me return to Earth. Let me show You what could have been if You had followed my leading." I hesitated, then looked up, trying to smile. "Hasn't that always been Your favorite method of teaching? Letting us have our way until we wind up proving Yours?"

His eyes sparkled at my little joke. I tried to hold His gaze but could not.

After another pause He finally spoke: "When would you like to begin?"

And that's how it started—how He gave me the opportunity to prove to Him, to you, and to all of creation, what could have been accomplished if He'd proclaimed His truth my way.

I'll say no more. Neither here nor at the end. Instead, I'll practice what He, himself, employs. I'll let the story unfold, allowing truth to speak for itself.

—J. Iscariot

CHAPTER ONE

T HE FIRST thing Rachel smells is smoke. That's how it always begins. Not the smoke of wood, but the acrid, chemical smell of burning drapes, melting carpet, smoldering sofa. The air is suffocating. Hot waves press against her face and mouth, making it difficult to breathe. Her mother stands before her in a white flowing gown. Flames engulf the woman's legs, leaping up and rising toward her waist where she holds little Rebecca. The two of them stare at Rachel, their eyes pleading for help, their faces filled with fear, confusion, and accusation as Rachel stands holding a lit candle in a small glass holder.

Mother and sister waver and dissolve, disappearing into the smoke. Suddenly Rachel is standing in the doorway of an upscale bathroom. The same bathroom she stood inside last night. And the night before. The marble tile is cool to her bare feet. There is no smoke now, only fog. So thick she sees nothing. But she can hear. There is the sound of splashing water. Someone in a tub. The room is filled with the sweet scent of rose bath oil.

A nearby dog yaps, its bark shrill and relentless.

A woman shouts from the tub, "Who's there?" Her voice is strong and authoritative, masking the fear she must feel.

Rachel tries to answer, but no sound comes from her throat.

"Who are you? How did you get in?" She hears the woman rising, water dripping from her body.

The dog continues to bark.

"Get out of here!" the woman yells. Water splashes. She swears.
The sound of a struggle begins. Someone falls, knees thudding into
the tub. There is the squeak of flesh against porcelain. Coughing,
gagging. A scream that is quickly submerged underwater, muffled
and bubbling.

Rachel hears herself gasping and grunting. She feels her own
hands around the woman's throat.

The dog barks crazily.

The last of the burbling screams fades. The struggle ends. There
is only the gentle sound of water sloshing back and forth, back and
forth.

And the yelping dog.

Rachel rises and turns, fearful of what she knows she will see
through the fog. As in the previous dreams, a bathroom mirror
floats before her. But this evening there is something different. This
evening there are letters scrawled across it in black cherry lipstick.
Her scrawling:

Tell Them

In the mirror she sees a tiny red glow dancing across her hand, the
hand that holds the burning candle. It's there every night, like a firefly.
But instead of her own frightened face staring back at her, she sees the
face of someone else: bald, white, and pale. A swastika tattooed on the
side of the neck. Man, woman, she can't tell. But it is leering. And it is
climbing out of the mirror toward her.

She screams and throws the candle at the reflection. The mirror
shatters, breaking into a dozen pieces, a dozen images of the face
sneering up at her. Until they change. Until they morph into different
faces. Froglike. Reptilian. Each climbing out of its broken shard—

snarling, reaching for her feet, clutching at her ankles until, mustering all of her strength, she wakes with a stifled scream.

Nineteen-year-old Rachel Delacroix lay in bed, heart pounding, T-shirt soaked and clinging. At first she thought it was from the water of the tub . . . until she realized it was her own cold sweat.

"Rachel?" Her father appeared in the doorway, his bald black head glistening in the streetlight from the hall window. The same window that held the broken air conditioner they could not afford to replace. "Are you all right?"

"Mmm?" she mumbled, pretending to be asleep.

"Was it—did you have another dream?"

She gave no answer.

"You're not taking your medicine, are you."

She remained silent, hoping he'd think she'd gone back to sleep.

"Rachel?"

More silence. She could hear him standing there nearly half a minute before he turned and wearily shuffled back down the hall to his room. Tomorrow was church and he needed to get his rest. Still, she knew full well he'd not be able to go back to sleep.

Hopefully, neither would she.

She opened her eyes and stared at the ceiling, then turned to the art posters on the surrounding walls—the Monets, the Van Goghs, the Renoirs. How often they gave her comfort. Even joy. But not tonight. Tonight, as in the past two nights she'd had the dream, they would give her nothing at all.

———————

It was barely past nine in the morning and the attic was like an oven. The Santa Anas had been blowing for several days, and Sean Putnam doubted the house had dropped below eighty degrees all night. That's why he was up here now—to save whatever was left of his paintings. To bring the canvases downstairs where it was cooler and the paint wouldn't dry out and crack. Over the past months he'd already thrown away dozens, mostly self-portraits; clear signs of what he now considered to have been his self-absorbed youth.

"Dad!"

He turned toward the stairs and shouted. As was the case with many Down syndrome children, the multiple ear infections had left his son hard of hearing. "I'll be there in a second."

"Well, hurry! We don't want to be late."

"I'll be right there."

"Well, hurry."

He quietly mused. Tomorrow would be Elliot's first day in middle school. A scary time for both of them. Yet it was all part of the plan he and Beverly had agreed upon. A plan conceived as the cancer began eating away and taking her. They wanted to make sure Elliot was prepared as much as possible to face the real world. Integrating him into the public school system seemed the best choice. They'd talked about it often during her final days. And it was the last conversation they had before she slipped into unconsciousness.

Now, barely a year later, he was making good on those plans.

"Dad."

"I'll be right there."

Elliot was nervous. He had been all week. That's why Sean had agreed to this trial run. That's why, though it was nine-fifteen on a Sunday morning, the two of them would pile into the old Ford Taurus and drive over to Lincoln Middle School. A rehearsal for tomorrow's big day. An attempt to help Elliot relax by eliminating any surprises.

Too bad Sean couldn't do the same for himself. Because he wasn't just anxious about his son. Tomorrow was a big day for him as well. He'd finally graduated from the Los Angeles Police

Academy, and tomorrow would be his first day on patrol in a black-and-white. That was the other reason he was up here in the attic. *"To put away childish things."* He wasn't sure where he'd first heard that phrase, probably from his old man. But it made it no less true. The days of being a long-haired art student had come and gone. Now it was time to be a man. To make the necessary sacrifices and take care of what was left of his family.

He quickly flipped through the remaining canvases until one slowed him to a stop. Not because of any artistic skill, but because of the subjects—six-week-old Elliot lying naked on his mother's tummy, his little fist clenched, nursing at her breast. It still moved him in ways he could not explain. Somehow, some way, he'd been able to capture the truth of that moment . . . mother and child lost in the act of life, their faces filled with contentment, glowing with an indefinable peace.

"Dad . . ."

He reached down and scooped up the canvas. "I'm on my way." He tucked the painting under his arm and headed back downstairs, where he would find someplace safe to keep it.

CHAPTER TWO

"I N THE time it takes me to say this sentence, two people in our world have died of hunger." Rev. Delacroix stood behind the homemade pulpit of oak-stained plywood and stared out at his congregation. There were fourteen of them this morning, their black faces shiny with sweat from the heat.

"And in the time it takes me to say this sentence, two more people in our world have died of hunger."

They were good folks. Some had been with him since he left the army and began this storefront church. Folks such as the Johnsons, who had sat in the same spot on those same folding chairs for more than a decade. Not only had he the privilege of baptizing their daughter, Sarah Johnson, his own daughter's best friend, but he'd also baptized their grandbaby, who Sarah now held in her arms—the poor child with scars from a cleft palate surgery gone wrong.

"And in the time it takes me to say this sentence, another two people have died of hunger."

As a congregation, they'd been through a lot: births, burials, factions, reconciliations. They'd not grown much in numbers, always hovering between one and two dozen, but they had grown in unity—an extended family with all the baggage, good and bad.

And these last two and a half years, when his own family had gone through its dark night of the soul, the church members were always there for him.

He looked at his daughter, who sat directly in front of him, just where her mother and little sister had once sat. Other than Jesus, Rachel was his only reason for living. No one gave him greater joy. And as he watched her struggle with her own guilt and demons, there was no one who so easily broke his heart. Behind her, in a beam of sunlight from the open door, sat a visitor—early thirties, startlingly handsome, and wearing a suit that no doubt should have paid several months' child support.

The reverend returned to his sermon. "And in the time it takes me to say this sentence, another two people have died of starvation." He leaned forward on the pulpit. "Are you bored yet? They're not. No, my friends, they're not bored . . . they're dead. In fact, while I've been standing here entertaining you, nearly two hundred seventy-five people have died of starvation."

Several of the members shook their heads.

"And you know what's sadder than that?" He waited until he had everyone's attention. "Most of us don't give a damn."

Their eyes widened in surprise.

He continued, "And you know what's sadder than that? Most of us are more concerned that I used that word than that two hundred seventy-five people have starved to death."

There was no sound, save for the oscillating fan pushing hot air back and forth across the room.

"Now, I know that language is inappropriate, but my dear friends, what has happened to us that we are more concerned about language than our fellow man?" He stepped in front of the pulpit and began pacing. "Did you know we have more than enough resources to feed the entire world several times over? Several times over!"

One of the Hartwell sisters nodded. "Hm-mm."

"In America alone we throw away three hundred sixty tons of food each and every day. Each and every day!"

Others shook their heads, expressing their dismay.

"And why? I'll tell you why." He stopped and faced them. "Because it's cheaper to throw away the food than to feed those starving to death. *Because it's cheaper!*"

He resumed pacing, his emotions rising along with the congregation's. "And some people have the gall, I say the *gall*, to blame God. 'Well, if God really loved the world, He'd do this. Or if God really cared, He'd do that.'" Delacroix shook his head. "Ingrates!" He wiped his face with a handkerchief and moved into the aisle. "God Almighty gave us His Son. His *only* Son. What more could He possibly do? What more could I possibly want? He poured out all the punishment that I deserve onto *His* boy so *I* could live! He gave up His only child for *me*. And I have the gall, I have the insolence to say He doesn't love me?"

"That's right," someone called out. "Amen," others agreed.

But Delacroix barely heard over the blood pounding in his ears. He knew full well the doctor's warning about his heart, the stress and strain he'd been under. But he also knew God deserved his best. "No!" he shouted. "Brothers and sisters, the question is not '*Why, God?*' The question is '*Why, man?*'"

"Amen. Preach it."

"Last Thursday night a prominent member of the Los Angeles Police Department was killed. A terrible thing, I don't deny it. But I tell you, you'd think it's World War III the way the media carries on. While all the time, right here on our own streets, in our own neighborhood, we lose young men, women, and children every week. Every week! Is that justice?"

"No," several called back.

"No, it is not. But does that mean we blame God?"

"No!" they exclaimed.

Delacroix nodded then turned to a frail, thirtysomething

woman who could have passed for fifty. "Sister Smith, we're so glad you found the strength to join us this morning."

She gave the slightest nod.

"It's been what, ten days since your baby was taken?"

Again she nodded.

He looked back to the congregation. "And did we see it on the television? Did we hear one snippet of it on the radio?"

The congregation responded, "No, sir. Hm-mm."

He continued, "And in the paper, I saw it with my own eyes. In the paper there were two sentences. *Two sentences.* And then they misspelled his name!"

The disapproval grew louder.

"Now, let me ask you, whose fault is that? Is it our Lord's?"

"No, sir!" they shouted back.

"That's right. It is ours. Now we can either sit here on our rear ends and blame God, or we can rise up, and in the name of Him who died for us, we can right these social injustices."

Applause broke out across the room.

"Let us be poured from the comfort of our cozy little saltshakers and become salt that changes the world. Let us seize our responsibility. Because it is our responsibility, brothers and sisters. Not the responsibility of those in the ivory towers of city hall. But ours! And we have the victory. In the name of Jesus Christ, the victory is ours!"

The room grew so noisy that he had to shout: "If we are serious in obeying our Lord and in serving each other, if we are serious in laying down our lives for one another as He did for us, then there will be no stopping us! We will change our neighborhood, we will change our city. And together, brothers and sisters, in the name of God Almighty, we will change our world!"

The congregation rose to its feet, clapping and shouting in agreement.

Rev. Delacroix wiped his face and looked upon them, feeling both a sense of satisfaction and sadness. It was one thing to inspire the people with fancy rhetoric . . . but quite another for them to actually put the words into action.

THE AC ON the third floor of the Parker Building was on the fritz. Again. No surprise. The aging eight-story edifice, in the heart of downtown Los Angeles, was a poster child for poor planning and shoddy construction. The slumping floors, cracked plaster, and cramped squad room were never-ending sources of bellyaching for the Robbery Homicide Division detectives. Within months they'd be moving into a new $437 million facility just across the street, where they'd be forced to discover an entire new set of problems to gripe about. Until then, this fifty-four-year-old structure gave them all the opportunity they needed.

But not today. Today grumbling was at a minimum. Even the trademark gallows humor was at an all-time low. Nor was anyone whining about being dragged into the unusual Sunday morning briefing.

RHD was made up of the Los Angeles Police Department's brightest and best. They were considered tops in the city, perhaps the nation. All of the twenty-four detectives had risen through the ranks, distinguishing themselves in their work until they were handpicked to join the special department. RHD investigated the highest-profile and most notable killings in the city. And they didn't come any higher-profile than the murder of Assistant Police Chief Margaret Hampton.

The briefing was led by Lieutenant Anderson, a slender man with a gray crew cut. Cowboy (aka Lawrence T. Riordan), the lead detective on the case, did his best to concentrate, but was frequently distracted by their special guest leaning against the sidewall. A fact not missed by his partner—the hawked-nosed, sardonic James Killroy. Just as Cowboy usually played the outspoken, good ol' boy from Oklahoma, you could always count on Killroy for his sly, acrid wit.

Nudging him, Killroy leaned in and whispered, "She's lookin' mighty hot, son."

"Shut up," Cowboy said.

"You know what they say, 'Fourth time's the charm.'"

"I'll cap you right here in front of the whole division."

"I mean, how many times can a woman say no before she finally takes a little pity on you?"

"Right here, on the spot," Cowboy said. "And with your popularity, there'll be no witnesses."

The witnesses, in this case, would be the entire RHD, all of whom had one reason or another to dislike Killroy. The "she" in the exchange was an attractive brunette in her midforties by the name of Dr. Sharon Fields. Relatively new in town, she was a noted psychiatrist with her own private practice who was occasionally brought in to help profile the more difficult cases. On three separate occasions Cowboy had tried to score with her and on three separate occasions she had shot him down. But persistence is a trait of all good detectives, and they didn't come any better than Cowboy.

Looking up from his notes, Lieutenant Anderson turned to her. "Dr. Fields, you have some updated info for us?"

She nodded and approached, expensive red pumps clicking on the worn linoleum. Her snug linen skirt said she still had a figure and knew how to use it. And if the subdued approval of the men didn't make it clear, Killroy sealed the deal with a whoop and a "Lookin' mighty fine."

She arrived at the podium and fixed her gaze on him. "It's obvious you haven't lost your eyesight, Detective—too bad about that body." The room gave a few hoots of their own as Killroy shrugged and Cowboy grinned.

She turned to the rest of the group and began. "It's been forty-eight hours since we contacted Quantico and the Feebs have been less then helpful."

McDoogle, a balding, ferret-faced man, called out, "So what else is new?"

The rest of the room agreed.

Cowboy watched as Fields pushed her thick, shiny hair behind a very delicate ear. "Here's my call," she said. "Despite what appears to be the obvious, I don't believe the murder had anything to do with sex."

"Whoa, hold the phone," Linda Preston interrupted. She was one of only three blacks and two women in the room. "Our first assistant female chief of police is killed, found stark naked, and you're telling us it's not sexual?"

Fields nodded. "There was no indication of sexual assault. No sign of penetration, no semen in or around the tub. Nor did the attack appear to be motivated by anger, which would indicate possible resentment of female authority. There were no marks on the body—just around the neck from the forced drowning. My evaluation is the motive was to kill and nothing more."

Several in the room exchanged glances.

Fields continued, "Nor was there any sign of robbery. All jewelry is accounted for and her pocketbook was left untouched on the bedroom dresser."

"So what are we talking about," Billings, the youngest and cockiest detective in the room, asked. "A vendetta? Organized crime?"

Lieutenant Anderson nodded at Cowboy and Killroy.

"Nothing along those lines," Killroy said. "Not yet, anyway."

"So it was a domestic," McDoogle said. "Somebody she knew."

Cowboy answered. "We're still checking on exes and past lovers, but so far nothing."

"If it was someone she knew," Preston argued, "why the broken lock at the front door?"

"To make it *look* like a burglary," Billings explained.

"Without taking anything to underscore the fact?" Cowboy turned to the youngster. "No offense, son, but I got mules back home smarter than you."

Killroy added, "And underwear a lot older."

"Okay," McDoogle said, "so far you've said what the motive isn't. Any idea what it is?"

Fields shuffled her papers. "Evaluating the information from both SDI and CSI, my guess is that you're investigating a hate crime."

"But you just said there was nothing singling her out for being a woman," Preston argued. "And she wasn't black, Jew, Hispanic—"

Killroy interrupted, "Forty-six-year-old white female and with a body like that—"

"—what's to hate?" McDoogle concluded.

"Exactly," Killroy agreed.

Preston ignored them. "So if it's not a hate crime because of her race or sex. . . ." She let the sentence hang.

"It's a hate crime because she's a cop," Fields said. She looked up from her papers, scanning the group. "It's a hate crime directed against you."

Except for a profanity or two, the room grew silent.

She continued, "And there's a good chance it will not be the last."

"You're saying somebody's got the hots for us?" Billings asked.

"Bring the mother to my door," Killroy said, "I'll show him a little heat."

The room agreed.

"What about the other details?" McDoogle asked. "Naked in the tub, the dead dog, the broken mirror?"

"I can't address the dog," Fields admitted, "but the broken mirror indicates our killer may at least have a conscience. It may be submerged, he may not even know it's there, but when he caught his reflection there was a good chance he didn't like what he saw."

Preston turned to Lieutenant Anderson. "You still want us to sit on the details?"

Killroy answered, "City sewage would have a field day—knowing they killed one of our own naked in the tub."

"Every punk and gangsta in the city would take credit," McDoogle said.

"Yeah," Cowboy agreed, "and by sitting on the details we'll have a litmus test to see who's really involved."

"Nice thinking," Billings scorned. "Your mule teach you that?"

Ignoring the comment, Fields addressed Cowboy. "You're right, Detective. Whoever did this will definitely want to be known."

Cowboy gave her a nod, and thought he caught her eyes lingering a moment longer than necessary. At least that's what he hoped. Apparently he wasn't the only one who noticed.

Killroy elbowed him and whispered, "Nice work, suck-up."

Without missing a beat, Cowboy leaned back to his partner. "DOA. Right here, right now."

The briefing continued another twenty minutes. But even as they sifted through the information, Cowboy knew he'd give the lovely Dr. Fields another try. Granted, he held the record in strikeouts, but just like Babe Ruth, the more you swung, the greater your chances for a home run.

"So LET ME get his straight, Mr. . . ."

"Miller," the good-looking man repeated. "Jude Miller."

The reverend continued, "And, Mr. Miller, you've come to my

church to tell me that God has given you a . . ." He hesitated, letting the visitor fill in the blank.

"A word. That's right, Pastor. A clear and unmistakable word from the Lord God Almighty."

Rev. Delacroix made no attempt to hide his skepticism.

"I have been called to assist your lovely daughter in becoming an influential messenger for our generation."

Delacroix continued sizing up the man, trying to determine if he was deranged or simply a con artist. With the fine suit and polished words, he suspected the latter. The neatly trimmed beard and chiseled features only confirmed his suspicion. He was about to say as much when he spotted the elderly Hartwell sisters lingering at the doorway just within earshot. No surprise there. Every church has them, the unofficial pipeline, the congregation's eyes and ears—even in matters where the congregation should be blind and deaf.

"Excuse me." He brushed past the young man. "I'll be just a moment."

He joined the women and smiled warmly. "Well, ladies, I trust you found this morning's message edifying."

"Absolutely, Reverend," Susan Hartwell, the older of the two, said. "We always do."

"Wouldn't miss it for the world," Ruth, her sibling, agreed.

"Good." He nodded. "Good." He stood a moment, letting the silence grow between them. The sisters eyed the handsome visitor, making it clear they were waiting for an introduction, a cue Delacroix ignored. "Well," he finally said, his smile unwavering, "I'm sure we'll see you both this Wednesday, then?"

"Absolutely," Ruth agreed. "Every time the doors are open."

His smile broke into a grin as he placed gentle hands on both of their shoulders. "That's wonderful," he said, easing them toward the door. "Don't know what I'd do without your faithfulness." Susan offered the slightest resistance, which Delacroix pretended not to notice. "How long have you two lovely ladies been attending services here?"

"Going on nine years," Ruth said, shading her eyes as they stepped into the hot sunlight.

"Nine years." Delacroix shook his head. "My, oh, my. How time flies. And to think you two haven't aged a day."

Ruth giggled.

"Now, Reverend," Susan admonished.

He feigned innocence. "What did I say?"

"You're s'posed to be a man of truth, remember?"

"Ah, but truth, like beauty, is in the eye of the beholder." He gave them a mischievous wink that caused them both to giggle. "Well, you two have yourselves a wonderful afternoon." He looked up at the sky. "And drink plenty of water. You know how this heat can be."

"We will, Reverend," Ruth said.

"All right, then, take care."

"We'll see you Wednesday," Susan said as they turned and started down the street.

Delacroix nodded and stood in the sun another moment. When he was sure they were on their way, he reentered the church. A quick glance revealed that only Samuel Burton, one of his elders, remained. He was across the room, retrieving the tiny plastic communion cups.

"They seem like good people," Miller said as Delacroix joined him. "Your whole congregation, they seem like good, decent—"

"Listen to me." Delacroix was suddenly very close and speaking with quiet intensity. "I don't know who you are or what you think you're doing—"

"I told you, the Lord spoke to me and—"

"Then He also told you my daughter is not well."

"She's had her setbacks."

"Setbacks?" Delacroix struggled to hold his famous temper in check.

Miller continued, "I only know that the Lord said she will have a ministry. That she will proclaim the gospel to millions and—"

"My daughter is incapable of speaking!"

Miller looked at him, not understanding.

"She can barely talk to those closest to her, let alone strangers. She tries, but she can't. Do you understand me?"

The visitor gave no reply. Apparently God had forgotten to inform him of that little detail.

Delacroix continued, "And you have the gall to tell me she'll be speaking to millions?"

"The Lord, the Lord works in mysterious ways."

"So do crooks and con artists, Mr. Miller. Now, I don't know what your game is, or how you know my daughter, but—"

"Are you telling me she's never had prophetic utterances? That the gifts of the Spirit have never worked through her?"

"If she had, it was a long time ago."

"So her gifts are dormant."

"They're dead. And that's how they'll stay, dead and buried."

" 'Quench not the Spirit.' Isn't that what Paul said to the Thessalonians?"

"No one is quenching the—"

"Look!" Suddenly a young woman's voice cried from inside the restroom.

Delacroix stopped.

"Look what you did!"

He turned and quickly headed for the lavatory, the visitor on his heels. When he threw open the door he saw Sarah Johnson and Rachel standing at the sink. Sarah, who was holding her baby, turned to him, her eyes filled with wonder. "Look . . . look what your daughter did!"

The baby squirmed and started to fuss.

At first Delacroix thought it was a trick of the light. Some shadow from the bare bulb above the mirror. But when he stepped closer, he saw something had changed. The purple, rippled scars above the child's mouth were gone. All signs of the cleft palate and its botched surgery had disappeared. His eyes darted to his daughter. She was as surprised as he was. And she was frightened.

"It's a miracle!" Sarah cried. "A miracle!"

Delacroix looked back at the baby as his own fears started to rise.

"Your daughter healed my baby! Praise Jesus, it's a miracle!"

Another moment passed before the stranger spoke, his words soft and reverent, just above a whisper. "And so it begins."

CHAPTER THREE

"Y OU BETTER hurry, we're gonna be late."

"We're not going to be late, son."

"Well, hurry, 'cause I don't wanna be late."

It was Monday morning, the first day of school. Officer Sean Putnam stole a look at his boy, sitting nervously in the passenger seat, his pudgy fingers adjusting the cuffs of his long-sleeve shirt. The Santa Anas were still blowing and the temperature was already into the seventies, but Elliot insisted on wearing long sleeves. Sean didn't push the issue. He knew his son wore them to feel safe. Somehow, the extra clothing, the covering over his exposed skin, made him feel less vulnerable.

Up ahead, the light turned yellow and Sean brought the car to a stop.

"You could have made it," Elliot said.

"We're not going to be late."

His son blew out a breath and pushed up his glasses.

Sean gave him another look. "You going to be okay?"

Elliot nodded.

"Remember, the kids may seem standoffish. Some of them may even make fun of you. But just like Mrs. Sanford said—"

"I know, I know, it's 'cause they're stupid." Before Sean could remind him those were not exactly the counselor's words, Elliot flashed that endearing grin of his. "Don't worry, I'll be my usual charming self."

"I'm sure you will," Sean said with a chuckle, "I'm sure you will." He turned and looked back out his window. Early morning was his favorite time of day—that first hour of sunlight when he saw things other people ignored. Even as a child he was accused of wasting time staring at the ordinary. But the low-angle light of morning brought out so many textures . . . the stucco of apartment buildings, broken and uneven sidewalks, the ripples of distant hills. Everything looked as if it belonged in a photo exhibit. Across the street, the bark of a large mulberry was a captivating study of light and shadow. And though its foliage had already called it quits for the summer (leaves in Southern California never change color, they just dry up and blow away), the low sunlight behind them created a magical glow.

He tapped his thumbs on the steering wheel and thought of checking the news. But the past few days had been so focused on the murder of Assistant Police Chief Margaret Hampton that he decided against it. The killing was just a little too close to home, at least for now. He adjusted the collar of his uniform and stole another peek at the buzz cut in his mirror. Yes, sir, it was a big day for both of them.

The traffic light changed and they started forward. Unable to restrain himself, he motioned to the blue nylon backpack at his son's feet. "You got everything? Paper, pens, that cool notebook we picked out?"

Elliot looked out the passenger window. "Yes."

"What about lunch? Do you have lunch money?"

"I packed my own."

The thought surprised Sean, then concerned him. "What did you pack?"

"Dad."

"I'm just asking. When did you pack it? I don't remember—"

"A few nights ago, okay?"

Sean frowned. "Elliot, I don't think—"

"Here, right here's good. Let me out here."

"But the school is another two blocks—"

"Right here is perfect."

Sean glanced about. There were only two other students on the sidewalk. Why on earth would his son want to be dropped off so far from—and then it dawned on him. Of course. Although it hadn't been that long ago since he'd been a teen (Beverly was still in high school when Elliot was born), he'd nearly forgotten. Of course. Parents were poison. Without a word, he pulled to the curb as Elliot reached for his backpack and made last-minute preparations.

"You have my cell, right?" Sean asked.

"Yes."

"And Aunt Traci's? If anything happens, she can be here in five minutes."

"Dad, I'll be fine."

Sean nodded. "Of course you will."

His son unfastened his seat belt, opened the door, and climbed out.

"Well . . . good luck," Sean said.

Elliot may or may not have grunted a response as he slammed the door and headed down the sidewalk. Sean started to call something through the open window, then caught himself. But his son had taken only a few steps before he turned and came back to the car. "Don't worry, Dad."

Sean grinned. "Oh, I'm not worried, son. You'll do great."

"No," Elliot said. "About you. Don't worry about you. You'll do fine."

Sean felt his throat tighten. "Thanks."

Without a word the boy turned and continued down the street.

Unable to contain himself, Sean called out, "I love you, son."

Elliot gave no answer. Nor did Sean expect one. But that didn't prevent him from repeating the phrase, softly and under his breath. "I love you."

RACHEL DELACROIX CRUMBLED another letter and tossed it into the wire wastebasket near her desk. She wanted to get every detail right—the smell of the bath oil, the barking dog, the woman in the tub, and the writing on the mirror:

Tell Them

Those were the words she'd seen again last night. She'd dreamed the dream four nights in a row now, but only the past two nights had she seen the writing. The dreams always started the same way—the smell of smoke, the choking haze, and the accusing glares of her dead mother and little sister. This was the prologue. The sign telling her to pay attention. Last night was no exception. But last night she'd seen something else, something even more unnerving than the writing and the images crawling out of the mirror. Last night she'd seen the face of the woman—under the water, her eyes bulging up at Rachel, bubbles escaping from her mouth in a final, desperate scream. It was the same face Rachel had seen on the news. The one belonging to the assistant police chief of Los Angeles.

She'd been reluctant to share the dreams. Who wouldn't be? But with the order written on the mirror, the appearance of the victim's face, and Sunday morning's healing of Sarah Johnson's baby, she felt she had little choice.

A pattern had begun to emerge.

That's how God spoke to her—in patterns. Life was normally random and chaotic. But when the Lord wanted to say something, she would begin seeing patterns. Sometimes unrelated events would catch her attention—a situation here, a spoken word there, and occasionally a dream. They never made sense at the beginning, but in time, as they started coming together, she'd see a pattern. The medication always blunted and blurred them, making everything smooth and homogenous. But when she stopped taking it, they returned.

The past few days were no exception.

Finally there was Mr. Miller's appearance. Despite Daddy's protests, she had immediately sensed a connection. Like roots hidden underground, she felt an intertwining of purpose, a quickening. There was certainly nothing romantic going on, she knew that. But when combined with the dreams and the healing of her best friend's baby, both his presence and prophetic words seemed to be important additions.

Gifts of the Spirit had never been uncommon in her family. Since she was a little child she remembered Daddy being called to lay hands upon the sick. Sometimes it worked. Most of the time it didn't. Still, as she got older, she noticed he brought her along more and more often.

"Where two or more are gathered . . ." he used to quote.

Maybe. But some in the church said other things. "She's got the touch," they would whisper to her mother. "An anointing," others agreed. And maybe she had. Back then when she prayed, she often felt her hands grow amazingly hot. But that was a long time ago. Before the fire. Before the killings.

Until yesterday. For months, she and Sarah had prayed dozens of times over the baby, and dozens of times nothing had happened. Until yesterday. Yesterday, when Mr. Miller had arrived.

Yesterday, when he had given what he claimed to be a word from the Lord. Yesterday, when for the first time in years, her hands felt like they were on fire.

A pattern was definitely forming. But she had to be careful. She knew the dangers of jumping to conclusions, of trying to force the pieces to fit. Patterns were like snowflakes. If you clutched them too hard, they were gone. But she also knew that Mr. Miller was right. She could not "quench the Spirit." She had a responsibility to share with others what the Lord had given her. Just as she had shared His gift in healing the baby, she would now share the information from her dreams.

Tell Them

She pulled another piece of paper from her desk drawer and started again. She would work until the letter was perfect. Then she would mail it.

———————

"So what's a nice-lookin' white boy like you droppin' out of college and bein' a cop for?"

"Art history wasn't my thing."

Officer Lucile Williams motioned to the passing homes and burned-out lawns. It was midmorning, and boys were already stripped down to their baggies and LA Lakers' shorts. Spider plants hung from porches, and scraggly geraniums spread their flowers across the rock-hard dirt of planter beds. "And South Central is your thing?" she asked. "Not that rookies get any choice. But why a cop?"

He gazed out his passenger window at two girls making a pastel chalk drawing on the sidewalk.

"Come on, 'fess up."

"I don't know," he said. "I just wanted to do something of value. You know, give something back."

"Horse pucky."

He cut a look to his partner. She was in her late thirties and just under six feet tall. She was hippy with a growing paunch, but he suspected there was still lots of muscle there. This was her tenth year patrolling the streets of South LA, and he could tell she was getting close to what the academy called "hitting the wall." Third marriage, bad back from years of carrying the mandatory equipment in her Sam Browne belt, resentment toward and from the very people she was trying to help . . . it was all adding up.

"Everybody wants to save the world," she said. "What else?"

He glanced back out his window. "My dad was a cop."

"Now we're getting to it."

"And his dad before him."

Williams chuckled as she turned the wheel and they rounded the corner. "Poor baby, didn't have a chance, did you?"

Before he could answer, they spotted a black Lexus double-parked thirty feet ahead. A dressed-down banger in white T-shirt and khakis, no older than thirteen and holding a skateboard, was slipping the driver a palm of cash. He looked up just in time to see the police cruiser. The fear on his face said it all.

"And away we go," Williams said. She reached over to give the siren a squelch as Sean hit the lights.

The boy leaped back from the Lexus. He dropped the board and jumped on, rabbiting down the street. But the kid wasn't their interest. The driver of the Lexus was the dealer. And with wheels like that, business was obviously good.

The car barely stopped before Sean was out, unsnapping his safety holster and drawing the Glock 22 issued to him by the academy. "This is the police!" he shouted as he quickly crossed in front of the cruiser and headed toward the Lexus. "Turn off the ignition and step out of the car." He knew Williams was already calling in the plates for outstanding tickets and warrants.

Inside the car, a dog began barking. The driver, no more than twenty with diamond-studded grillz across his teeth and more ink on his arms than the *LA Times*, poked his head out the window. "What seems to be the problem, Officer?"

"Step out of the car."

The dog continued barking.

"I'm sorry, what did you say?"

As Sean approached the vehicle, the tinted back window behind the driver rolled partway down to reveal an angry pit bull.

"I'm just taking Beauty here for a ride." The driver motioned to the dog, who was not only barking ferociously but squirming to get out.

Suddenly Sean's focus was split, his concern now divided between the young man and the dog. "Step out of the car!"

"What you sweatin' me for, man?"

From the corner of his eye, Sean spotted neighbors rising from their porches, opening screen doors to take a peek . . . as the animal's rage grew by the second.

"Restrain your dog!" Sean shouted. "Keep the animal inside and step out of the vehicle!"

The dog gave a violent lunge. It was nearly halfway out. Sean spun his gun to the animal.

"You're gonna shoot Beauty?" the kid cried. "You're gonna kill my dog!"

Sean hesitated, unsure what to do—before him was an enraged animal about to attack, a young man no doubt armed, and neighbors watching his every move.

"Putnam!"

He glanced over his shoulder to see Williams stepping from the cruiser.

"Lower your gun!"

Was she kidding? Didn't she see the situation? One or two more lunges and the dog would be free.

"Put the gun away! You will not shoot that dog!"

Confused, he threw her another look. She was serious. Suddenly he understood. Of course. He wouldn't shoot the dog. He quickly reholstered his gun and pulled the Taser from his belt.

"No!" Williams shouted. "Return to the car!"

"But—"

"Now!"

He heard neighbors calling, felt his body prickling in sweat, tingling with adrenaline.

"Now!"

Reluctantly, he started backing up.

"That's a good boy," the kid shouted over the barking. "Listen to Mommy."

Sean headed back around the cruiser and arrived at his open door just as the animal broke loose. It fell to the ground with a grunt and charged.

"Get in!" Williams shouted as she scrambled to her side.

Sean jumped in and shut his door just as the dog arrived, leaping at the glass, barking, snarling.

"What were you thinking?" she yelled.

"It's a dog!" Sean shouted.

"You know how much paperwork there is in shooting a dog?"

The animal jumped onto the hood, its claws scratching the paint, bracing itself on all fours, barking through the windshield, saliva flying.

"I could have Tasered it. I still can if you—"

"And have animal rights all over our butts? Honestly, did your momma have any children who weren't brain-dead? This is LA, college boy. Better to Taser the kid than the dog!"

There was the chirp of tires and puff of blue smoke as the Lexus sped off.

Sean watched in disbelief as it disappeared down the street, the dog still on their hood inches from his face, as it continued barking, snapping, and snarling. Apparently there was a lot more to learn than what the academy had taught.

CHAPTER FOUR

"*T*HERE SHE *is!*" one of the weaker ones cried.

"Where?" the kid asked. "I don't see—"

"*She's coming out of the house!*"

The stronger ones scooted him down in the seat, hiding him behind the steering wheel of his rusting Malibu. They'd been parked here all morning, ever since they'd discovered her address. But they would not step onto her property. They hated her, but they would not approach her.

"Let me do her now," the kid whispered. "I could drag her into the car, kill her, and nobody would—"

"*Silence,*" a stronger one ordered. "*She's one of His.*"

"She's just a chick."

"*We must not approach.*"

The kid scowled. "If you hate her so much, how come you want to protect her?"

"*We are not protecting her, we are protecting ourselves.*"

The kid scoffed. For a moment they thought he'd reach for the door handle, but he didn't. They'd trained their host too well for that. Instead he simply waited as they studied and evaluated her. It was imperative to know your enemy. And she was their enemy.

She had seen them. In the bathroom. She was a witness. And that made her dangerous.

They watched as she stepped from her porch onto the sidewalk. She turned, moving away from the car, and they felt a sense of relief. It's not that they were afraid of her. How could they be? Like most Inferiors, she had no idea of her authority.

But she was still a threat.

On the other hand, her presence heightened the risk, raised the stakes, which made the game a bit more dangerous. And they liked games. As long as they won. And they would win. She would be destroyed. They'd been promised. Not yet, but soon.

RACHEL FELT A wave of uneasiness and glanced over her shoulder. There was nothing there. Just the usual cars and vans— some carefully detailed, others thrashed and sun-faded. She shrugged it off and continued down the sidewalk. She'd missed this morning's mail and was heading to the nearest drop box to send off the letter. The Santa Anas blew into her face, making her skin itch and her eyes water. This was the season of crazies and craziness. When civil people struggled to maintain their civility. When those with abnormal wiring worked just a little harder to keep from shorting out. And when Rachel Delacroix prayed to keep the balance she'd fought so intently to regain during her stay in the hospital.

She knew Daddy would not approve of the letter. He hated the police. Well, not hate. Christians don't hate. But if they did, he'd have his reasons. More than once he'd been arrested for nothing except being black at the wrong place and the wrong time. There were always stories circulating the community about harassment, false arrest, verbal and physical abuse. Some of them true. Some of them created or embellished for effect. But you couldn't deny the frequent questionings, the shakedowns, or the ominous thumping of helicopters at night, their blinding lights scouring the streets, the yards, and sometimes blazing through living room windows. If her father didn't hate the police, he at least didn't trust them.

That's why she wouldn't tell him about the letter. It wasn't a lie; she simply didn't tell him. It's also why she'd not put a return address on the envelope. Yes, she had obeyed the dream. Yes, she would share her gift with those who could use it. But no one needed to know its source. If her father did not trust them, she saw no reason why she should.

She approached the corner and gave a start at the Doberman suddenly barking and leaping to the end of his chain. More and more folks were doing that. Besides window bars and security screen doors (standard-issue among South Side residents), they were getting themselves dogs and tying them up in their front yards.

Beyond the yard lay a cinder-block wall, tagged by so many gangs it was hard to see the beige paint underneath. And beyond that, the strip mall, complete with a 7-Eleven, Bernie's Tacos, a Laundromat, Blockbuster Video, and there, at the far corner, the drop box. There were only five or six cars in the lot, along with a police cruiser, the sun glaring off its shiny black-and-white paint. She glanced at the envelope in her hand:

Los Angeles Police Department
Murder Investigation Bureau
Los Angeles, CA

She'd been worried about the address. Besides not having a street name, much less a street number, there was no zip code. She'd tried looking for the address in the phone book, but there were so many utility and public services it was hard to find anything. And even it if was delivered to the right address, who knew if there really was such a thing as a "Murder Investigation Bureau"?

She looked back to the police car. They'd know. The cops inside or at the 7-Eleven or wherever they were would know what to do with it. She'd just hand it over to them and they would deliver it to the right department. After all, it was sealed and had a stamp on it.

Of course, it would be hard on her. There were few things as painful as approaching total strangers. The fact that they were cops didn't help. But if this is what the Lord had wanted, she would obey.

IT WAS GETTING close to quitting time and Sean was grateful his partner called in another Code Seven for a meal break. There had been no other incidents except a few traffic violations and one domestic disturbance. Still, he figured the escapades of his first day would spread through the station like wildfire.

"Probably will," Williams agreed as she started on her second taco. "But it's a good story. One for the grandkids. Not like mine." She reached for more hot sauce and poured out a healthy portion.

He gave her a look.

She shrugged. "Thank God for Prevacid." Taking a bite, she added, "You'll be on it soon enough yourself."

He nodded, remembering his old man's stash of Rolaids in the kitchen cupboard.

"Your first day," he said, "it was tough?"

"Got caught in a crossfire." She took another bite. "Some kid popped another over dissing his tennis shoes."

"How'd it turn out?"

"Not good."

Sean shook his head, reaching for another tortilla chip. "Over a pair of tennis shoes."

"Don't you go judging, white boy."

"I wasn't—"

"'Course you were. You'd be a fool not to."

Sean bit into the chip, unsure how to respond.

"You got to remember, down here these people got nothin'. You criticize somethin' like their clothes, you criticize them."

Sean looked on, listening.

"You tell some kid his pair of two-hundred-dollar jumpers are crap—it's the same as me callin' your momma a whore."

"It's not worth a shooting."

"'Course it is. On the streets all you got is your reputation. You take that away from these kids, you take away their identity."

Sean remained quiet, realizing he was out of his depth. He reached for another chip just as a pretty young woman in her early twenties entered. There was an effortless beauty about her that even the plain, yellow summer dress couldn't hide. She was tall and lean, but not boney like those he'd seen sitting on the curbs, the tweekers who chose meth over food. She was more fashion-model lean. And she was frightened. He could see it in her breathing and how tightly she clutched the letter in her hand. Their eyes connected, and she quickly looked away. Then, after a breath for courage, she approached the table and held out the envelope.

Williams wiped her mouth. "What you got there, sugar?"

The young woman glanced down. Sean and his partner traded looks. The woman forced her eyes back up to Williams and motioned for her to take the envelope.

"Fan mail?" Williams asked, reaching for it.

The woman tried to smile but didn't quite succeed.

Williams read the address and asked, "You want me to deliver this for you, is that it?"

She gave a nod and another attempted smile. She started to glance at Sean, then thought better of it.

"Anyone in particular?" Williams asked.

She shook her head.

"All right, we'll see what we can do."

The girl nodded, turned, and quickly walked toward the door. Sean watched after her. Despite the painful shyness, there was a nobility about her. And something else. A lack of pretension, a type of—well, he could think of no other word for it but . . . trueness.

He looked back at Williams, who was holding the envelope up to the light. "Hmm" was all she said before tearing it open.

"What are you doing?" Sean asked.

"It's addressed to the Murder Investigation Bureau." She pulled out a single piece of typing paper. "As far as I know there is no such bureau."

"Right, but . . ." He fell silent as his partner began reading. What little he could see through the paper showed neat and precise handwriting.

Suddenly Williams swore, then scooted across the booth's seat. "Let's go, partner."

"What's up?"

She rose and called over to a squat Latino who was wiping down the counter, "Gotta catch some bad guys, Bernie."

He nodded.

She hiked up her pants and turned to Sean. "You got a twenty?"

"Sure." He glanced down at the meager food of four tacos and coffee. "Shouldn't we have a bill, or—"

"Twenty," Williams repeated as she headed for the door.

Reluctantly, Sean dug out a twenty-dollar bill, tossed it on the table, and followed. As he stepped outside he was hit by the hot, dry air.

"There she is." Williams motioned toward the girl who was just leaving the parking lot. "Miss?" she called. "Miss?"

The girl stole a quick look over her shoulder, then picked up her pace.

"What's going on?" Sean asked.

Again she called, "Excuse me!"

The girl broke into a run.

"Go get her," Williams ordered.

"What?" Sean turned to his partner. "What's she done?"

"Maybe nothing, maybe accessory to murder. Go."

He turned back just as the girl disappeared behind a cinder-block wall.

"Go!"

Sean began pursuit, the tools on his belt—the gun, Taser, flashlight, baton, radio, and handcuffs hitting his hips and thighs with every stride. He rounded the corner and ran directly into a Doberman that leaped at him until it was brought up short by its chain. It barked and snarled, bringing back all-too-recent memories.

The girl ran some thirty yards ahead.

He started again and shouted, "Stop!" Following protocol, he began to identify himself as the police. But given the situation—a lone white cop chasing a pretty black girl through the hood—he thought better of it and simply repeated, "Stop!"

She darted left, into a yard.

He continued after her, hoping his partner wasn't putting him through some sort of rookie hazing. He arrived at the yard and cut into the driveway. The cement was broken with ankle-high weeds pushing their way through the cracks. He heard the slap of a gate and spotted a swaying eight-foot-high wooden fence at the back of the yard. He ran past a white Escalade and reached the gate. Throwing it open, he saw her running down the alley. More dogs had started barking. He continued pursuit. The alley was walled in by leaning fences, detached garages, and giant oleanders, their pink and white clusters drooping on spindly stalks. Even here, even now he was struck by the beauty of the mottled light and shade.

She was twenty yards ahead when she veered to the left and yanked at one of the gates. It was locked.

"I'm not going to hurt you," he yelled. "We just need to talk."

She scampered onto a garbage can. Reaching up, she grabbed the top of the fence and pulled herself over. Sean arrived just as she dropped to the other side. He tried the gate, then turned to the garbage can and hoisted himself up. But the lid could not support his 185 pounds, and it crumpled beneath him. Before he could leap off, both he and the can tumbled to the ground. He scrambled back to his feet, grabbed the top of the fence, and pulled himself up and over. He dropped into a backyard of mostly dirt. What clumps of grass existed had been neatly mowed. He caught a glimpse of the yellow dress darting around the front of the house. He continued, reached the front yard, and turned just as the front door slammed shut. He ran to the porch steps and took them two at a time. Breathing hard, he knocked on the steel screen door. "Police! Open up!"

There was no response.

He banged on the screen again. It rattled against the door. "This is the police. Open—"

A bald man, well cut and in his forties, opened the door. He wore a white shirt and black slacks. "Yes?"

"You have somebody inside that we need to question."

The man pushed up his glasses but said nothing.

"A young lady just entered your house and we need to speak to her."

"Is she under arrest?"

"No, no, we just have some questions."

"I see. And do you have a warrant to enter my home?"

"Well, no."

"So she's not under arrest and you don't have a warrant."

"Right, but—"

"Then I suggest you stop beating on my door and quit harassing me."

"But she's a suspect in—"

"And if you don't mind, I'd appreciate you stepping off of my porch."

"But—"

"Have a good day, Officer." Before Sean could respond, the man closed the door in his face.

The rookie stood blinking, then he knocked on the screen again.

No answer.

He turned, surveying the neighborhood. An elderly couple next door was watching from their porch.

He called to them. "Do you know who lives here?"

They said nothing.

"I'm asking you who lives here."

He was met with blank expressions.

Suddenly his radio squelched and he heard Williams. "Putnam. Putnam, you there?"

He pulled the radio from his belt. "Yes."

"What's your ten-four?"

He stepped back and looked at the black, wrought-iron numbers above the door. "Twenty-three fourteen."

"Twenty-three fourteen what?"

"Um." He looked up the street but could see no sign. "Uh . . ."

"Never mind," the voice sighed. "I'll find you."

———————

"I say we haul her butt off to jail right now."

Cowboy frowned. "Let's not be too hasty, partner."

Killroy snapped shut his notebook. "Come on, man." He motioned to the letter on the coffee table in Rev. Delacroix's living room. "The information in there screams of her being an accessory, maybe the actual killer."

"I know, I know," Cowboy said, rubbing his head. He turned

back to Delacroix. "You sure she won't talk to us? I mean, things are kind of suspicious here."

Delacroix looked almost amused as he rocked quietly in his overstuffed green chair. There was a coolness about him, but something more. A dignity. He'd obviously had his experience with cops and was not intimidated. Earlier, after the arriving officers, some white rookie and a woman veteran, radioed the information, Cowboy and Killroy were there within twenty minutes. And although Delacroix had originally shut the door in the rookie's face, he had the good sense to admit the detectives, knowing if he didn't, they'd come back with a search warrant and flip the place.

It was quite a home. Like every South Central residence Cowboy had ever visited, there was plenty of poverty—yellowed light switches, threadbare carpet, cracked plaster puttied and painted over so many times its lines looked like shiny scar tissue. There was no money here but, like Delacroix, the place had class. Clean, neat as a pin. And artwork. There were modern art prints on several walls. Even the small table by the door had some weird, African sculpture thing. The place wasn't Bel Aire, but it wasn't exactly the ghetto, either.

Killroy sat beside Cowboy on the worn sofa, pretending to get more and more worked up. "And don't forget she resisted arrest." He jerked his thumb toward the porch where the rookie stood outside with his partner. "The kid chased her halfway through the hood."

Cowboy nodded thoughtfully before turning back to the father for help.

But Delacroix remained unimpressed. "All three of us know running from an officer is not the same as resisting arrest. And as for your good-cop, bad-cop routine, honestly, gentlemen." He shook his head.

"What do you mean?" Killroy demanded. He turned to Cowboy. "What's he saying?"

The reverend answered. "What he's saying is, Keep your day job, fellas, 'cause you'll never make it as actors."

The veins in Killroy's neck bulged. "You know we should arrest you, too. Right here, right now."

Delacroix opened his hands. "Please do. Attendance at my church is low; we could use the publicity. And with the hundred grand settlement for violating our civil rights, my daughter could finally go to a decent college."

Killroy swore. This time Cowboy suspected it was not an act. Turning back to Delacroix, he tried again. "If we could just ask her a few questions."

"I told you, she doesn't speak to strangers."

"Yes, that's what you said." Cowboy glanced down at his notes. "Some sort of trauma."

"Her mother and little sister were killed in a house fire."

"She won't speak to anyone?"

"It's not a matter of won't. It's a matter of can't."

"Except to you."

"Except to individuals she trusts. She has an uncanny instinct about good and bad people."

"And she doesn't trust us?" Killroy asked.

Delacroix simply repeated, "She knows good people from bad."

Before they could respond, the front door opened and the rookie stepped in.

"What's up?" Cowboy asked.

"May I"—he turned to Delacroix—"would it be possible to use your bathroom?"

"Can't it wait?" Killroy snapped.

The kid hesitated.

"Go ahead," Delacroix said, motioning. "It's just down the hall."

The kid looked at Killroy, who glanced away, then at Cowboy, who nodded impatiently.

"Thank you." He passed between them, offering a quiet apology. "Sorry."

Once he was gone, Killroy pointed at the letter on the table. "And these . . . dreams. You're trying to tell us she's what, psychic?"

"I'm telling you her dreams are from God."

Killroy snorted.

Delacroix added, "Just like Jacob, Daniel, Joseph, Peter—"

"And you really expect us to buy that crap?" Killroy said.

"I really don't care what you buy, Detective."

Still acting as the voice of reason, Cowboy said, "You have to admit it does sound pretty odd . . . I mean, *if* any of the details of her dream are actually true."

"Oh, they're true, all right," Delacroix said. "Rachel doesn't lie."

"Let me guess," Killroy said. "She can't do that, either."

Delacroix simply looked at him. "She can, but she doesn't. My daughter is the most honest person you'll ever meet. To a fault. She thinks that being good is all that's necessary for her survival in this world."

"And you don't?" Cowboy asked.

Delacroix turned to him. "You tell me, Detective. From what you've seen out there, you tell me."

———————

"And Elliot's okay?" Sean spoke into his cell phone.

"Everything's fine," his sister answered. "Relax."

"It's just, it's his first day of school. I wanted to be there, you know, to pick him up and everything."

"He understands. He's fine," Traci repeated. "He's out back playing with Andrew."

Sean nodded and glanced around the tiny hallway where he stood. Like the rest of the house, it was worn but immaculate. Amid one or two pieces of African art, a half dozen French Impressionist prints hung on the wall. The bathroom had been in use, so while he waited, he'd quietly put in the call . . . away from his partner and out of earshot of the detectives.

"You want me to get him?" his sister asked.

"No, I'll be there." He glanced at his watch. "Soon . . . I hope."

"You want dinner?"

He was absentmindedly examining the Van Gogh print before him. It was the 1885 *Still Life with Open Bible.** "No, uh, I think we'll go out. You know, celebrate. First day on the job, first day at school."

"All right. See you when you get here. And Sean?"

"Yeah?"

"Relax."

"I am relaxed."

"Right. I just hope you're a better cop than a liar."

"Good-bye, Traci." Sean slipped the phone back into his pocket just as the bathroom door opened. He turned to see the girl he had chased down the alley. When she saw him, she froze.

"Sorry," he said. "I didn't mean to startle you. I just have to . . ." He motioned toward the bathroom.

She glanced down, then away, anywhere but at him. Again he was struck by her presence. Despite the fear, there was that . . . nobility, like some African princess.

"I, uh"—he cleared his throat—"I was admiring your prints."

She gave no response.

He nodded to the wall. "It's quite a collection."

She hesitated, almost glancing up.

---

* To view this painting, go to http://www.vangoghmuseum.nl/vgm/index.jsp?page=3450&collection=1297&lang=en.

Encouraged, he motioned to the print behind him. "This Van Gogh here is interesting. Did you know he painted it right after his father died?" He glanced at her, saw her eyes flicker. "That explains why the candle in the candlestick is no longer burning. And the giant Bible that fills the frame, that was his father's, too. He was a minister."

She gave the slightest nod.

Pleased, he turned to the print and pressed on. "He was trying to symbolize both the death of his father and the rejection of the man's overbearing faith. That's what this little trashy pulp novel on the corner of the table is all about."

He turned back to the girl, surprised to see she was looking directly at him. And frowning.

"What?" he asked.

She glanced away and shook her head.

"You disagree?"

She nodded.

"Why's that?"

She hesitated, then cautiously moved past him to the print. Reaching up, she tapped the top of the Bible.

He looked at the print, then back at her.

She tapped harder.

"I'm sorry, I don't—"

"Iss . . ." The sound caught in her throat and she tried again. With difficulty she forced out the word, "Isa . . . iah."

He squinted back at the print. Just above her fingers were the letters *ISAIE*.

"Yeah, you're right. Could be Dutch for Isaiah. It's in the Bible." She nodded. "Fifty . . . three."

"What, is that like a chapter or something?"

She nodded.

It was his turn to frown. "All right. Isaiah fifty-three. What does that mean?"

She scowled again, then started to speak. "It . . . means—"

"Well, well, well, what do we got here?" They both turned to see the bigger of the detectives, the one called Cowboy, standing at the entrance of the hallway. "She showin' you her etchings, son?"

The girl tensed and stepped back.

Spotting her discomfort, the man opened his hands and smiled. "Come on, darlin', I ain't gonna hurt you."

Despite his southern charm, she backed away.

"We just wanna ask a few questions, that's all."

Her eyes darted to Sean, as if looking for help.

"Just come on into the living room for a few minutes. Chat with me and your dad."

She turned and, without a word, briskly moved down the hall.

"Miss?"

She entered the last room and shut the door.

"Miss?"

He was answered with the soft click of a lock.

He swore, then turned to Sean. "Well, at least you two were hitting it off."

Sean shrugged. "I was an art history major in college."

"You don't say." Cowboy couldn't have sounded less interested, until he noticed the prints along the wall. "And all this crap is—"

"Mostly French Impressionism. Late eighteen and early nineteen hundreds."

"Hm," was all the man said as he took a moment to evaluate them. Then, with a grunt, he added, "Leave her your card."

"Pardon me?"

"They gave you a business card, didn't they?"

"Yes. At orientation."

He continued with exaggerated patience. "Then take it out of your billfold, turn it over, and very neatly write your cell phone number on the back of it."

Sean pulled out one of the new business cards, complete with his name and badge number on it, and quickly jotted down his cell number. He looked up and glanced around. "Where do I, where should I—"

Cowboy turned and headed back toward the living room. "You're a bright boy, Picasso, you figure it out."

Sean looked at the girl's closed door, thought better of it. He turned to the prints behind him, then carefully slipped the card into the lower left-hand corner of the Van Gogh frame.

"Let's go!" Cowboy called.

"Yes, sir." Sean hesitated, turned for the bathroom.

"Now."

He looked longingly toward the facilities, knew they were no longer an option, and turned to join the big man in the living room.

CHAPTER FIVE

S O YOU'RE telling me this selective mutism stuff is for real?"
Cowboy asked.

"Oh, yes, very real," Dr. Sharon Fields said. She sat on the edge of her Plexiglas desk, holding the girl's letter in her hands.

"She can't talk, even if she wants to?" he asked.

"They usually speak to their parents and select individuals, but for the most part, the children are simply unable to verbalize to others."

"Children? She's nineteen."

Fields shook back her shiny, dark hair, letting it fall onto some very delicate shoulders. "Sometimes it continues into adulthood. And sometimes"—she sighed sadly—"it's intractable."

Cowboy shifted in his chair, trying not to stare at the lovely long legs before him. He had come to her Century Plaza Towers office to get some insight on the Delacroix girl and the letter. If anyone could help with this stuff, Fields could. Of course, he was hoping for other possibilities as well, perhaps a late-night study of the case over dinner, a drink or two at her place afterward. And it wasn't just wishful thinking. The signs were all there. He was a detective, for crying out loud, he knew how to read people. At least he thought he did. For months he was certain she'd been sending out signals that she was interested. But whenever he made his move, it seemed the signals changed, the rules shifted. Game over.

And it was making him just a little bit crazy.

He focused back on his notes. "This stuff is caused by what— her old man beating her, sexual abuse, what?"

"No. Studies indicate it is not the result of abuse." He was staring at her legs again. She waited until he looked back up and then, with emphasis, added, "And nothing sexual."

He returned to his notes, scowling hard.

"That's why I don't think we're dealing with selective mutism—at least not the textbook variety. This seems more connected to the trauma of losing her mother and sibling. You say she was institutionalized?"

"Eighteen months. Just got out this spring."

Fields nodded, then rose from her desk, crossing to a file cabinet. "You mentioned there was an abundance of artwork in the house?"

"Mostly French Impressionistics."

"Impressionism?"

"Right. Why, is that something?"

"It might provide an outlet for her feelings. With her past trauma and all the repressed communication, she may be looking for ways to connect with the outside world."

"She was definitely connecting with the rookie."

Fields nodded. "They had some chemistry?"

"Like dogs in heat." He immediately regretted his crassness.

She paused, as if considering the comment.

He quickly changed gears. "Back to these so-called dreams." He motioned to the letter she still held in her hands. "Could they be real?"

"I'm afraid the paranormal is way out of my field."

"She just doesn't seem the type, you know? Sneaking into

some high-profile cop's home and killing her." He shook his head. "I don't think the girl has it in her."

"Maybe she doesn't." Fields crossed around her desk and sat back on the edge. "At least the part you've seen. At least the part she's aware of."

This time he was careful to keep his eyes locked on hers.

She continued, "But from what you've told me, there could be lots more going on under the surface."

"Meaning?"

"Meaning she could be the murderer without even knowing it."

He glanced back at his notes, careful not to stop at her legs on the way down. "And the dreams are what, like her repression coming out?"

"A strong possibility, yes." She gave what might have been a sigh. "Repression comes in many different forms. Wouldn't you agree?"

He looked up. Her hazel green eyes were fixed on his. He may have nodded, he wasn't sure.

She continued, "Sometimes it's more powerful than we care to acknowledge even to ourselves."

He swallowed.

"The important thing is that we find ways to release it, to uncage the animal trapped within."

He swallowed again, though his mouth had gone dry. Somewhere, in another world, he felt his cell phone vibrate. He tried ignoring it. It vibrated again.

"Is that your phone?"

"I'm sorry?"

She smiled. "Your phone?"

"Oh, right." He reached for it, silently cursing his luck as he pulled it from his jacket. He watched sadly as she rose and returned to the file cabinet. "What?" he demanded.

"You still there?" It was Killroy.

"Yes, we're evaluating what could be crucial information."

"So, you score yet?"

Cowboy watched as Fields worked the files. "These things"—he cleared his throat—"take time."

"Amateur."

"I'm sure you didn't call to give me a pep talk."

"No, sweetheart. What I got you're gonna like a whole lot more."

"I'm listening."

"We lifted the girl's records from the mental motel."

"How?"

"Some parolee who works at the hospital wants to stay out of jail."

"And?"

"She's the killer."

Cowboy turned his head, shifting the cell to his other ear. "Talk to me."

"She's the one who set the fire and offed her mom and little sister."

"*She* killed them?"

Fields glanced up from her work.

Killroy answered. "Her words to the letter. 'Course, the old man tried to cover for her, but—"

Cowboy finished the thought, "It didn't stop her from going psycho."

"Guilt, the gift that keeps on giving."

"And now she's out six months and back to her old tricks."

"With some new and creative twists along the way."

"Any other activity?" Cowboy asked. "Before? After?"

"Clean as a whistle—just the capping of our lovely Assistant Chief Hampton."

Cowboy rubbed his head.

"You're the lead on this one," Killroy said. "What do you think? Take her in?"

"On what, a dream? Info illegally taken from her medical records? The DA will kick her 'fore we even get her processed. Every civil liberty org in the state will be on our backs. Lawyers will have to take numbers."

"And the righteous reverend will do all he can to help."

Cowboy scowled hard at the floor.

"So, what's your call?" Killroy asked.

"My call is we keep an eye on her and turn up the heat."

"I figured you'd take the gutless route."

"What would you do?"

"Same."

Cowboy nodded.

"Well, good luck on your hunting expedition there. And take notes. I like details."

"Thanks." Cowboy reached up and disconnected his phone, still thinking.

"Sounds like important news," Fields said. She was still at the files, her back to him.

"Yeah." He tapped his phone, thinking.

"About the girl?"

"Yeah."

She turned those hazel green eyes back on him. "So what can I do? What would you like from me?"

He blinked. "You don't suppose we could," he cleared his throat, "pick up this conversation a little later, do you? Maybe over a nice dinner or something?"

She hesitated. "Are we talking work or pleasure?"

"Oh, work. Definitely work."

She turned back to her files. "I'm sorry to hear that."

"Or not. I mean, it doesn't have to be."

She looked back over her shoulder. "Why, Cowboy, are you asking me on a date?"

"No, of course not." He tried to chuckle, but it came out more of a cough. "I mean, unless you want."

"I think that would be"—she turned back to the files—"interesting."

He couldn't believe his ears. "Fine. Well, that's just fine. Why don't I pick you up at, say, seven?"

She turned to him, startled. "Tonight?"

"Or tomorrow. I mean, whatever's good for—"

"Actually, I think seven would be perfect." She turned back to her files.

Cowboy sat stunned over his victory, amazed at how easy she'd been to play. But even now, as he sat staring at that lovely body, he couldn't help but wonder just exactly who had played who.

———

DELACROIX WAS LIVID. If there was room in his tiny nook of an office to pace, he would have. But with Rachel, Jude Miller, and himself holed up behind the thin door separating his office from the sanctuary, there was barely room to move. Not that there was much more room in the sanctuary. The place was packed. The Wednesday night service had been over nearly half an hour but virtually no one had left.

"You've turned this place into a carnival," Delacroix growled.

"Have I?" Miller calmly scooted aside a stack of 8½ x 12 flyers on the desk and sat. "Is that what you call a church full of people needing the touch of God?"

Delacroix snatched up a flyer, one of hundreds Miller had passed out since last Sunday's service, and read: "Bountiful Blessings. Receive all God wants you to have! Favor, health, wealth, and prosperity!"

"Did I miss something?" Miller asked.

"How about salvation? How about giving your life to God?"

"I thought you worked that in nicely."

"Worked it in? That was my entire message!" He slapped the paper with the back of his hand. "I didn't touch on any of this."

"Maybe you should have."

Delacroix shot him a look.

Miller shrugged. "You can't catch fish without bait."

"And now they won't leave." Delacroix nodded toward the door. "Despite what I say, everyone's hanging around, just in case."

"The night's young."

Delacroix's rage pounded in his ears. He looked at Rachel, who stood to the side examining her hands.

"Has your church ever been so full?" Miller asked. "And, not to be indelicate"—he motioned to the two baskets overflowing with money on the bookcase—"when was the last time you saw an offering that size?"

"I have a day job as an accountant! Every cent this church raises goes right back into the community."

"Of course it does. And look how much more the community could be helped."

Delacroix's jaw tightened as he struggled to rein in his temper.

Miller made the task no easier. "Think of it. A church that would actually give the people what they want."

"The gospel is about meeting people's needs, not pandering to their wants. God is not our errand boy."

"You saw their faces, Reverend. So much suffering out there, so much need." He turned to Rachel. "And you have the power to help. To be God's blessing to His people."

She looked up from her hands, then timidly turned them to her father. The palms were flush with blood, just as they had been Sunday. Just as they had been so many years before. Delacroix felt his own face growing hot, his stomach tightening.

Miller also saw her hands and added, "Would a loving pastor deprive his people of that? When there is an outpouring of God's power, would you dare quench His Spirit?"

There was the phrase again. The one Delacroix had wrestled with ever since Miller accused him of it Sunday. As a pastor, the last thing he wanted to do was stand in the way of the Holy Spirit. But as a father, was he not also obligated to protect his child? He shook his head. "No. I will not quench the Spirit. But neither will I let you exploit my daughter—not until she's ready." He scooped up his Bible, preparing to leave.

"And when will that be, Pastor? A year? Five years? How many people will suffer, how many people will go untouched by God's loving hands before *you* decide your daughter is ready? Your *fully grown* daughter who, as you've seen, God has already commissioned to begin His work?"

Delacroix opened the office door. "Let's go, Rachel."

She obediently joined him, and they stepped out into the crowd. Heads turned, and conversations slowed to a stop. He placed his hand on the small of her back and guided her toward the rear exit, smiling, nodding to those he saw, many he did not know. The people parted and returned his greeting with nods of their own, all the while stealing looks at Rachel, who kept her eyes to the floor.

Spotting his elder, Samuel, he called out, "Would you mind locking up for us?"

The white-haired gentleman nodded while also sneaking a peek at Rachel.

They arrived at the dented fire door, with Miller directly behind them. As always, the door stuck slightly and Delacroix had to throw his hip against it. They stepped into the evening air that was still hot from the Santa Anas. They passed a pair of Dumpsters that smelled of rotting produce and eventually reached his faded gray Honda. He stooped down to unlock Rachel's door.

"Reverend . . ."

Turning, he saw Deborah Douglas and her mother hobbling from the building. The older woman had been struck down with a stroke more than a year ago. She could barely walk, and the left side of her face hung limp and useless. Deborah, her daughter, was a thin, nervous woman in her fifties who accompanied her mother wherever she went.

"Could we talk with you a minute?"

Delacroix softly spoke to Rachel. "Get in the car, child." She did as she was told. Before closing her door, he looked up, all smiles, to the mother and daughter as they arrived. "What can I do for you lovely ladies this evening?"

"It's Momma," Deborah said. "She's getting worse and I was wondering if"—she stole a look at Rachel—"well, if you two wouldn't mind praying for her. You know, asking the Lord if He'd see fit to heal her?"

"I'd love to," Delacroix said, checking his watch. "But right now is not a good time. Maybe I could swing by your house later this evening and we could—"

"Just a quick prayer, Reverend. It'll only take a minute."

He glanced over at the building. The church door had not been shut, and several of the congregation filled the opening.

"Daddy." Rachel's voice was barely a whisper.

He looked down and saw her motioning to her palms. He nodded but, without a word, closed her door. "I'm sorry, ladies. It will have to be another time."

"But, Reverend—"

He started for the driver's side, where Miller was already standing. "I really am sorry. But right now just isn't good. Call me at home and we can schedule something." Joining Miller, he unlocked and opened his door. "See what you've done?" he whispered. "See their disappointment?"

"What I've done?" Miller made no attempt to lower his voice.

"It's not what I've done, Reverend." He dropped his head and looked through the open door at Rachel. "It's what you're *not* doing."

Delacroix kept his voice low and even. "I'm not letting you turn my daughter into a sideshow freak."

Miller did not back down. "You're quenching the Spirit, Reverend. For your own selfish purposes."

"'Selfish purposes'?" Delacroix practically hissed.

"What would you call it?"

"My church is not a circus! My daughter will not be—" He stopped, hearing the passenger door creak open. He turned and saw Deborah and her mother stepping back as Rachel rose from the car. "Rachel?"

She was breathing hard and appeared nervous, clear signs she was frightened. But she did not look at him. Instead, she reached for Mrs. Douglas.

"Rachel?" Delacroix repeated. "What are you doing?"

The old woman's eyes glistened with moisture as she lifted her face to the girl.

"Rachel?"

Ever so gently, Rachel placed her hands on the woman's sagging mouth and cheek. She closed her eyes and began to silently move her lips.

Delacroix had seen enough. He started around the car until Miller grabbed his arm. He spun back to Miller, glaring at him, but was stopped by the compassion in the man's eyes. He turned to his daughter, hesitating, unsure. He glanced at the church. People were slowly spilling out into the parking lot. He turned back to Rachel as she continued praying, her eyes closed, her face knotted into a frown. And then, to his amazement, he heard her begin to speak. She was praying out loud . . . in front of all these people. She said only two words, but they were clear and distinct.

"Jesus . . ." She clenched her eyes tighter. A moment passed before she finished. "Please."

Everyone waited, seeming to hold their breath. But there was no change in the woman.

Finally, sadly, Delacroix resumed his walk around the car and joined his daughter. "It's okay," he said gently. "You tried."

Rachel nodded and opened her eyes. They were shiny with emotion. She lowered her hands from Mrs. Douglas's face and whispered, "I'm . . . sorry." The old lady nodded, tears brimming in her own eyes.

Deborah reached out to take Rachel's hands into hers. "It's okay, sweetheart." She gave them a squeeze. "You did what you could."

Rachel nodded and wiped her eyes. Then slowly she turned and reentered the car.

Delacroix crossed back to his side, addressing Miller. "See what you've done? Now I seriously suggest you find someone else to—"

"Sweet Jesus!" Deborah cried.

Both men turned to see the younger woman clenching and unclenching her fists. She looked across the car to Delacroix. "My arthritis . . . it's gone." She wiggled her fingers in astonishment, then turned to her mother. "Momma, it's gone. My arthritis is gone!"

People at the church door began to murmur. Deborah turned to them. "It's a miracle!" She raised her hands, opening and closing them. "My arthritis, she's healed my arthritis!"

"Praise God!" someone shouted. They started toward the car. "Hallelujah!"

A dread began filling Delacroix's chest. Dread mixed with awe, anger, and confusion. He felt Miller taking his arm, helping him into the car. "Go."

"What?"

"Always leave your audience wanting more."

Delacroix took his seat, frowning.

"I'll handle it from here. Right now, take your daughter home and get some rest." Miller reached for the car door and before closing it added, "Buckle in, Reverend. It's going to be one unforgettable ride."

Chapter Six

SHE IS *surrounded by fire. It hisses and crackles and pops. The hot air burns the back of her throat, making her eyes water as if she's standing in the midst of a strong Santa Ana.*

"Rachel."

She turns to see Momma holding little Rebecca. The woman reaches toward Rachel's forehead the way she always does when pushing the bangs out of her eyes . . . until suddenly the mother and little daughter erupt into flames.

"Rachel!"

Their hands reach to her, pleading for mercy as their faces are lost in the fire. Everything is smoke. Swirling smoke becoming a thick, impenetrable fog. Rachel sees nothing . . . but she can hear. Music. Soft and floating. The sound of a flute. She turns toward it and realizes she is kneeling. She feels cool sheets against her bare knees and the back of her feet. She hears the rustling of a blanket, a pillowcase. A groggy male voice mumbles, "Who's . . . there?"

She tries to answer, but no words come.

The flute grows louder.

The voice gives a start and is suddenly wide awake. "Who's there?" It throws aside the covers. "I said, 'Who's—'"

There is the faint ring of steel, like a sword pulled from its sheath. Then a slicing sound. The voice cries, and a struggle begins. The flute grows forceful, urgent.

Horrified at what she hears, Rachel tries backing off the bed, but she cannot move. She is frozen, a witness to the sounds in front of her but also, she knows in her gut, a participant. More slicing as a different type of scream rises. Moist gurgling. Grunts and gasps. Blind panic. Another slice. More screams. And another, until the struggle subsides, until the last of the cries fades into an airy, bubbling wheeze.

Now there is only her heavy breathing. And, of course, the flute, harsh and demanding.

She is finally able to move and crawls backward until she reaches the foot of the bed. She slips off it, bare feet touching cold, hard wood. She stands but nearly falls as her right foot gives way. It's clumsy, as if half-asleep. She stretches her hands into the darkness, limping three, four, half a dozen steps before touching a wall. She runs her fingers over smooth wallpaper until they strike what feels like a picture and dislodge it. She fumbles but is unable to prevent it from falling to the floor, its glass frame shattering. She freezes, holding her breath. But everything is silent.

Except for the flute.

She gropes along the wall, sees the flickering firefly dancing on the back of her hand. Her good foot steps on a shard of broken glass, and it slices through the pad of her big toe. She winces but continues along the wall until she feels the coolness of a metal light switch. Gratefully, she flips it on. The light is blinding. Shielding her eyes, she looks down and sees the broken picture frame from the wall. It is a painting: Édouard Manet's The Fifer.* *The child in it wears red pants, a black jacket, a funny hat, and a white sash stretching from his right shoulder to the center of his waist. Attached to the waist is a brass case for*

---

* To view this painting, go to http://en.wikipedia.org/wiki/The_Fifer. The painting is kept at the Musée d'Orsay in Paris (the same place as *The Clown Cha-U-Kao* by Toulouse-Lautrec).

the flute. The flute she is hearing. The flute that the boy's fingers, now alive, are playing.

She watches them fly across the holes, the child's eyes distant and concentrating. But they are not a child's eyes. They are reptilian, identical to those she's seen in the mirror of her other dreams. They shift until they are fixed directly upon her. She sucks in her breath and backs away.

He plays faster, louder. Blood appears at his throat. It streams down his jacket toward the white sash. Faster and faster he plays. Manically. The blood reaches the sash, narrows into a tiny stream that begins forming letters. Handwriting. Her handwriting. Letters that become words:

Tell Him

But not once. The words spell themselves over and over again on the sash, moving until they reach the bottom:

Tell Him
Tell Him
Tell Him
Tell Him
Tell Him
Tell Him
Tell Him

They thicken, spreading into one another until the entire sash is soaked. Bloodred. The flute grows impossibly shrill as the red spreads, filling her entire vision. There is only the flute and the color, music and blood, until, with all of her effort, she starts herself awake.

Rachel lay in bed, catching her breath, waiting for the music to fade. As in her last dreams, the request could not have been clearer.

It had changed slightly. "Tell Them" had become "Tell *Him*." But there was little doubt who was meant. The young policeman had such good eyes—clear and sensitive. The type that could be trusted. The type she caught herself thinking about more than once—that had left her insides just a little bit warm and buttery.

She knew she could refuse the dream. "The spirits of the prophets are subject to the prophets." It was a verse Daddy had taught her from First Corinthians long ago. She had free will. She was not a robot. And sharing the first dreams had led only to trouble. Still, there had been those two wonderful healings—Sarah's baby and Deborah Douglas's hands. The pattern was definitely taking shape. And though it confused and frightened her, if this was the path God wanted her to travel, this was the path she would continue.

She pulled aside her bedsheet and sat on the edge of the mattress. She was surprised to see she still wore last night's clothes—her white capris and baby blue blouse. Apparently she'd been so overcome from healing Deborah Douglas and so exhausted from the emotion that she'd forgotten to change. She didn't like that. She'd fought too hard to get back on her feet and regain control. She didn't like that at all.

The house was silent. No sound or movement except for the wind outside and the dancing shadows of tree branches through her window.

Tell Him.

She took a breath, rose, and padded across the rug of flickering shadows. Wedged in the frame of her dresser mirror was the card the young policeman had left for her. It would be difficult, she knew that. But the request had been clear.

With her pulse quickening, she pulled the card from the mirror, turned, and entered the hallway. She passed Daddy's room and could hear his soft snoring. Given their last run-in with the police, he would not be happy. But she had made the choice to

"Yeah, I guess."

"Yeah, it better." Cowboy looked toward the kitchen.

"I mean, probably. I'm not sure."

Cursing, Cowboy reached for his glasses. "Talk to me."

"We've got a lot more information this time. A description of
room—a bedroom."

Cowboy rubbed his head in frustration.

"The floor, the music that was playing, even the artwork on
wall."

Sarah reentered, bottled water in hand. Not the end of the
d, there was still a chance . . . until he noticed her hair. It was
up and neatly pinned.

This better be important, kid," he muttered. "Real important."

enter God's mysterious current, and it was important to let Him
take her where He wished.

She crossed the living room and stepped into the small
kitchen. There was still the faintest smell of fish from last night's
dinner. She snapped on the light and winced at its glare. With
card in hand, she reached for the cordless phone on the wall. It
would be difficult, but not impossible. She'd talked to him once
already. She noticed her hands were damp—either from fear or
the terror of the dream. Either way, the room felt hot and stuffy,
so she headed for the porch.

She quietly unbolted the doors, pushed open the screen, and
walked to the edge of the steps, where she sat. The night air was
warm and filled with smoke from a fire up in the Santa Monica
mountains. The scorching winds had obviously been too much
for some unbalanced soul whose tendency was toward arson. She
hugged her knees trying to calm herself, working up the courage.
Over the wind she heard the faint pounding of rap music; a handful of barking dogs; and, of course, a distant siren, always a siren.
She also heard Daddy's car in the driveway, its engine clicking as
it cooled down. She frowned. What church member had needed
his help this time of night?

Tell Him.

She looked back down at the card. Then, with forced resolve,
she raised the phone and with trembling fingers dialed the number.

IT HAD BEEN a long and expensive night for Cowboy—though
he hoped it would soon be worth every penny. Truth be told, he
might have overextended himself a bit by taking Dr. Fields to the
Saddle Peak Lodge. "The most romantic restaurant in Southern
California," the magazine said. But it was the chance of a lifetime,
and he wasn't about to blow it by being too thrifty.

So, after a brief lie to get reservations—something about classified police work for which the city of Los Angeles would be eternally grateful—and a quick stop at Sears to get a clean shirt, he was off to the races. Still, no matter how fortunate he considered himself, it was impossible to stop the tally from running in his head:

- $ 12.95 for red roses, courtesy Ralph's Supermarket (whose source he hoped she wouldn't notice);
- $ 52.00 x 2 for the New Zealand elk tenderloin;
- $170.00 for a red blend wine, something called Justin Isosceles;
- 20 percent for tip (it would have been 10 percent, but the clever waiter returned the change, pretending there had been a mistake);
- $6 for valet parking;
- (He didn't bother to include gas from her Wilshire town house all the way out to Calabasas).

Nevertheless, the investment was paying off. She'd invited him up to her place for drinks. Thanks to the cognac and his smooth moves, she'd begun to respond. They were kissing on what she called the "divan" (though to him it looked a lot like a sofa). He'd just removed his glasses and loosened his tie, and she'd just let down that thick, gorgeous hair when he heard the guitar rift of "Hotel California" from the Eagles.

She opened her eyes. "Is that your cell phone?"

"Yeah," he murmured against her neck. "Don't worry about it."

She hesitated, but he was persistent. Thanks to his skills, any ground he'd lost was quickly regained. She closed her eyes and was again responding appropriately . . . when his cell rang again.

With one hand under her back, he fumbled in his pocket with the other to find the phone's off switch. But unlike his teen daugh-

ter who lived with her mom back in Austin, he di[d] phone's intricacies by touch and had to squirm to snug-fitting pants. By the time he had it up to h[is] had ended.

So had the mood.

"Must be important," she said coolly.

"Nothing that can't wait." He peered at t[he] vainly to make sense of the blur without his g[lasses] the essence. Every moment, she drifted furth[er] Giving up, he tossed the phone on the coffe[e] her. "Now, where were—"

Again the tune played.

Angrily he sat up and reached for it. Pr[essing] he knew by heart, he barked, "Yeah?"

"Detective, um, er, Cowboy?"

"Who is this?"

"Patrolman Putman."

"Who?" He shot a look over at Fi[elds] straightening her blouse.

"Sean Putnam," the voice said. "Pic[ked]

The name stirred a vague memory[.] did you get this number?"

"Division gave it to me."

Fields rose from the sofa or d[ivan] it, and Cowboy looked after her,[.] He tried getting her attention, bu[t] kitchen.

"It's about the girl."

He slumped back into the cu[shions]

"The girl. She had another d[.]

"What girl? Who are you—

"The suspect. South Centr[al]

"Can't this wait?"

CHAPTER SEVEN

"T HIS IS stupid," their host complained as he stopped to rub the cramp out of his hand.

"*Patience,*" a stronger one ordered. "*You are almost through.*"

The kid wiped the sweat off his face with his sleeve and resumed drawing the bare hacksaw blade back and forth across the bolt. It had not been hard slipping the blade between the door and the jamb, but the repetitive motion was taking its toll.

They'd chosen the north entrance to Parker High School. The doors faced away from the street, and they could work unnoticed for hours unless some vagrant was unfortunate enough to walk by. Originally they wanted to bust out a window and crawl through, but after visiting the school that afternoon (disguised as a lost electrical repairman) they saw that each of the windows had alarms. Of course, there would still be motion detectors inside, but they'd chosen the door closest to the band room. The kid would be in and out before the police ever arrived.

Earlier they'd swung by the thrift store on South Vernon and purchased a man's extra-large white dress shirt, which the kid cut and tore to look like a sash. They'd also found an old lady's hat that he was able to fold and tape to look like the cap in the picture. This would be their final stop.

At last the blade broke through the bolt and he yanked open the door. He stepped inside and immediately set off the motion detector—a loud, pulsing buzzer. Ignoring it, he limped down the hallway, arrived at the band room, and pulled out a hammer from the pocket of his baggy jeans. The first two blows only spider-webbed the door's wire-meshed glass. The third shattered it. And the fourth allowed him to push away the glass, work through the wire, and reach inside to open the door.

"Let's go." The alarm was getting on their nerves.

He raced to the instrument lockers at the back of the room and threw open door after door until he found a small case. He unsnapped the latches and raised the lid to discover a shiny, black clarinet.

"No." A strong one snapped. *"Find another."*

He tossed it aside and opened more doors, working his way down the row until he spotted an even smaller case.

"Yes. Open it."

He did. It was just as they'd hoped, a flute.

"Now the uniform. Quickly."

He closed the case and darted with it to the uniform room. The place was a giant walk-in closet with more than fifty black uniforms, each with shiny brass buttons running down its front.

They pointed to the largest. *"That one there."*

He yanked it from the rack.

"Just the coat."

He nodded, slipped it from the hanger, and let the pants fall to the floor. Turning, he limped back through the band room, through the broken door, and down the hallway. Within a minute he was outside, climbing over the fence to the street where he'd parked his Malibu.

"You were marvelous," they cooed. *"Glory will soon be yours."*

"Yeah." The kid grinned. He opened the door and climbed inside.

They smiled. Inferiors were so easy to manipulate.

"She's gonna like this, isn't she?" he said. "She's gonna like it a lot."

They remained silent. No need to give credit where it wasn't due. After all, they were the ones taking the risks, doing the work. Still, she'd be dealt with soon enough. They hated sharing their power with anyone.

He dropped the car into gear and they took off.

"Lights. Don't forget your lights."

He snapped on the lights as they headed toward the 10 freeway. Next stop, Santa Monica, home of Deputy Chief Robert Wilson. They approached the entrance ramp and he reached into his pocket, running his fingers over the cold, serrated blade of a hunting knife. A smile spread across his face as he pressed the accelerator to the floor and they shot onto the freeway.

"DAD?" SEAN FELT the bed jostle. "You awake?"

Someone was on Beverly's side. Funny, after all this time he still considered it her side. And more often than not he felt guilty when he woke and discovered he was taking his half out of the middle.

"Dad?"

"I'm awake," he mumbled.

"Movie's in. I got coffee going."

Consciousness slowly blossomed in his brain. Sunday morning. *Star Wars.* With effort, he pried open his eyes—well, one eye—enough to tell there was still no sunlight in the room. "What time is it?"

"Almost six. Come on."

He felt the covers peeling back and grabbed for them but was too late. "All right, all right," he groused. "Give me a minute."

"Well, hurry!" The bed bounced again as Elliot hopped off and crossed to the door. "It's Episode Four, *A New Hope*. Luke finally gets to meet Obi Wan."

"I know," Sean answered, pumping as much civility into his voice as he could at six in the morning.

And he did know. After seven or eight viewings of the entire series, he knew them by heart—down to the last cheesy bit of dialogue. Still, all the books on fatherhood, courtesy of his sister and other well-meaning friends, said these were the times to cherish. Because, according to one text: "As the male adolescent matures, he will enter a season in his life where he finds the company of his parents less desirable." Sean knew they were on the cusp of that season and he didn't want to seem unapprecia-tive. But lying there in the dark, he had to admit that part of him would not mind if, at least for this morning, it came a bit more quickly.

So, with that cheery bit of guilt for motivation, Sean dragged his feet over the side of the bed and sat up. The air was dry and cold. Elliot had the AC turned way up again. On more than one occasion, they'd talked about the waste of energy (actually, the waste of money), and Sean would mention it again when the time was right. But not now. His son was too excited.

"Dad . . ."

"All right, all right." He rose, found his cargo pants on the floor, slipped into them, and searched for his flip-flops. It had been three days since he'd contacted the detective at Robbery Homi-cide Division about the girl's dream of Manet's *The Fifer*. And for three days he'd kept his ears tuned to the news and police reports, waiting to hear of another high-profile murder. Fortunately, there was none. Plenty of violence and a few killings—it was that time of year—but nothing remotely resembling her dream. That was good news. Especially for the girl.

Oddly, and more times than he could count, his mind had drifted back to her. Not just because of her beauty, though it was exceptional, but because of that face. It seemed so true. In some ways it reminded him of the Madonna and Child paintings he'd studied in school. Despite her fear, her face was an open book, filled with an innocence that both attracted and concerned him. He'd heard it in her voice as well. Despite the difficulty she had speaking to him in the hallway and more recently explaining her second dream to him over the phone, there was no guile, no irony. Just plain, soft-spoken truth.

He grabbed a UCLA Bruins T-shirt from a chair, gave it a sniff, and slipped it on. He'd no sooner pulled it over his head than his cell phone rang from its charger on the dresser. Wondering who would be calling at this time in the morning, he crossed to it and flipped it open. "Hello?"

"Picasso?"

He had his answer. "Yes?"

"Hate to ruin your beauty sleep, but I need your butt out here at Santa Monica."

"Pardon me?"

"Thirteen fifty Pearl Street. We just lost another one: Robert Wilson."

"Dad," Elliot called from the living room.

"Who?"

"The deputy chief of your bureau, dipstick."

Sean closed his eyes.

"Get over here and see if he matches what the preacher kid told you."

"But"—Sean cleared his throat—"it's my day off."

The voice chuckled. "Yeah, right. I'll see you in twenty." The phone went dead.

"Hello?" Sean stared at the display, then hit redial. He hesitated a moment, then slowly disconnected.

"Daaad . . ." Elliot moaned from the other room.

Reluctantly, he punched number two on his phone's speed dial and waited for his sister to pick up.

———

THE SMELL HIT Sean the moment he stepped into the modest, three-bedroom home. It was like cheap hamburger opened after the expiration date. But it was more than a smell. It was a taste. It lingered at the back of his tongue. Hamburger plus something else—tangy, metallic, like sucking on a copper penny. He felt himself starting to gag and he wanted to spit, but of course he did neither. Not with half a dozen patrolmen, detectives, and LAPD criminalists passing back and forth from the hallway. They wore face masks and white latex gloves. Despite the activity, no one spoke. He stood in the living room, unsure what to do.

"You're late."

He turned to see Killroy pass him as he headed into the hallway.

"I had to drop off my kid."

"You're old enough to reproduce?" Killroy shook his head. "Another reason for passing out condoms in elementary schools." He disappeared into the farthest bedroom.

Sean stood, unsure whether to follow or stay where he was. From day one, the academy drilled into their heads the dangers of contaminating a crime scene.

Cowboy helped make up his mind. "Picasso!" The man's voice bellowed from the bedroom. "Get your sorry butt in here."

Sean quickly strode down the hall. With each step the smell grew more pungent, the taste more tangible. He entered the room and collided with a Special Investigation Division officer who carried a white paper bindle, no doubt holding fibers or hair. The officer muttered a curse at him as she passed and headed out into the hallway.

The bedroom was spacious, with royal blue wallpaper covered in tiny lotus blossoms. The furnishings were eclectic—heavy Spanish American, Early Colonial, on-sale Ikia. A large photograph of a sailing yacht hung on one wall, a silk screen of bamboo trees hung on the opposite. Every light in the room was on, but the drapes had been pulled to prevent the sun from destroying any DNA. To his left an officer was painting the wall around the bronze light switch. The fact that he was wearing goggles and special gloves indicated he was using Ninhydrin, a solution for capturing fingerprints on the more porous objects. To his right, another detective was carefully sketching the scene.

And in the center, sprawled on the bed, was the star attraction, South Bureau Deputy Chief Robert Wilson. His face was dark and bloated, difficult to recognize. On his chest he wore a black uniform coat with brass buttons. A darker stain ran from his throat and spilled down a white sash stretching diagonally from his shoulder to his waist.

Cowboy stood beside the head of the bed, tie tucked into his shirt, hovering over the corpse. Like the others, he wore a face mask and latex gloves. He spoke without looking up. "Over here."

Sean approached. Besides the copper and hamburger taste, there was now a putrefying stench not unlike an outhouse. He felt his face breaking into a cold, clammy sweat.

"See this?" Cowboy motioned to the body's left forearm. It was bent, slung across the chest and reaching toward the side of the face that was partially covered in a crumpled sheet. "See all these cuts?"

Sean noticed the increased saliva in his mouth and swallowed.

"Defensive wounds."

He nodded. The egg and sausage McMuffin he'd wolfed down on the way over was starting to churn.

"So what does that tell us?" Cowboy asked.

Sean wanted to answer but felt it better to swallow back the brine filling his mouth.

Cowboy replied. "It tells us he put up quite a fight."

Sean nodded as he reached up, discreetly covering his mouth and nose.

"And the throat." Cowboy pointed to a tarry black gash in the part of the neck that was not covered by the sheet, his finger precariously close to the wound. Sean swallowed again, burping back sausage. "You can tell by the way the tissue is torn here and here that the knife was serrated. Could be military. We'll know when SDI gets back with the results. And this . . ."

But Sean no longer heard. He turned and bolted into the hallway. With luck he'd make it to the bathroom in time. But where was it? He tried the first door, a closet. The next led to a bedroom. He turned back to the hallway just in time to lean over and retch. Once. Twice. He heard officers swearing as he wiped his mouth and started to rise, then doubled over again, heaving a third time. He rose and wiped his mouth again as a female officer passed, with the encouraging comment, "You're cleaning that up, you know."

He nodded and leaned against the wall.

"Quit screwin' around," Cowboy shouted. "Get back in here."

He hesitated, unsure if he should first clean up the mess.

"Picasso!"

He headed back into the room.

Cowboy was on the other side of the bed. "What do you make of this?" he asked.

Sean moved to join him, giving the bed a wider berth.

Without glancing up, Cowboy said, "Should have got yourself a face mask. They were on the porch."

"That's all right." Sean cleared his throat. "I'm fine."

"Body gets like that after a couple days. All bloated and everything from the bacteria."

"Two days?"

"Or three. Coroner will let us know." Cowboy pushed his finger into the gash of the throat. "If you're interested, you can get a rough approximation of the time by how developed these maggots are. Flies lay them in the open wounds within the first—"

"That's okay." Sean turned away. "I'm good."

"Just tryin' to further your education, son."

"Thanks." He swallowed back another wave of nausea.

Cowboy motioned to the sash and coat. "Best guess is these were put on him after the kill." He turned to Sean. "This all the stuff she described to you?"

"Yeah. Could be."

"Could be?"

"No, I mean, yeah. They were in the painting she saw in her dream. Édouard Manet's *The Fifer*."

"Fife? That's like a flute or something?"

"Yeah."

Carefully, Cowboy pulled back the crumpled bedsheet that had been hiding the right side of the face as well as the opposite arm, which was bent at the elbow, its hand next to the head. In it was clutched a bright, silver flute. Although it had fallen slightly to the side, it was a clear and obvious attempt at duplicating the pose in the Manet painting. "So what do you think?"

A heavy sadness pressed in on Sean. "Yeah," he quietly answered.

" 'Yeah,' what?"

"It's like the painting she described. Someone was trying to imitate the painting."

Cowboy took a breath and blew it out. "That's what I figured." He turned and called across the room to his partner. "Killroy?"

"'Sup?"

"Looks like you and me got another house call to make."

"BUT THE DREAMS," Rachel repeated. "And Sarah's baby and Deborah Douglas's arthritis."

"I understand." Her father kept his eyes on the street as he drove. "And maybe in time. But not yet. And not in the manner that this Jude Miller keeps proposing."

"Why not?"

Delacroix turned to her in surprise. "'Why not'?"

She stared at him, waiting for an answer. How like his wife she was—the regal countenance, the persistence that bordered on stubborness. And, of course, the naïveté. Just like her mother, Rachel had no clue how deceptive the world could be. Particularly when it came to men such as Jude Miller. He answered, "Mr. Miller wants to turn God into a commodity. He says he's all about serving the Lord, but the truth is he's all about the Lord serving him."

"And others," Rachel insisted.

Delacroix scoffed.

"I know he seems a little . . . smooth. But haven't you seen his eyes? He really does have a heart for people. Can't you see that?"

Delacroix listened for any signs of attraction in his daughter's voice. Miller was certainly handsome and charming enough. But she'd seen through his slickness. And to Miller's credit, not once during their times together had Delacroix spotted him looking inappropriately at her. Still, he was concerned about the man's other interests. He carefully chose his words. "What I see is someone who wants to exploit and use God. Someone who wants to exploit and use *you*."

She said nothing.

He stole a glance at her before continuing. "Sending out flyers, advertisements. Treating your gifts like they're some sort of product to market."

"Haven't you always said we should be good stewards of the Lord's gifts?"

"Of course, but that's not the same as—"

"Isn't that all he's doing? Helping me be a good steward?"

"You're not ready for that, child. Not yet."

"Then when?"

He hesitated and gave no answer. She'd barely been out of the hospital six months. And despite the therapy, despite her assurances, he knew she still blamed herself for the fire. She was on the road to recovery, but had a long way to go. They drove in silence. When he glanced over, he saw her examining her hands. "Is it happening again?" he asked.

Without a word, she showed him. Her palms and fingers were scarlet red.

"When did it start?"

"Soon as we got in the car."

He reached over, and she gave him one of her hands. It was on fire.

"I know you're afraid for me," she said.

"You're barely on your feet."

"I know, but"—she nodded to her palms—"maybe God knows something we don't."

He said nothing.

"I can't be your little girl forever, Daddy."

Again he remained silent. To their left he saw a young family—husband, wife, and a baby daughter. The father was dressed in slacks and a white shirt. The mother wore a short-sleeved blouse, beige skirt, and heels.

He glanced back at Rachel. She was testing her palms with her fingers.

Up ahead, he spotted a young woman in her twenties, also in

heels. And beyond her an elderly couple shuffled along—he in a worn houndstooth sport coat, she in a faded print dress. The church was two blocks away; up one block and left on Rucker. And although part of him secretly hoped for another crowd (it felt good preaching to a full house), another part was uneasy. Very uneasy.

They approached the intersection, and he noticed the number of cars on Rucker. The street never had that much traffic, especially on Sunday. When it was clear, he turned. The sidewalks were filled with people, and every parking place had been taken. Wednesday night's service had been packed. From what he saw, this morning's would be even bigger.

"Is all of this"—Rachel's voice started to sound thin—"for us?"

He looked ahead to the church. People had spilled out onto the street. "Not for us," he said. "For you." He glanced over to see her swallowing, gazing back down at her hands. He turned to the street, surveyed the crowd, then made his decision. He picked up speed and drove past the alley that lead to his parking spot in back.

"What are you doing?" she asked.

"I'm taking you home."

"But the service, the people—"

"They can wait. It's not time. This is not God's will."

"How can you say that?"

He was directly in front of the church now, staring straight ahead so no one could catch his eye.

She held out her palms. "What about these?"

He glanced at them, searching for an answer.

"Look out!" she cried.

An SUV had suddenly stopped in front of them. He hit the brakes, tires screeching, missing it by mere feet. He watched in frustration as passengers began unloading. From the edges of his vision he saw heads turning. Someone called out, "Reverend?"

"I'm taking you home," he repeated.

"But—"

"The service will be a few minutes late. Nobody will mind if—"

The loud rap on his window startled them both. "Hey, Pastor." He turned to see Jude Miller standing outside, face beaming. Delacroix reached for his window and rolled it down.

"Some turnout," Miller said.

Delacroix motioned to the SUV. "Would you tell those folks to please—" That's when he spotted the photographer, some white kid in his twenties. And the girl, a stick-figure blonde, same age. "Who are they?"

"*Hawthorne Tribune.* I tried getting the *Times*, but no luck—at least this week." He raised his hand and motioned for the couple to join them.

"You called the press?" Delacroix asked.

"Of course. Don't want to hide that light under a bushel." He lowered his head and called through the window, "Morning, Rachel."

Without a word, Delacroix dropped the car into reverse. He looked over his shoulder and eased backward, trying to put enough space between himself and the SUV to move around it—until a car pulled up from behind, giving him no room to maneuver.

Delacroix waved his arm. "Back!" he shouted to them. "Back up!"

The car didn't budge.

"Just be patient," Miller said.

He continued inching backward until their bumpers nearly touched. Then he turned, put the Honda into drive, and cranked the wheel hard to the left.

"Pastor Delacroix?" The blonde was approaching.

There still wasn't enough room to pass the SUV. He tried again, dropping into reverse, this time tapping bumpers with the car behind him and drawing a concerned honk.

"What are you doing?" Miller asked. "You're not leaving? People came a long ways to—"

Delacroix rolled up his window and shifted into drive. This time he successfully pulled into the opposing lane—though by now he had everyone's attention, including the kid who was busy firing off photos.

"Reverend?" Miller called.

"Daddy?"

He began pulling away when a black-and-white slid around the corner in front of him, lights flashing. It gave its siren a *squelch* for good measure as it skidded to a stop fifteen feet ahead. For the briefest moment he thought of backing up and driving down the lane in reverse, until he saw the bright lights of an unmarked police car in his rearview mirror, racing up from behind.

Unbelievable.

"Daddy?"

The two patrolmen up front were out of their cruiser, guns drawn, positioning themselves behind their respective doors. "This is the police," a beefy, bald one shouted. "Turn off your ignition and step out of the car."

"What's going on?" Rachel cried.

"Just sit tight, child." He glanced back in the rearview mirror, saw the two detectives who had been at their house last Monday also climbing from their car. Guns were raised as they cautiously approached—the hawk-nosed one on Rachel's side, the good ol' boy on his.

"What's the problem, Officers?" Miller called to them.

"Step away from the car," the good ol' boy ordered.

"I don't understand. What's the—"

"Now! Step away!"

"Okay, okay," Miller said, backing toward the curb.

Hawk Nose was the first to arrive. He tapped on Rachel's window. "Open the door and step out of the car, miss."

"Daddy?" Her voice was high and trembling.

He hesitated, evaluating the situation: the patrolmen up front, the detectives behind, and, of course, the crowd.

The detective rapped harder. "Miss, step of the car."

Good Ol' Boy appeared at his door and also knocked on the glass.

Rachel turned to her father, eyes wide in fear.

Seeing no alternative, Delacroix reached to the auto lock and unlocked her side. She'd barely unbuckled before Hawk Nose threw open the door. She cried out as he took her arm.

"Hey!" Delacroix shouted. "Hey!"

But his door also opened and Good Ol' Boy grabbed him.

"Let go of me!" He unbuckled his seat belt. "Let—" Before he knew it, he was yanked out of the car and suddenly found himself transported back to Iraq. Instinctively, he grabbed Good Ol' Boy's wrist and twisted it, breaking his grip on the gun, while spinning around to deliver an elbow to his larynx.

"Daddy!"

Her scream stopped him midaction. He turned and saw her, face down on the hood, hands shoved behind her back. The image struck hard, shocking him back to reality. Realizing his mistake, he threw up his hands. "Sorry!" he shouted. "I—"

It was the right response, but a little late. The detective landed a punch into his kidney, then another into his stomach, doubling him over. He heard the scuffling of feet, the shout of the approaching patrolmen, then felt a baton slamming down onto his right shoulder.

"I'm sorry!" he yelled.

The baton struck again, dropping him to his knees.

"I said, 'I'm—'"

This time the butt of the stick smashed into his face. Delacroix heard Rachel scream but could not move. Nor did he remember falling unconscious to the pavement.

CHAPTER EIGHT

THE ELEVATOR wheezed to a stop and, after an eternity, the doors rattled open. Cowboy guided the handcuffed girl by the elbow. He could feel her trembling. Without a word, they moved down the hallway of blue green fluorescents, tan peeling paint, and pipes that had rusted orange. The basement, which housed the interrogation rooms and was seldom visited by the public, smelled like a mixture of dank concrete and disinfectant. They passed an open door to one of the small rooms where McDoogle and his partner were questioning a suspect. Both detectives stopped and watched as the suspected cop killer shuffled past. She did not look up.

Thirty minutes earlier, Cowboy had observed her in the holding cell, her arms wrapped around herself, huddled in the corner, lips perpetually moving in what must have been prayer. It struck him as odd. The guilty and hardened cons were always the most relaxed. Some actually slept. It was the innocent who were the most frightened. And when it came to being frightened, this girl won the prize. Granted, it was no cakewalk being tossed in with hookers, tweekers, and the usual degenerates, but this one ... talk about fresh meat in a shark tank. The vermin smelled fear the moment she entered the cage and they wasted little time closing in . . . until they smelled something else as well—the acrid odor of urine. Peeing her pants may have been embarrassing, but it also proved to be her saving grace, protecting her from the predators.

Now back in the hallway, Cowboy opened one of the heavy wooden doors and ushered her into the room. It was furnished with a battered table and two wooden chairs, just this side of being antique. There were no windows, and one of the two over-head fluorescents was flickering, about to go out.

"Can I get you anything?" he asked.

The girl didn't answer. No surprise there. She hadn't said a word since the arrest. Not a peep in the car or during processing. That's why he'd called Picasso . . . again. It had taken some danc-ing, but not much, to pull the kid from his current assignment and temporarily join them at RHD. The boy certainly didn't com-plain. Why would he? Robbery Homicide was only for the best of the best, and only after proving themselves a good ten, fifteen years. But this case had major juice upstairs, and once Cowboy explained the kid was the only way to reach the killer, the rest was history.

He pulled a chair out from under the table. "Have a seat. We'll get somebody here you can talk to in a minute."

The girl slumped into the chair, once again wrapping her arms around herself.

"You cold?" he said. Not that he particularly cared. Still, he felt compelled to ask.

There was a knock at the door, and he turned to see Sharon Fields. She wore a white blouse and a navy blue, Hillary Clinton power suit. Although the wardrobe was designed for respect, it was cut just low and tight enough to cultivate other interests as well. She traded looks with the girl, gave a nod to Cowboy, then stepped back into the hallway.

He turned to the girl and said, "Sure I can't get you anything?"

Again, no response.

"Just sit tight. Somebody will be with you in a minute." He turned and headed for the door, adjusting his thinning hair in the small glass window before stepping out. Fields stood a dozen feet down the hall, leaning against the wall, reading a file. "Thanks for coming down," he said.

She looked up. "That's quite a zoo you've got upstairs."

"More photographers?"

"You should be so lucky. I counted three, maybe four news vans."

He swore quietly.

"Arresting an African American pastor and his daughter on their way to church. Too bad you couldn't drown a few puppies and kick a baby along the way."

"We have evidence."

"That's right. She dreams."

Cowboy refrained from comment.

She didn't. "I hope you like fame. Because this time tomorrow you and your partner will be household names."

He sighed heavily.

Fields returned to her folder. "Where is your charming sidekick?"

"Over at the DA's, convincing him to file charges."

"And the reverend?"

"He struck an officer. Clear case of resisting arrest."

"Or protecting his daughter."

"We have witnesses."

"Members of his congregation."

Cowboy gave another sigh.

"You got some bad juju here, my friend."

He nodded. "Yeah."

"Shall I go in now? See if she'll take the test?"

"Let's wait for the kid."

"And he's . . ."

"Upstairs changing into civvies. The moron came wearing his uniform. Not exactly the human touch we were looking for."

Fields nodded. She ran her hand through that thick, beautiful hair and leaned against the wall with a sigh of her own. Any other time, Cowboy would have found it sexy.

———————

"Are you going to be okay?" Sean asked.

The girl stared down at the test booklet Dr. Fields had given her moments before.

Now it was just the two of them in the tiny room. Cowboy and Dr. Fields had stepped out in the hall to wait.

"You don't have to take it if you don't want to. It's strictly volunteer. But Dr. Fields, she thinks it will help."

She looked at Sean across the table with a gaze so innocent that he nearly glanced away. But he held his ground until she swallowed and opened her mouth. "I feel . . ." Her voice clogged and she tried again. "The doctor . . . we have a connection."

"A connection?" Sean said. "What do you mean?"

She frowned and shook her head, indicating she didn't know or couldn't explain.

"And you're okay with taking the test?"

She nodded.

"Good," he said. "Good." He knew they were on shaky ground. So far the girl had still not requested a lawyer, which was just fine with Cowboy.

"Make sure she doesn't ask for one," the detective had warned Sean. "If she brings in a suit, we won't get anything."

Dr. Fields had agreed, but for different reasons. Like Cowboy, she was interested in justice and, of course, in stopping the killings. But she also was concerned about the girl. And the more information she had on what was going on inside her head, the better her chances were of helping her.

Sean still wasn't sure what to believe about Rachel. With her sketchy past and the details from her dreams, the evidence was piling up. But he doubted she was lying. If she was the killer, she probably didn't know it. He had no proof. Only her face and those eyes. It was a weak argument that he knew came from being too soft and sensitive. But after watching his own son struggle for so many years, it was the only argument he had. Nevertheless, he'd done as he was told. He had convinced her to take the test—something called the MMPI, or Minnesota Multiphasic Personality Inventory.

"I'll, uh"—he rose from his chair, feeling her eyes watching his every move—"I'll just be outside. When you're done, let me know, okay?"

She nodded and looked down at the booklet.

"If you need anything, I'm just around the corner." Without looking back, he stepped into the hallway. Cowboy and Dr. Fields stood a few yards away.

"Nice work," Cowboy said as he joined them. "Glad you found something you couldn't screw up."

"Any problems?" Dr. Fields asked.

Sean shook his head. "No."

Apparently the answer wasn't as convincing as he hoped, and Cowboy pursued. "Except?"

He glanced up. Both Cowboy and Dr. Fields were staring at him. He cleared his throat. "Except she doesn't seem the type, that's all."

"You mean a serial killer?" Cowboy said.

"Well, yeah."

"They usually don't," Cowboy said. "At least not these." He nodded to Fields to explain.

"Sociopaths are seldom who you expect them to be," she said. "That's part of the game."

"Sociopath?" Sean asked in surprise. "Her?"

Cowboy answered. "She killed her old lady and her sister."

"She was acquitted."

"So was O.J."

Fields continued, "Sociopaths are masters of disguise. And since, unfortunately, they're incapable of feeling emotions, they have to learn to fake them—often better than most of us are able to exhibit them."

"Like one of those Photoshop pictures," Cowboy said. "So perfect you get the feeling they aren't real."

Sean scowled.

"They practice it from childhood," Fields explained. "While the rest of us learn appropriate social behavior from conscience, a sociopath has to mimic those feelings to convince others they're actually experiencing them."

"You're saying they don't have *any* conscience, no emotion?"

"None."

"That's why they kill," Cowboy said, "so they can feel something."

Fields shook her head. "That's a misconception. It's not the killing that excites them. It's the game. Most never commit violent acts. They just want to play. And win. Without emotions, their lives are boring. There is no joy except for competing and winning. They don't have to be killers. They can just as well be a coworker who sabotages your career to get ahead. Or a lover who cheats to see if they can get away with it. Or the driver who cuts you off on the freeway without a shred of guilt."

"That could be half of LA," Sean said.

"Actually, it's one out of every twenty-five people in the United States."

"You're kidding," Sean said. "One out of twenty-five?"

"Four percent. And the figure's doubled since the nineties."

He shook his head. "I had no idea."

"Most people don't. The truth is, we have more sociopaths in the United States than anorexics."

Sean took a moment to digest the fact. There was so much he didn't know. In college he was egocentric enough to think that only artists could appreciate life with all its nuanced intricacies. But during his months at the academy, he'd learned there were others who understood the vast range of human experience. For cops, it often meant delving into the underbelly of humanity. This was what his father saw and lived with every day, what he kept hidden when he came home from work. And why, Sean guessed, that after school one afternoon, he had found him hanging from the rafters in the garage.

He motioned toward Rachel's room. "So you think she's, that she's a—"

Fields shook her head. "I don't know. Her acute shyness—"

"Which could be real or make-believe," Cowboy interrupted.

Fields nodded. "Maybe. And the matter of the dreams . . ." She took a breath and let it out. "I don't know. But it's obvious somebody's playing a game with us."

"And enjoying it," Cowboy said.

The elevator at the end of the hall came to a sighing stop. The door rattled open, and out stepped a handsome black man in his early sixties. He wore a three-piece Armani suit complete with handkerchief, silk tie, and a golden watch fob. In his hand he carried a shiny alligator-skin briefcase that perfectly matched his alligator boots.

"Well, my children, which one of you is responsible for trampling all over the civil rights of my client?"

Sean recognized him instantly: Anthony T. Hathaway, champion of the poor, defender of the downtrodden, and media hound whose efforts made him an icon for any citizen of Southern California with a television set.

Cowboy stepped away from the wall. "Mr. Hathaway, so nice of you to slum it and join us."

"Where is she?"

Cowboy motioned toward Rachel's room. "In there, taking an entrance exam."

Hathaway continued forward, shaking his head. "Amazing. There's simply no end to your arrogance, is there? I don't suppose you bothered her with inconsequential details like the Miranda rights, reminding her she can ask for legal representation?"

"We did bother."

"And?"

"She doesn't speak."

Hathaway gave him a withering look. He arrived at the room and turned toward it. "Ms. Delacroix, my name is Anthony Hathaway. I am here to inform you that you are now free to vacate these lovely premises."

"Whoa, whoa, whoa." Cowboy started toward him.

Hathaway answered without the courtesy of a look. "I have just conferred with the district attorney's office."

"Yeah, and?"

"And your partner, Mr. James Killroy"—he spoke the name with the same pleasure as smelling raw sewage—"was unsuccessful in rewriting the American Constitution, thereby allowing my client to continue practicing its provisions."

"Meaning?"

Hathaway turned to him. "Meaning, my dear detective, one of you will escort this lovely lady up to the lobby, where a Mr. Jude Miller patiently awaits. Another will direct me to her father, whose future the DA was less enlightened about. And the third member of your little club will provide me with some coffee—black, three sugars, no cream."

FIVE MINUTES LATER Jude Miller was standing beside Rachel. "Sorry you can't see your father," he said. "But Hathaway's the best there is. Your dad will be out in no time." They entered the elevator, and he pressed the button for the parking garage. "Assaulting a police officer, that's tough. But we'll get him out, don't you worry."

Rachel nodded and turned, catching a glimpse of Sean staring after her. He looked away, obviously embarrassed as the elevator doors shut. He was a good man. Whatever he'd been through— and she sensed it was a lot—it had left him kind, tenderhearted. Not at all what she sensed in the others. She knew he still didn't trust her or her gifts—which was okay, sometimes she didn't trust them herself—but she knew he was good.

The patterns and connections had continued to grow, like threads of some giant tapestry appearing, then disappearing, then reappearing until an overall image began to form. That's what she'd sensed from Dr. Fields. A thread. She suspected it had to do with the woman's profession . . . like the other doctors who had worked so hard with her in the hospital, who tried to help her overcome her guilt, who explained how lots of teens burn candles in their bedrooms—though they never had an answer when she said Momma had strictly forbidden it. Still, they had tried. The same was true with Mr. Miller. She glanced at him as he checked his text messages. She knew there was a little too much flash for his own good. But she also knew there was a connection—a thread in the complex weave. Not a bright one, not like Sean, but as with Dr. Fields, an important one.

The elevator doors rattled opened to the underground garage. A black Lincoln Town Car was parked in the handicap zone to their right. Mr. Miller glanced up from his phone and started toward it. Rachel followed, confused. As they approached, a young driver close to her own age and wearing black pants and a white shirt, tie, and a cap scrambled from behind the wheel and opened the back door.

Mr. Miller finished his text and, when he saw her puzzled expression, chuckled. He motioned her toward the door and said, "You gotta play the part to be the part."

His explanation did little to help. They arrived, and she lowered her head down for a look—tinted windows, polished wood, soft, black leather seats.

Mr. Miller rounded the car to the other side. "Hop in."

She looked to the driver, who touched his cap. "Ma'am."

Ma'am? They were the same age.

"Meter's running," Miller said. He opened his door and ducked inside. "And believe me, with this chariot, every minute counts."

She finally climbed in. The car smelled of leather and cherry tobacco. Not smoke, just tobacco. On the seat in front of them hung a small plasma screen TV. Between them was a console with glowing ruby red buttons. The driver shut her door. But instead of a *clunk* or a *thud*, she felt as much as heard a quiet *woosh*. She turned to Mr. Miller, who watched with amusement.

"What," he asked, "you don't think God deserves the best?"

She didn't know how to respond.

He reached for the small cabinet of inlaid wood in front of them. "Statesmen, rock 'n' rollers, movie stars—they all ride like this. Don't you think servants of the most high God deserve to?" He opened the cabinet's door to reveal a minirefrigerator. "What would you like—Diet Coke, Seven-Up, juice, water?"

She shook her head as the car started forward. Mr. Miller grabbed a bottle of apple juice and shut the refrigerator. His phone buzzed, and he pulled it from his jacket. Checking the number, he dismissed it.

Rachel motioned to the car. "What . . . where did this . . ."

"We had a little impromptu street meeting after you and your father were arrested." He opened the bottle. "I said a few words and the people felt a need to help financially."

She frowned. He took a healthy swallow of the juice. "They know what you've done, Rachel. They see how you're standing up for Jesus, and they want to be a part of it. You can't deny them that."

The car emerged from the garage, and she was momentarily blinded by the late-afternoon sun. But the vehicle had barely crested onto the street before it lurched to a stop. Shading her eyes, Rachel saw a dozen people standing in front of them. One or two were photographers. The rest looked like normal, everyday people. The driver honked and began inching into the street where she saw not a dozen people, but thirty or forty. They swarmed around the car, men and women of all ages.

"Look at them," Mr. Miller said. "All these people. Every one of them desperate for a touch from God."

She turned to her window. Several were trying to peer inside.

"A touch only you can provide."

She looked at him.

"It's true. You know that. You've known it for years."

Someone banged on her window, and she spun around to see a pair of wizened hands cupped against the glass. An old woman had spotted her and shouted, "Rachel! Rachel!"

She stared at the woman's eyes. So anxious. So needy. Her face slipped away and was replaced by another—a young girl who was equally anxious, equally needy.

"I know you're afraid," Mr. Miller said. "I know how unworthy you feel. But doesn't God use 'the foolish things of the world to confound the wise'? Doesn't He use the 'poor in spirit' to proclaim His kingdom?"

More banging. She turned to see a meth addict, his face ravaged with acne from an insatiable hunger for sweets, his skin

stretched over bone, hair dry like straw and falling out. So desperate. So in need of God's touch. And less than six inches from her.

"The Lord won't force you, you know that. It must be your
decision. Not God's. And not your father's."

Her eyes began to burn with moisture. Was it possible? Had
the time really come?

"Remember the parable of the talents?" Mr. Miller asked. "The
good servant who loved the Lord and invested all his talents for
Him? And the fearful servant who was so afraid of Him that he
only invested one?"

She understood exactly what he meant. It was only her fear
that was holding her back.

Behind them, an older man tried crawling onto the trunk
of the car. He was that desperate. For what? For her? No. For
God. For God's touch. And maybe, just maybe, she was the
one to provide it. She saw a young mother holding her baby
above the crowd. The child's face was covered in scar tissue.
Birth defect? Accident? She didn't know. But she did know she
could help.

"I won't lie to you, Rachel. It will be difficult. At times exhausting. But since when has the Lord's work ever been easy?"

She swiped at her eyes and nodded, remembering her father's
own heart attack from the stress just a few years ago.

The car picked up speed and began pulling from the crowd.

Quietly, Mr. Miller quoted, "'The Son of Man came not to be
served, but to serve.'"

She turned and looked out the back window. So much need.
So many people desperate for His touch. As she watched, the pattern grew clearer.

"God will still love you," he said. "Regardless of your decision.
But it must be *your* decision. Not God's. Not your father's. But
yours."

She felt tears spill onto her cheeks. Their car was half a block from the garage, and stragglers were still trying to keep up, still calling her name.

"So what will it be, Rachel?" Mr. Miller's voice grew even softer. "What is your decision?"

She wiped her face and continued looking out the window. And then, almost indiscernibly, Rachel Delacroix began to nod.

PART TWO

PART TWO

Chapter Nine

S EAN SAT inside a cramped cubicle of Robbery Homicide Division, staring down a chipped mug holding the world's worst coffee. Apparently there was a grudge match between his side of the room, RHD 1, and the other side (cleverly named RHD 2) over whose turn it was to brew the joe. And since neither side agreed, that left a jar of stale instant coffee someone had appropriated from the brass upstairs. Better than nothing. Except the microwave in the kitchen was broken and the hot tap water had the taste and consistency of chlorinated sludge. You could forget about the milk or creamer, since RHD was made of real men (and real women). The same went for the sugar. There was, however, some artificial sweetener. Unfortunately, the faded pink packets were decades old and had gotten wet sometime in the eighties, hardening them into prepackaged granite.

Still, some drug was better than no drug. And well into his second shift without a break, Sean needed all the caffeine he could get. Manning up, he raised the mug, closed his eyes, and took another gulp. For a moment he thought he'd gag, but after a full body shudder he managed to hold it down.

Setting the mug just out of reach (lest there be any accidental sippings), he returned to the mound of paperwork before him. It

was important they study and catalog every piece of evidence re-
trieved from tossing Rev. Delacroix's house. They were coming up
to the forty-eight-hour mark since his arrest, and if they couldn't
find something to stick, the DA would kick him back onto the
streets before the end of the day.

Of course, Sean knew Cowboy and Killroy were using him to
do the grunt work—filling out the files, forms, and inventories
every detective loathed. But what did he expect? After all, here
he was at RHD with the best and brightest, the place every rookie
dreamed of. He also knew he'd be back on the streets as soon as
the case was done. So until then, he would treasure every over-
worked minute of every grueling day.

"Hey, Picasso."

He looked up to see Cowboy grinning down at him over the
partition.

"Got everything cataloged?"

"Uh, no." Sean scratched his forehead and sneaked in a rub at
his aching eyes.

"How 'bout them pictures?"

He glanced at the pile of artwork they'd confiscated from the
house. "Not yet."

"So what are you doin', son?" The seasoned vet raised his voice
so those in surrounding cubicles could hear. "Just sittin' around,
gettin' off on the porn?"

"No, sir, it's not porn."

Cowboy motioned to the top print, Édouard Manet's *Olympia*,
a well-padded courtesan staring brazenly at the viewer. She wore
only sandals and a bracelet. "Sure looks like porn to me."

"Actually, this one is pretty famous. It's—" His cell phone rang,
Elliot's *Star Wars* theme. What was his son doing calling him in
the middle of a school day?

Cowboy leaned farther over the cubicle to get a better look at
the print. "You don't find this sort of stuff . . . interesting?"

"No, sir, not in the way you're implying." The phrase was too highbrow, and he immediately regretted it. The theme continued to play.

"You gay, son? You know you can tell me."

Sean's face reddened. He was unsure how to respond. The phone continued. He wanted to answer it but knew better.

"That your girlfriend calling?"

"No, sir, I don't have a girlfriend."

"Then you *are* gay."

He heard the chuckles from surrounding cubicles. The phone stopped.

Cowboy continued, louder. "You got no girlfriend. You don't like pictures of naked women. Son, maybe it's time you just admit it and come out of the closet."

"No, sir."

"No what?"

"I . . . do like looking at girls."

"Well, good for you, son. That's a step in the right direction. Ain't that right, boys?"

More chuckles. A voice added, "You go, girl."

"Yes, sir." Cowboy nodded. "Just stick with us. We'll get you straight in no time."

"Sir, I'm really not—"

"Killroy's down at the Wilson autopsy. I want you to join him."

Memories of his last encounter with the corpse surfaced, heightened by the taste of RHD's coffee. It must have shown on his face because Cowboy was grinning again, obviously pleased at the reaction. "Or," he added, "you could go door-to-door with me, looking for witnesses."

"I'd . . . prefer that."

"Well, all right, then." Cowboy turned and started for the exit. "But remember, I'm straight, so no hanky-panky, you hear?"

"Yes, sir."

"Meet me down at the car in five." With that, he was gone.

Sean sat, looking at his paperwork, then the Manet print. Finally he dug into his pocket, pulled out his cell phone, and hit redial.

Elliott picked up on the first ring. "What?"

"Hey. Is everything all right?"

"Sure. Why?"

"Didn't you just call me?"

"Yeah."

"Well . . . why?"

"I don't know. I guess to tell you everything's all right."

Sean leaned back in his chair. "Oh. You just wanted to talk?"

"I gotta go."

"Sure, okay." He waited a beat, then added, "I love you, Elliot." But his son had already hung up.

The only reply came from an adjacent cubicle, "Give him my love, too, sweetheart," followed by a handful of smooches sounding throughout the room.

———

"OKAY, OKAY, SO we're down to three. Is that right, is that where we are?" The young PR executive was named Timothy. He wore designer jeans, an aqua blue T-shirt (tailored with sleeves cut at midbicep), and a pair of $250 Zara loafers (no socks). He stood by the projection screen looking calm and cool, but Rachel could tell by the way he clutched and reclutched the back of the leather chair in front of him that his mind was racing a thousand miles an hour.

Mr. Miller was seated to her left. Sarah Johnson, along with Sarah's sleeping baby, were at her right. They sat in a dimly lit boardroom halfway down a long, polished conference table that showed every smudge and fingerprint.

"That's right," Mr. Miller answered the young man. He read

from the notepad in front of him. "'Feel Good, Feel God,' 'Yours for the Asking,' and"—he flipped the page, trying to make out his writing in the faint light—"'Expect . . . Expect . . .'"

At the other end of the table another executive was standing. She wore blunt-cut bangs the color of ink and a sleeveless maroon blouse that showed off her skinny arms. With the single keystroke of a laptop computer, she brought the final slogan up on the projection screen. Gold, three-dimensional letters swept in from all sides:

Expect God's Best

Everyone stared.

The young man cleared his throat. "So, what do you think?"

"I don't know," Mr. Miller said, tapping his tablet with a pencil. "From what you've shown us, this last one comes the closest."

"That's right." Timothy nodded. "I agree."

"But to be honest, I was expecting something . . . more."

"Yeah, I know, I know. Trust me, I know." The young man cut a look to his associate. "All the good ones have been bought up aeons ago."

"Registered?" Mr. Miller asked.

"Trademarked or copyrighted," the girl said. "We could look into purchasing them if you want, but that could get pricy. Particularly if—"

"Wait a minute," Sarah interrupted her. "You mean people can buy and sell words?"

The girl cranked up a polite smile for her but made it clear she felt no need to answer.

Mr. Miller turned to Rachel. "So what are your thoughts?"

Rachel hesitated. She'd grown comfortable enough around Mr. Miller to speak, but certainly not in front of these two executives. She reached for the tablet in front of him and wrote: "Do we really need this?"

"A slogan?" Mr. Miller asked.

She nodded.

"Absolutely."

Timothy explained, "We already have a felt need, which is the first step in any campaign."

Mr. Miller nodded. "Sickness, poverty, disease . . ."

"Plus a common enemy."

Rachel frowned.

"The police," the woman answered. Rachel turned, trying to see her face past the projector's beam. "You've got yourself a real David-versus-Goliath thing going. What the cops have done to you, your father. I mean, talk about gold."

"She's right," Timothy agreed. "We've got a fantastic situation that no amount of money can buy. And we'll play it as long as it's got legs. But we also have to create a brand to identify you—so when people see the slogan, they'll think of you."

Rachel's frown deepened. She started to write, but Mr. Miller saved her the trouble. "I know, it's the Lord we want them to think about. I absolutely agree."

She looked at him, waiting for more.

"But it's what I've been saying—they can't see God, they can't touch Him." He continued a bit more gently, "But they can see *you*, Rachel. They can touch God through *you*."

She searched his face. Even in the dim light there was no missing his sincerity.

Timothy spoke up. "It's a noisy world out there, Ms. Delacroix. The average American is hit with thirty-five hundred messages a day—*thirty-five hundred*. If we want them to pay attention to yours, you've got to be heard over all that noise."

Mr. Miller gave her a nod, and she continued listening.

"In this age of mass marketing there is no better way to be heard than creating your own brand. Whatever words you pick will be how the people connect to you . . . and God. Whether it's through social networking on the Internet, the billboards we've suggested, the free Bibles, or the banners we'll be hanging at your events—whatever words we choose, when people see them, they'll think of you."

Mr. Miller agreed. "Like it or not, it's the only way to compete in today's market."

"And if I may," the girl behind the projector said, "we want to do more than compete. We want to dominate. You and God should be on people's minds more frequently than Starbucks, Wal-Mart, even McDonald's."

Timothy nodded. "And study after study, billions of research dollars insist that branding is the next step."

Rachel listened intently. She understood what they were saying. With so many other messages competing for attention, how could the average person even hope to hear God?

Mr. Miller's cell phone rang and he pulled it from his pocket. "Hello?"

Rachel continued staring at the screen. This was the twenty-first century's method of communication. And if this was how people communicated, wasn't it necessary for God to speak to them in a language they understood?

"Now?" Mr. Miller glanced at his watch. "It's not even noon. They have until the end of the day." He listened and answered, "No, I'm not complaining. Actually, it's to our advantage; we'll make the five-o'clock news." He turned to Rachel and winked. "Right. Thanks." He disconnected and turned to her. "That was our friend at Parker Center."

She waited hopefully.

"Your father will be released at three o'clock this afternoon."

Rachel beamed and Sarah hugged her in excitement.

Mr. Miller smiled. "I told you we'd get him out." He turned to Timothy. "Who do you know that's good with hair and wardrobe?"

"We've got friends who do the stars," Timothy said.

"Best in the business," the girl added.

"Great. Bring them in."

Timothy hesitated.

"Just put it on the bill." Giving him no time to reply, Mr. Miller turned to Rachel. "We've got three hours to make you look ravishing."

Ravishing? She tried to repeat the word, but it stuck in her throat.

He smiled. "Don't get me wrong; you look great now." He leaned past her to Timothy. "Doesn't she look great?"

"Great," the young man repeated, giving her a thumbs-up.

"But great doesn't cut it. Like we said, our message has to be heard above all the others. It has to be bigger, brighter, and louder."

Something about the phrase left Rachel just a little unsettled, though she couldn't put her finger on it. She glanced at Timothy, who was already on his cell making a call. Then to the girl who was doing likewise at her end of the table. She looked back to the screen:

Expect God's Best

She turned to Mr. Miller, who examined the message with growing satisfaction, then to Sarah, who was doing the same. Finally, she settled back into her chair and took a deep breath. If this was what was needed, this is what she'd do.

───────

"NICE WORK BACK there, son."

Sean gazed out his passenger window at the stop-and-go traffic on Fourth Street. Any moment he expected Cowboy's compliment to be followed by one of his zingers.

"Got to say I'm real proud of you."

Sean repositioned the cup of ice against his swollen eye.

"You say your old man is a cop?"

"Was," Sean muttered.

"Well, it shows. The way you handled yourself back there, you might have the right stuff after all."

Sean continued waiting. A verbal slam had to be there somewhere. But there was nothing. As far as he could tell, the man was serious. How was that possible? After all that went down that morning, was he actually getting a compliment? From a seasoned vet?

Initially, things had started off well enough, going door-to-door through Deputy Chief Wilson's Santa Monica neighborhood with something called a six-pack—a cardboard holder featuring six different photographs, one of them of the suspect. They showed it to neighbors and asked if any of the faces looked familiar. Of course, several had recognized Rachel Delacroix from the news reports, but no one could say she'd been in the area. Nevertheless, it didn't stop them from knocking on door after door after door. When they'd finally finished, they broke for lunch.

"Not exactly the excitement you see on TV," Cowboy had said as they entered a pizzeria on the Third Street Promenade.

"No, sir," Sean agreed.

"A real detective, a good one, is just somebody who wears out his soles while wearing down the odds." He liked the phrase so much, he repeated it. "Wearing out your soles while wearing down the odds."

The man was full of such profundities. And stories. Sean figured they'd grown a bit over the years, but he still listened politely. They ordered at the counter—a salad for Sean, and three large pieces of pepperoni pizza with a side of ranch dressing for Cowboy. Once they filled their drink cups they headed for seats at the rear of the restaurant.

"Always eat with your back to the wall," Cowboy said. "That

way you can keep an eye on the place in case something comes down. A good cop is always aware of his surroundings; remember that. And he knows how to use those surroundings to his advantage."

Sean nodded. He knew all about being "aware of his surroundings." At least in that aspect his artistic training came in handy. Even there at the pizzeria he was acutely aware of the ghetto blaster playing outside; the smells of grease, garlic, and table cleaning solution; even the dust motes glowing in the sunlight streaming from a dirty window above the door.

"And rule number one, everybody lies. Everybody." They pulled out their chairs and sat. "You gotta develop cop eyes. You gotta stop seein' everyone through them Joe College, rose-colored glasses of yours."

Once again Sean had to nod. Underneath all that country boy charm, Cowboy had some pretty good insights. Though the man did love to hear himself talk.

"'Course, the biggest headache you're gonna run into is the paperwork." He dipped one of his pizza pieces into the ranch dressing, folded it in half, and took a sizable bite. "Prelim reports filed within three days, then the sixty-dayers." He continued chewing. "And keepin' up that Murder Book." He reached for his soda and took a gulp. "Every little observation, every little scrap of evidence you find, it all goes in there." Another dip, another bite. "I mean, everything."

Sean continued listening as he spotted a young Latino with a pockmarked face and hooded sweatshirt sitting near the restroom.

"And politics." Cowboy fought a string of cheese that wouldn't let go, then gave up and shoved the rest of the piece into his mouth. "All I can say about the politics is make sure you got plenty of Chap Stick for all the butt kissing you'll have to do."

Sean continued to watch the Latino as the kid scoped out each customer who entered. He was obviously on the make. And by the look he gave an older man in a Kings' hockey jersey across the room, he had an accomplice.

"And SID?" Cowboy snorted in disgust. "You know, back in '06, I asked the Scientific Investigation Division to analyze some blood for me. A big-time murder. Syndicate thing."

Sean nodded, watching as a buff forty-year-old in black T-shirt, gym shorts, and flip-flops entered. The Latino kid glanced over at his partner in the hockey jersey and shook his head. They were looking for an easier mark—most likely someone they would follow to the car, intimidate, and rob. Sean's vision began to narrow, his pulse quickened.

"Anyways, 'cause I didn't 'yes, ma'am' and 'no, ma'am' like she wanted, I got the results back, all right—three years after the murderer was convicted. Can you believe that? Three years?"

Sean shook his head in sympathy as another customer entered and approached the counter—silver hair, white tailored shirt. Definite money. Both the kid and his partner stirred, showing interest.

Sean had two options: tell Cowboy or handle this on his own. But after being held captive in his car by a dog in the hood, hurling at a murder scene, and having his sexuality questioned at RHD, he figured it was time to start proving what he was really made of. He pushed away from the table and rose. "Excuse me," he said, "I need to wash up."

Cowboy nodded and reached for his drink as Sean crossed the room toward the kid. He doubted there would be any drama. He'd just swing by the table and casually put the fear of God into him. Cowboy would take note, Sean would explain, and the rookie would finally have something up on the scoreboard.

He arrived at the table. The Latino stared down at his plate, pretending not to notice.

"Excuse me," Sean said.

The kid glanced up, all cool with attitude.

Sean reached into his pocket to pull out his badge. "I'm with the Los Angeles Police De——"

The kid's eyes widened and he went for his own pocket.

"Hold it!" Sean ordered. "Stop!"

But the kid didn't stop until Sean, with catlike reflexes, pushed the table into him. But the kid also was quick. He dropped his hands under the table and flipped it at Sean.

"Picasso . . ." Cowboy's voice was far away.

Sean stumbled back from the impact and reached for his Glock. But he was unfamiliar with his new chest holster, and the gun stuck as the kid reached back into his pocket. With no other option, Sean leaped at him. He landed hard and they toppled to the floor, rolling with fists flying. Sean landed one into the kid's throat and another to the side of his head while catching one in the eye and several in the gut. There was no pain, not yet, just gasping for air and struggling for position. Both seemed intent on throwing a chokehold, their feet scrambling for traction on the tile wet from spilled soda. Sean landed the heel of his palm into the kid's nose. He felt the cartilage snap, heard the youth yell. The pain gave Sean time to move behind him and put him into a hold, subduing the kid, who kicked and bucked, swearing through spurting blood.

Trying to catch his breath, Sean searched for Cowboy until he spotted him standing next to the man in the hockey shirt.

"What are you doing?" the kid shouted, blood and spittle flying.

Sean gulped for air. "You're under arrest!"

"I'm a cop, you idiot!" The kid spat, reaching for his pocket until Sean shoved his face into the floor, pinning his arm behind him, which produced another tirade of oaths. With his free hand, Sean reached into the kid's pocket and pulled out a Santa Monica detective badge.

"We're on stakeout, you jackass!"

Sean looked up at Cowboy and the man in the hockey shirt. Both watched with fascinated interest.

The kid shouted into the floor. "The guy at the counter!"

Sean turned to the counter, but the man with the gray hair and white shirt was gone. He turned back to Cowboy, who looked on, cocking his head as the man in the hockey shirt folded his arms, shaking his own head in amusement.

That had been thirty minutes ago. Now, after cleaning up, Sean was back in Cowboy's car, nursing his bruised eye, and heading to Parker Center to witness Delacroix's release.

"Yes, sir," Cowboy said as they turned onto the 10 Freeway. "You might a got a detail or two wrong in procedure, and I'm sure you'll get a little howdy from Internal Affairs, but if I ever need somebody to watch my back, I wouldn't be entirely opposed if it was you. Where'd you learn to fight like that?"

"Like I said, my old man was a cop."

Cowboy slowly nodded. "Yes, sir . . . wouldn't be opposed at all."

"SO WHAT DO you think of the little dog and pony show, slugger?" Killroy asked.

"Slugger," of course, meant the question was directed to Sean. He'd been back to RHD all of fifteen minutes before word spread. And "dog and pony show" referred to the sight before them just outside Parker Center—part news conference, part pep rally—all surrounding the release of Rev. Delacroix.

"Why is it so important we stand here?" Sean asked, surveying the crowd of close to 250 people. "So they can look at us and gloat?"

Cowboy, who was fighting against the wind to keep his comb-over in place, replied, "You got the 'look at us' part right. We want 'em to know we're here."

Killroy coughed up a wad of phlegm. "And that we're not going to be forgetting anytime soon." He glanced around for a place to spit, found a large concrete planter, and used it.

"Classy," Cowboy said.

In response, Killroy cleared his throat and spit again.

They'd been enduring the hot Santa Anas for nearly thirty minutes, waiting for Anthony T. Hathaway's rhetoric to run down. And then another thirty for him to answer questions. To the attorney's left stood Rev. Delacroix. On the other side was his daughter. Her eyes never left the ground, and, to be frank, Sean's eyes barely left her. She wore a tailored silk dress, royal blue, with scoop neck, pearls, dangling earrings, and hair that fell in soft ringlets around her shoulders. Despite her slight unsteadiness in high heels, this sophisticated woman was anything but the waif he'd helped in the interrogation room just forty-eight hours earlier.

"Close your mouth, son," Cowboy said, "you're representing LA's finest."

Sean glanced away.

Eventually one of the reporters in the crowd directed his attention to Rachel. "What about the young lady? How does it feel to have your daddy a free man?"

Her eyes darted up. She glanced at Hathaway, then at another well-dressed man to her right, a spokesman named Jude Miller. Taking his cue, Miller moved to the microphones, subtly forcing Hathaway to the side.

"I think it's safe to say we are all very, very pleased that Rev. Delacroix has been released."

"Were you surprised?" another reporter asked. "Rachel, were you surprised at how quickly he was freed?"

"No," Miller replied. "None of us was surprised."

"Let her answer," another said. "Why weren't you surprised?"

Hathaway moved toward the microphones, but Miller refused

to relinquish it. "For those of you familiar with Ms. Delacroix, you know how extremely shy and modest she is in front of crowds." Rachel continued staring at the ground. "And as to why we weren't surprised—just let me say that when this young lady prays, she's used to getting answers." He turned to her. "And you prayed for your daddy, didn't you? Real hard."

She glanced up, obviously caught off-guard.

"That's right," a supporter in the crowd called out. "I've seen what happens when she prays."

"Amen!" another agreed.

"Amen, indeed." Miller chuckled. "I see several of you who attend her church are here with us today."

There was a handful of acknowledgments and a spattering of applause.

Miller continued, "And as you know from the miracles we've witnessed, the healings we've experienced—well, we've simply come to expect God's best. Isn't that right? When Rachel prays we expect God's best."

More applause.

"How's that tie in with the dreams?" a woman reporter called out. "Do you know who's going to die next?"

Rachel shifted, obviously uncomfortable with the question.

Miller replied, "That's really not why we're—"

"Let *her* speak," the first reporter said.

"She's the one with the dreams," another called.

"As I've explained, Ms. Delacroix is not—"

"What about the murders?" the woman reporter asked. "They say you saw things only a witness would know."

"Or the actual murderer," another called out.

"Watch your mouth," a hulking black man warned.

"Why don't you ask something nice?" the woman beside him agreed.

Rev. Delacroix, who'd been a poster child of patience, pressed his way to the microphones. "Listen, people. As Mr. Miller said, my daughter is not comfortable in crowds. But I can assure you this, there is no more kind and loving person on the face of this earth than—"

"You never thought she might be involved?" the woman reporter interrupted.

The question surprised him.

"What are you saying?" another supporter demanded.

"How else would she know the details?" the first reporter said.

The big black man growled, "God told her, you idiot. Ain't you been listening?"

Others agreed.

Sean watched as the friction grew.

"Please. . . ." Rev. Delacroix raised his hands, but it did no good. Hostilities had flared up and were growing hotter by the second. Cameras turned toward the crowd.

"She's got the gift!" a woman called out. "Isn't anybody paying attention?"

"Rachel, we love you!" another shouted.

More applause.

"Rachel, pray for me!"

"What about your past?" a younger reporter called. "Your time in the mental ward?"

"We love you!"

The younger reporter continued, "The rumors about killing your mother"—someone gave him a push, but he held his ground—"killing your little sister." Another push. This time he pushed back. "Watch it!" Another shove. "I said—" Someone threw a fist at him. He returned it. Others in the crowd tried to separate them. Another fist flew. A scuffle began, and people moved in. More pushing and shoving, more punches thrown.

Sean tensed, unsure what to do.

"Easy," Cowboy said. "Let the uniforms handle it."

And they did. The two officers stationed on either side of the podium drew their batons and moved in. They didn't swing the sticks, merely used them as bars to push their way toward the skirmish. Most people stepped aside, except for the individual who foolishly attacked, screaming something about God's holy prophet. He was dropped to his knees by a single blow. Outrage spread through the crowd. Others moved in, shouting at the officers, pushing until another crowd member was clubbed. And then another. The scuffle had turned into a brawl—supporters against press, police against supporters, each moment growing uglier than the last until, suddenly, over the noise, Sean heard Rachel's voice:

"Please. . . ."

He turned to see her standing at the microphones, her face filled with concern, her voice thick and husky. "Stop."

Heads turned to the podium as the skirmish quickly calmed.

"Please. . . ."

The cameras spun back around to her. Rachel took a breath and swallowed. Then she spoke again, her voice trembling. "I . . . just, I just want . . ."

The crowd grew silent. No one spoke, no one moved. Only the click of cameras filled the air.

She took another breath and tried again. But her voice would not cooperate. It had clutched into a whisper, barely discernible. ". . . to help." She looked at the microphones in front of her and was suddenly lost, unsure what she was doing. She stepped back, lowering her head, wobbling slightly in her heels. The reverend was immediately at her side as Miller beat Hathaway to the microphones.

"Did you hear that?" he shouted. "Did you hear what she said? She just wants to help." His intensity grew. "She just wants the best for us. Do you understand? That's Rachel Delacroix, ladies and gentlemen, someone who just wants us to have God's best!"

Several in the crowd started to clap; others cheered.

"That's all she wants for us: to expect God's best! That's it. Expect God's best!"

CHAPTER TEN

—————

Rev. Delacroix sat in the empty classroom. He had taken off his glasses and was rubbing his temples. The headache that had started early that morning had grown no better. The clock above the door clicked, and he looked over to see it had jumped another minute. It was now seven forty-one in the evening. Less than twenty minutes before the show.

And that's what he called it: "the show."

Jude Miller was still wrong. Delacroix was sure of it. Well, mostly sure. The piling up of events before and after his time in jail certainly had him thinking. Miller was wrong . . . but maybe Rachel wasn't. She *was* growing up. She'd certainly shown backbone by contacting the police on her own about the dreams. Twice. And he'd been more than surprised when, two weeks ago, she'd stepped up to the microphones and addressed the crowd outside Parker Center. Granted, she had spoken only a few words, but for her it had been revolutionary. His little girl had spoken to an audience of strangers.

Of course he knew this day would come. In one way or another. Even after the fire. There was a calling upon her life, and nothing would change that. But he had never expected it to arrive so abruptly. And certainly not like this. He heard the clock click again but did not bother to look. He closed his eyes, recalling the conversation they'd had with Miller just nine days earlier in the living room.

"It's a school cafeteria," Miller had argued. "It holds no more than four hundred people, tops. She spoke to nearly that many at the press conference."

Delacroix sat in his green easy chair, pretending to hear him out.

"And it's not like she'll be there by herself. I'll be right beside her the entire time. I'll do the talking, I'll do the explaining."

Rachel interrupted from the sofa. "Unless you wanted to, Daddy. Maybe you could give some sort of sermon or—"

"No," he answered curtly. "I will not be a part of this."

"A part of what?" Miller said.

"Of your showmanship. Of your exploiting."

"Exploiting what?" Miller asked. "The gifts God has given your daughter?" He pulled up a rocker and sat facing her father. "She has been given a mighty gift, sir. And He's called upon her to use it."

Delacroix remained silent, expecting there was more. He was not mistaken.

"And what is your response to that call? To act as the miserly steward? The one in the Lord's parable who buries his talents and refuses to invest them in God's glory?"

"If that's my choice, what is it to you?" Delacroix leaned forward in his chair. "You're right. I am the steward. And it is my obligation to protect the very talents you're speaking of."

"Daddy . . ."

"To make sure my girl is not exploited by snake oil sellers and con artists."

The men held each other's gaze, the room charged with electricity. Until Rachel cleared her throat and spoke. "Except . . ."

They turned to her.

"Except it's not your talent, Daddy. Not anymore."

The muscles in his jaw tightened.

She looked down at her lap and continued softly. "Maybe Mr. Miller is right. Maybe it's time I stop hiding my light under a bushel." She looked back up, imploring, but also building resolve. "Maybe it's time I put that light on a lamp stand for all to see."

It had been quite a declaration. Yes, she was indeed growing up.

The classroom clock gave another click. He looked across the desks to where she sat, her own eyes shut. If he was nervous, he could only imagine what she was feeling. Still, in the end, it had been her decision. And though he vowed to have no part of it, here he sat in the empty classroom, waiting, listening to some hand-clapping gospel choir as its music drifted down the hall from the cafeteria.

He still didn't trust Miller, no farther than he could throw him. But he also agreed with his daughter's perception. There was something deeper about the man, as if he were on a mission. Despite the questionable means, his commitment was obviously sincere. Delacroix couldn't deny that. And since when did the Lord only use perfect people with perfect means? Wasn't everyone just a little schizophrenic, a combination of flesh and spirit, clay and holiness, pure and profane?

He slipped on his glasses. "Rachel, how are you feeling?"

She opened her eyes, took a breath, then nodded. And that small, insignificant gesture pulled his heart up into his throat. Like her mother, there seemed no end to her courage. Or her faith. She would be obedient regardless of the cost.

"If I can just look into their eyes," she said. "It's like when I see their needs, then I feel God's love for them and I'm okay."

"That's how you were able to pray out loud over Deborah Douglas?"

She nodded. "And speak to the crowd at the police station. It's weird, but when that happens, it's like I'm not there anymore and I'm all right."

As a pastor, Delacroix knew exactly what she meant. It was the times he'd come home from work dead-dog tired and someone needed him for a late-night visit, or when the least likable person in the congregation needed his help—those were the times God's power seemed to surface out of nowhere, enabling him to do the impossible. And that's what his daughter was hoping to do now: the impossible.

He cleared the tightness from his throat. "I'll be ten feet away, just off the platform."

She nodded.

He heard the clock click and turned: seven forty-eight. Twelve more minutes.

Looking for something to do, he rose and stuffed his hands into his pockets. He strolled to the desk with the crackers, cheese, and vegetables. He stooped down to the cheap Styrofoam cooler underneath and pulled out a water bottle. The music grew louder as Sarah Johnson opened the door and entered. Like Rachel, she'd also purchased a new dress. It was long, lavender, and a bit too revealing for his tastes, but not as gaudy as his daughter's tightly fitted, apple red gown.

"The cafeteria is packed!" Sarah exclaimed. "They're having to bring in extra chairs!"

Delacroix shot Rachel a look. The news was supposed to be encouraging, but he knew it would have the opposite effect. Still, his daughter remained calm and poised. The fear she faced must have been overwhelming, but she refused to show it.

"Can I get you guys anything?" Sarah asked as she crossed to the table and scooped up a handful of carrot sticks.

Rachel shook her head. "I think Mr. Miller has everything covered."

Sarah nodded, munching on the carrots and glancing at the clock. "Just ten minutes to go."

Delacroix scowled at her, hoping to dampen her enthusiasm. But the girl never bothered to look in his direction. Once again his mind drifted, this time to another discussion.

"And I have your word there will be no press?" he had asked.

"None," Miller promised. "I'll have our people screen everyone." The term "our people" referred to the ushers and volunteers, mostly from the church, who Miller had been training. "She'll be completely protected, you have my word."

Delacroix said nothing, though he still considered Miller's word a bit slippery.

"I'll be by her side the entire time. I'll say a few words, make the invitation, and then our people will help those who need prayer to come forward. All she has to do is pray with them; that's it. She doesn't have to say a word, she doesn't have to do a thing. All she has to do is obey whatever the Lord tells her."

"To obey whatever the Lord tells her." That was the wild card. And what frightened Delacroix the most. Because he knew that's exactly what she would do.

"Did you see Sarah's nice work?" Rachel's voice pulled him back from his thoughts. He looked up to see her showing off her long, porcelain fingernails. "Aren't they gorgeous?"

He'd seen them earlier, thought them as gaudy as the dress. But he nodded and smiled, touched at his daughter's obvious attempt to make Sarah feel a part of the proceedings.

"I made a couple of mistakes," Sarah said with a shrug. "But I'll get better."

"I think they're perfect," Rachel said, holding them up to the light. "Don't you think they're perfect, Daddy?"

"Yes." Delacroix said. "They're very nice, Sarah."

"Thanks." The girl practically glowed from the praise.

Delacroix gave her another smile, then looked back at the clock.

THEY WERE TWO blocks away, circling the school for the third time, when he turned the wheel hard to the right and tried to approach.

"What are you doing?" they demanded.

"I want to get closer."

"No. This is as far as we are allowed."

"What are you afraid of?"

A stronger one bristled. *"We are afraid of nothing."*

"I want to kill her and I want to kill her now."

"Patience and obedience. Your time will come. But there are other matters we must first attend to."

"But you hate her as much as I do."

It was true: their hatred was no less than his—and in some ways, similar. He hated her because of her race, because his people's rights were constantly being stripped away and given to her kind. They hated her because she was not only an Inferior, but also a child of the Enemy, given privileges that should have been theirs.

"Turn around," they ordered.

He gripped the wheel tighter and accelerated. "No, I'm going into that school and—"

They clenched his gut and he gasped. He tried to fight as they pulled him down into that dark place where he was kept whenever they took control. Of course his struggle was laughable. He may have had free will once, but his constant relinquishing of control over the years had reduced his resistance to child's play.

At first their occupation had been subtle. The original cluster was cautious, gradually taking ground by twisting his awakening sexual desires. The first time he had been eleven years old. That's when he'd found his stepdad's secret stash of DVDs. Eventually he graduated to the Internet and indulged in its unlimited perversions. Soon he could not get enough. And though some part of him always knew it was wrong, especially the torture and snuffing scenes, he continued to feed his hungers, devouring everything he could find . . . until he was no longer devouring, but was being devoured.

Nevertheless, watching a host enslave and destroy himself was a minor amusement. To turn that self-hatred outward and destroy others with it, that was their real joy. And they found it by introducing him to the local chapter of skinheads.

He'd always been the runt of the litter—which was the best his drugged-out mother could say about him when she was coherent enough to say anything. But with them he found acceptance. At the meetings no one cared about his shyness and awkward social skills. No one made fun of his pronounced limp, courtesy of another stepfather, a Bible thumper whose idea of not spoiling the child by sparing the rod included powerful swats of a two-by-four to the soles of his feet—except for that one blow that missed and broke his ankle. (It had been allowed to heal "naturally," avoiding expensive ER bills and any inconvenient visit by Child Protective Services.) The point is, he may have been a loser physically and emotionally, but when he attended the secret meetings with the older kids and tatted-out adults, he belonged.

As his hatred grew, others joined the cluster, weak ones, strong ones, convincing him to feed his rage as it—as *they*—took more and more control. Soon he was terrifying younger blacks and border jumpers at school, leaving piles of burning excrement on their porches, eventually breaking windows and slashing tires. It felt good, but not good enough. The hatred grew so addictive that he graduated to more exciting crimes, violence more liberating, acts of rage no longer confined to minorities. And the time in juvie, the psychiatric hospital, even with the court-assigned shrink, proved that no one could break their hold. Their infestation was so thorough that he no longer knew where he left off and where they began. Somewhere, deep inside, the spark of free will still burned, but he no longer knew how to access it.

And if they did their job, he never would.

———————

SEAN PULLED INTO the parking lot of Jefferson Elementary, where a banner reading EXPECT GOD'S BEST! was strung between the posts of a covered walkway. It was the end of his second week with RHD and, though he was grateful to get away from the paperwork (his partners had several more cases backed up than this one), he wasn't crazy about deserting his son again. Of course, it didn't matter to Elliot. The kid was twelve. What did he care about not having a father around to nag him over homework and any of those other bothersome details distracting him from his latest X-Box?

But Traci, who was always cheerful in volunteering to look after her nephew, had started showing concern. "Is it going to be this way all the time?" she'd asked. "Aren't you entitled to have a life of your own?"

He didn't have the heart to tell her that the first unofficial question asked of RHD applicants is, "So, why do you want a divorce?" Nor did he feel inclined to mention that first-time spouses are often referred to as "starter wives." But making RHD would be a long ways off, ten to fifteen years, *if* he was lucky. For now he'd enjoy the make-believe promotion and continue the grunt work that tonight included surveillance at this South Central religious service.

He opened the door of his Ford Taurus and was immediately struck by the music—a gospel choir accompanied by organ, electric guitars, drums, and tambourines. Even from the distance he could feel the joy. Pretty refreshing compared to the gut-thumping rap he was usually subjected to in these parts. He crossed the parking lot and joined a small crowd that had not yet entered the building. Knowing it was a church service, he'd chosen to wear a sport coat and tie. Because of the heat, everyone else had dressed in shirtsleeves and cargo shorts.

"Excuse me?"

He turned to see an earnest-looking young man in glasses approach. "Are you with the press? I'm sorry, the media is not allowed."

Sean shook his head.

"Are you sure?"

"Yes, I've just come to watch."

The kid eyed him suspiciously. As the only white man in the crowd, Sean understood. For whatever reason, the kid finally nodded. "Well, okay, then."

"Thanks." Sean continued moving through the crowd until he entered a hallway just outside the cafeteria. He was surprised at the large number of wheelchairs along the wall. He expected a few invalids to show up, but this looked like a convention. To his immediate right he spotted a petite, young usher in black slacks and a white shirt. She was motioning to her empty wheelchair and shouting over the music to an elderly woman with a cane, "Are you sure you don't want to use this?"

"I'm fine, sweetheart," the woman called back. "It's just a little arthritis in the knees."

"Are you sure? We rented these as a courtesy to our older attendees. If you want, I can wheel you right to the front."

"To the front, you say?"

"Yes, ma'am."

"Well, then"—the old woman flashed a toothy grin—"what are we waiting for?"

They both laughed as the girl took her cane and helped her into the chair.

Impressed at the thoughtfulness, Sean continued to the cafeteria doors. When he opened them, the music crashed over him like a giant wave. The band stood to the left of a ten-foot-long platform near the front of the cafeteria. The choir of nearly two dozen stood to the right. What the singers lacked in pitch, they made up for in volume . . . and energy. Their faces beamed as they clapped and swayed and waved their hands, repeating the same phrase over and over again. How different this was from the church of his childhood. The "Perma-Press Presbyterians," his dad used to call them. For Sean, going to church had always been like visiting a museum. But this was more like a party. And the audience seemed just as enthusiastic as the singers. What faces he saw in the dim light were smiling, practically glowing with joy. Several were shiny with tears that he suspected were not from sadness.

At the back, where he stood, were several more people in wheelchairs. They had been stopped and were being interviewed by ushers with clipboards. Curious, he eased closer to a conversation between one of the teens and a man in his seventies. But the music was too loud to hear. Only after the usher had patted the old gentleman on the hand and rose did Sean signal for her attention. "Excuse me!" he shouted. "Excuse me?"

She turned to him.

"I'm just curious." He motioned to the clipboard. "What's that for?"

"Oh, this? It's a questionnaire."

"A questionnaire?"

"To see if they're really sick. To discuss the details of their ailment."

Sean nodded at their thoroughness.

"And to see if they're feeling the anointing."

"The what?"

"You know," she said with a grin, "to see if they're feeling any 'Holy Ghost goose bumps.'"

"Oh," Sean said. "Why is that important?"

"So we know how close to put them to the front."

He nodded, though he still didn't understand. She smiled and returned to her work, scouting for another person to interview. He continued through the crowd toward a sidewall, garnering more than a few looks. It was impossible not to feel awkward. With his sport coat and tie, not to mention self-conscious stiffness, he felt not only overdressed but overwhite. The guitar and drums pounded away as the choir continued to repeat the chorus. Though it was 180 degrees different from the angry, thumping rap music he'd heard on the street ten minutes earlier, he was struck by certain similarities. Both had a powerful impact upon the senses and the emotions. And both had a nearly hypnotic quality that drew in the listener. The difference, of course, was that one produced a sense of peace and joy, the other offered discontentment and rage. So similar and yet so different.

He arrived at the sidewall just as the crowd broke into applause. He turned and saw a spotlight catch Jude Miller stepping onto the platform. The man wore an expensive suit that shimmered in the light. "Hey there!" he shouted through a wireless headset. "Welcome! Welcome! So tell me, are you happy to be here tonight?"

"Yes!" the crowd shouted back.

"I mean *really* happy?"

"Yes!"

"And are you expecting God's best?"

"Yes!"

"Good. Because that's what Rachel is all about." He motioned to a banner hanging from the ceiling beside the band. "*Expect God's Best.* Is that why you're here?"

"Yes!" they yelled, several throwing in amens and clapping.

He cupped his ear, pretending he hadn't heard. "Why are you here?"

The crowd shouted back, a jumble of voices.

He laughed and repeated, "Why are you here?" He helped in the response, "To expect God's—"

"Best!"

"To expect what?"

"God's best!"

"That's right," he said with a chuckle, "that's right. Now, before we get started, so we don't interrupt the flow of the Spirit, I have to share a little something with you." Then, pretending to forget, he asked, "What are you here for again? To expect what?"

"God's best!" the audience shouted, then laughed and applauded.

He laughed with them. "That's right, that's right. Now, we all know Rachel's giving God all she has. Wouldn't you agree? I mean, just look around you—this auditorium, this choir, the band—she's paid for it all, right out of her own pocket. And we also know how shy she gets in front of people. I mean, I saw her a few moments ago and the poor girl was petrified."

The crowd understood, nodding, a few shouting encouragement.

"And yet she's here tonight, isn't she? She's here ready to give you everything she has."

More agreement and more applause.

"And the opposition she's having to face? Gracious me, is there a one of you who has not seen what the devil is throwing at her? How the law enforcement officers have treated her? How they've treated her own father?"

More agreement and shouts.

"And still she's here, giving her all. Just like God, she's determined to give you her very best."

Louder applause.

"And I trust, I *know*, you will want to do the same for her. I mean, here's this shy young girl facing impossible odds from every side, facing the very devil himself, and yet she comes here to you tonight, asking only that you receive."

He took a step forward, lowering his voice, becoming more intimate. "But I'm going to ask you to do something else. Just as she's giving you all that she has, just as we're expecting to receive God's very best, I want you to do something, too. I want you to give *your* best. I want you to sow seed into her life, to invest in the work she's doing for the Lord God Almighty. Will you do that for me? Will you do that for her?"

The group shouted in affirmation.

"Will you do that for the Lord?"

"Yes!"

"I said, will you do that for the King of kings and Lord of lords?"

"*Yes!*"

"I know you will. Because you're God's people. And God's people never let Him down. Now I'm going to ask this choir here, I'm going to ask this lovely choir—aren't they beautiful?"

More applause.

"I'm going to ask this lovely choir from Redeeming Glory just down the street to sing one more song for us. And I'm going to ask our dedicated young ushers here to pass those buckets around. See those buckets in their hands? And I want you to dig deep. Dig deep for God's glory. I'm not going to tell you how much to give. That's between you and the Lord. Just give Him as much as you think He deserves. That's all. Not a penny more than what He deserves. 'Cause when you dig deep, the devil we'll defeat. You hear what I'm sayin'? Dig deep and the devil we'll defeat!"

More clapping and shouts.

"And don't put it off. Don't think you'll mail it in tomorrow or the next day. 'Cause there may not be a next day. The way they're treatin' this young woman and her family, this may be your only chance."

The crowd shouted in both concern and approval.

"Because delayed obedience is *dis*obedience. You understand what I'm saying? Delayed obedience is *dis*obedience!" He turned to the choir. "Now, Mrs. Ellis, how 'bout one more song for us? Will you do that?"

The choir leader nodded and the audience broke into applause. The drummer kicked off four beats and another song began—as loud and pulsing with joy as the others—while giant red and white buckets, sporting the smiling face of Colonel Sanders, began making their rounds.

RACHEL'S FATHER WAS outraged, and he shouted over the music, "He didn't say anything about this!"

Rachel remained silent as they stood out of sight behind the band, under the green glow of an EXIT sign, watching the buckets being passed. People were already pressing down the contents so the money and checks wouldn't spill over.

"This isn't what we agreed to! You don't have to go on!"

But she did have to go on. She knew that. It was all part of the pattern. She still had no idea what it was, but she knew this was part of it.

"Just say the word. I'll go up there and tell him—"

"No, Daddy. It's okay." But of course it wasn't okay. Just as she knew she had to go on, she knew something wasn't quite right. She closed her eyes, searching in vain for some direction, some leading, but it was impossible to sense anything over the noise and commotion.

Eventually the music dropped into a vamp, a pulsing throb, and Miller stepped back into the light. "Are you ready to receive God's best?" he shouted.

"Yes!" the audience cried.

"I said, are you expecting God's best?"

"Yes!"

"Then, my friends, beloved saints of God, here she is, the Lord's very hands reaching out to us. Brothers and sisters, join with me and welcome . . . Rachel Delacroix!"

The sound of her name startled Rachel and she opened her eyes. She saw Mr. Miller motioning to her as heads turned and the crowd cheered. What slim grasp she had on God's will began to evaporate. She watched Miller stride to the edge of the platform, spotlight following. He stretched his arm toward her, and she felt her stomach tighten into a knot. But she had to do this. Steeling herself, she took a breath for determination and, despite Daddy's protest—"Rachel, no!"—she released her father's arm and started toward the platform. Her movement was restricted by her long gown, and she was still a little unsteady in her heels, but she continued forward—three, four, five steps. She noticed her legs becoming heavy, but she pressed on. She looked at Mr. Miller, who stood just a few feet away, still grinning, still holding out his hand. The next step grew even heavier, and the next nearly impossible, until her legs quit working altogether. But she would not be stopped.

If I can just look into their eyes . . . when I see their needs I'm okay.

Summoning all of her will, she turned to the audience and looked for a face. There was a young mother in the second row clutching a three-year-old. Rachel immediately sensed the child was unable to speak. She sensed something else as well—the wagging tongues of relatives. *"Is he deaf? Retarded? That's what happens when you sleep around."*

Dear God . . . The mother's lips moved in what Rachel knew to be prayer. *Please help us . . . please, Jesus. . . .* Rachel could not hear the words, but she knew the thoughts. And as she watched the young woman, the tiniest flicker of purpose began returning.

When I feel God's love for them, I'm okay.

She forced her eyes to another face. A middle-aged wife clinging to her husband who'd just been diagnosed with pancreatic
cancer. *Please, Lord, he's all I got. Please, please have mercy on
us. . . .*

Heat began spreading through Rachel's body—a warmth
flowing from her chest and into her arms, through her legs. The
fear was still very present, but there was something else now.
Something greater.

From the corner of her eye she saw Mr. Miller step off the
platform to help her up the steps, but she remained focused on
the faces, feeling their needs, hearing their prayers. As she did, her
legs grew less and less heavy until she was finally able to move.
She started up the steps, looking down to make sure she wouldn't
trip. But when she looked back up, the spotlight glared into her
eyes and the faces disappeared. She raised her hand, shielding
her eyes, but there was only light—blinding light and a faceless
crowd.

Miller turned to them and shouted, "What are you expecting?"

"God's best!" they cried.

The fear returned, washing over her like ice water. The heat in
her arms and legs disappeared, replaced by a freezing, paralyzing
dread.

"You're expecting what?"

"God's best!"

They were on the stage now, Miller holding her arm. She
turned to him for help, saw his smile, heard him telling her, "Isn't
this great? You're doing great!"

She tried to answer, but the cold had squeezed the air from her
lungs. She could only stare, her eyes wide in panic.

Still smiling, he took her right hand and turned it over.

Please, God, she prayed, *I can't do this. Stop him!*

But God did not answer. Instead, Mr. Miller held her palm

toward the sea of faceless strangers. "Can you feel the heat?" he shouted to them. "Does anyone feel the anointing?"

"Yes!" a voice yelled. It was close by, front row. Through the glare of lights, Rachel saw movement, a form rising from a wheelchair. The silhouette clapped her hands, shouting, "They're gone! They're gone! My pain is gone! I'm healed!"

But she was wrong. Rachel sensed it immediately. The bunions on the woman's feet, the ones plaguing her for years, were still there.

"I'm healed!" The woman was practically jumping. "I'm healed! I'm healed!"

The faceless crowd cheered, and a wave of dizziness struck Rachel.

More movement in the front row, to her left, someone standing. "Thank You, Jesus!" a man shouted. "Sweet Jesus! Thank You!"

And another beside him. "Glory to God! Hallelujah!"

The crowd roared.

The stage shifted. Rachel staggered and it shifted again, more violently. Her knees gave way and she began to fall, helplessly, embarrassingly . . . until she felt a hand grab her other arm. She turned to see her father. She couldn't speak, she didn't have to. He knew. He wrapped a protective arm around her waist and half-guided, half-carried her toward the steps. The faceless sea grew angry, shouting its concern and disapproval. But it didn't matter. He'd come to save her. Strong and steady, Daddy's arms helped her down the steps and toward the exit.

"It's okay, child. You'll be okay, you're all right. . . ."

She tried to nod but could not. Her legs were rubber, no longer having feeling as the edges of her vision turned pale, then white, then to nothing at all as the roaring sea faded into silence.

CHAPTER ELEVEN

RACHEL SMELLS *the fire but can see only thick, impenetrable smoke.*

"Momma!"

There is no answer, just the popping of wood and hissing of curtains as they continue to burn. But there is another sound. Children playing. And the gentle lapping of water. She squints, peering through the smoke. But she is mistaken. It is not smoke. It's a thick ocean fog that is quickly dissolving. She looks down and sees she is kneeling in sand. And instead of her mother's dark, sculptured face, she looks upon a pasty white girl with wavy brown hair. The child rests on a beige towel, eyes closed, and she is wearing a brown-and-white-striped blouse with a chocolate brown skirt.

The red firefly darts about Rachel's hand. She waves it aside and notices she is holding an ivory comb. She reaches for the girl's hair and begins to tenderly run the comb through it. An open parasol rests against the child's hip. Beyond her feet a white bonnet lies in the sand.

Suddenly there is a cry from above. At first Rachel thinks it's a seagull. But when she looks up, she sees the dark form of a man silhouetted against the moon and stars. He is falling toward her.

She lurches backward, rolling to the side just as his body strikes the sand. There is a sickening crack of bone and the oaff of air rushing from his lungs.

She scrambles back to the man to help. His eyes are open but he is not breathing. Only then does she recognize his face. He is the police detective, the skinny, mean one with the hooked nose. Blood, the thickness of her little finger, streams from his mouth. Something grazes her head and she ducks. She sees it is the white parasol gently floating down and landing upon him, rocking back and forth until it settles exactly where it had been with the little girl—the little girl who has now been replaced by the man.

Rachel rises to her feet and drops the comb. It clatters to the concrete. Concrete? She looks around. She is no longer on a beach, but in the courtyard of some apartment complex. There is a swimming pool immediately to her left that is littered with dead, floating leaves. She looks up, but instead of the moon and stars, she sees balconies looming from all sides. She searches the courtyard, spots an exit at the far corner. She turns back to the detective. Now he is dressed like the little girl, wearing her striped blouse and brown skirt.

Rachel begins backing away. Spotting movement, she turns to see her reflection in one of the apartments' sliding glass doors. She is shorter than she remembers, and she has a limp. Her face ripples, becoming the reflection of the boy with the shaved head and swastika on his neck.

She turns toward the exit and begins running along the edge of the pool . . . until the reflection leaps at her from the glass door. It hits her with such force that they both tumble into the pool, spinning and swirling. She kicks and thrashes but they are so intertwined she can't tell her arms from his arms, her legs from his legs. She fights and struggles for the surface but has no idea where it is. Her lungs begin burning for air. Each spin binds their clothes tighter, binds them tighter. She panics—squirming, punching, lungs on fire, head growing lighter and lighter until suddenly . . .

Rachel woke up, gasping for breath, drawing in deep lungfuls of air to cool the flames. Her bedsheet was wrapped around her, sodden with sweat, as tight as any straitjacket.

SEAN HEARD THE cell phone ringing. But it had been another twenty-hour day and he couldn't seem to open his eyes. He was surprised by the feel of something on his chest until he finally managed to pry open one lid and saw Elliot, facedown in a pillow, his right arm slung across Sean. Poor kid. He must have had another nightmare. It had been fourteen months since they'd buried his mother, and the dreams came less frequently. But when they came, they were just as traumatic.

Despite the ringing, Sean closed his eyes and savored the moment. He knew these times were coming to an end, and he wanted to enjoy whatever was left of them. Unfortunately, Elliot had other ideas.

"You gonna answer that or what?" his son mumbled.

Sadly, Sean removed Elliot's arm, rose, and shuffled toward the dresser, arriving at the same time the phone stopped ringing. Just as well. He turned and started back to bed.

"Hit send," Elliot muttered.

"What?"

"Send, hit send."

"Right." Sean turned back to the phone, scooped it up, and peered at the display's blue blur. Unable to make out the number, he pressed send and waited. He threw a glance to Elliot. The boy was breathing heavily, already back to sleep.

"Hello?"

He recognized her voice and felt a little jolt of pleasure. "Hello, hi," he said. "This is Officer Putnam." There was no response. "You called?" Still nothing. "Hello? Did you—"

"I . . ."

"I'm sorry? Hello?"

"I had another one." Her voice was thin and wavery.

"Another dream?" Sean glanced over to his pants on the chair. His pen and notebook were in the pocket. "Are you saying you had another dream?"

Silence.

"Hello?" He started toward his pants. "Are you saying you had another dream?"

More silence.

"Hello, did you say—"

Her voice was so faint he barely heard. "Yes."

———

Dr. Sharon Fields came at Cowboy with a spinning back fist. He easily ducked and countered with a hook to the left side of her protective headgear—not hard, just enough to remind her he knew the sport. Actually, for a woman her age, she was surprisingly agile, throwing front kicks to the chest and even trying once or twice for his head. Agile and aggressive. What she lacked in experience she made up for in determination.

Earlier, when she'd learned they both kickboxed (Cowboy for years and Fields for the past six months), it had been her idea, actually her *insistence*, that they come down to the gym and work out. Of course, Cowboy's strength and experience were much greater, but he was impressed with her tenacity. To see the little lady tear after him was kinda cute and very sexy.

It was 8:45 A.M. when Killroy and Picasso came to brief Cowboy on the girl's latest dream. He'd wanted to show off Fields's verve, and, of course, his own prowess, so he continued the workout as they filled him in. When they'd finished the briefing, Cowboy wasted little time in needling his partner. "So how many bodyguards you requesting?"

Fields came at him with a crescent kick, which he easily side-stepped.

Killroy forced a yawn. "Yeah, I'm crappin' my pants."

"Wouldn't that be skirt, partner?" Cowboy kept a careful eye on Fields as she circled. "And should I tell the coroner to only photograph from the waist up? Or do you want everyone to know that you went out like a real girl?"

Fields moved in, landing a hook kick to the side of his head followed by a half swing. He stepped back, shaking off the blows, then looked at her with a grin. She grinned back, bouncing, ready for more.

Killroy turned to Picasso. "And you say it was all in the painting?"

"Actually," the kid answered, "*she* said it was from the painting. Edgar Degas, *On the Beach, 1876.** She recognized it before I did."

Fields attacked again, looking for an inside kick. But she mis-judged the distance and came too close. They fell into a clinch until Cowboy grabbed her arms and held them to her sides so she couldn't move. When he'd proven his superiority, he released her and pushed her back. She was not happy.

"So what do you think, Doctor?" he asked.

She was breathing hard, dabbing sweat from her forehead with her glove. But still determined. "I think she's raised the stakes on you boys. You haven't been able to bust her, so she's taunting you by taking greater risks."

"But," Picasso ventured, "would she be that obvious?"

"Considering the incompetence you've displayed so far, why not?"

"Suggestions?" Killroy asked.

"Go on the offense," Fields said.

---

* To view this painting, go to http://www.nationalgallery.org.uk/paintings/hilaire-germain-edgar-degas-beach-scene.

"And pull the press down on us again?" Cowboy shook his head. "We need something a little more stealth and perp-friendly."

"Have her come see me, then." Fields started for him again, but he anticipated the move and she bounced back.

"How's that going to help?" Killroy asked.

"I know sociopaths."

"You ran the MMPI on her," Cowboy argued. "You said the results were inconclusive."

"The results were inconclusive because the test was never concluded. Hathaway interrupted it with his Johnny Cochran routine. She wants to get caught, I'll help her get caught."

Cowboy paused a moment, adjusting his gloves. "You think she would—"

Fields raced at him, throwing another spinning back kick. She barely brushed him and he took advantage, moving in, countering with a straight knee to her stomach. She doubled over with a gasping cry.

He was immediately struck by guilt. "Hey, I'm sorry. You okay?"

She stayed bent over, trying to catch her breath.

Feeling very much the bully, he approached. "Listen, I didn't mean—"

She bobbed up, caught him with a liver shot, then a right to his head. She finished the assault with a spinning kick that sent him staggering backward until he stumbled and hit the mat rear first.

He sat a moment, stunned.

"Atta baby!" Killroy said, clapping. "Beautiful!"

Still catching her breath, Fields bent over, hands on her knees. "The girl . . . likes to play games." She took two more breaths, then rose and crossed to Cowboy. "But she also wants to get caught." She offered him her hand. "All we have to do is learn her rules and help her lose."

Cowboy looked at her hand. She offered it with a nod. At last he took it and she pulled him to his feet.

CHAPTER TWELVE

J ude Miller was better than Delacroix had imagined. Right there on the platform at Jefferson Elementary, he had been able to spin catastrophe into victory. Without missing a beat, the man had played the sympathy card and played it like a genius.

"Do you see how much she loves you?" he'd shouted to the audience after Rachel had left the stage. "Did you see how that shy, timid young lady was willing to sacrifice everything she had for you?"

They had seen.

"And the power? My, oh, my, is there anyone here who did not feel the anointing, who did not feel the presence of the Lord God Almighty?"

They had felt it.

And still he continued. "If ever there's proof that 'the spirit is willing but the flesh is weak,' it's in this sensitive, sweet girl with the very power of God flowing through her. And if there's anyone here, I say *anyone* who wants their money back, who wants a refund from the Lord, just come on up and I'll give it to you right here and now." He scanned the crowd. "Anybody? Is there anybody at all?"

Of course, there had been no one. And as he continued to speak, Miller convinced them they had just seen the first, fledgling steps of a great movement of God. And because they had helped that night to launch the movement, they would share in its future glory.

He was good. There was no doubt about it. And word quickly spread.

Meanwhile, Rachel grew even more determined. No surprise there. She was a survivor. She always had been. In less than a week she was back on her feet. But not for herself. It was never for herself. It was for something greater.

"If they're God's gifts, Daddy, He expects me to use them."

And that's what made arguing with her so impossible.

"I have to be a good steward."

The reasoning was getting old, and it irritated him. But it was no less true. Despite their disagreements and their opinions about Jude Miller, truth was truth. His daughter had a gift, and she was its steward. In the long run, roadblocks and difficulties such as Jefferson Elementary proved nothing. Wasn't it the Scriptures themselves that said "Count it all joy when you encounter various trials . . . so that you may be mature, complete, and not lacking anything"?

That's what was happening to his daughter. Before his very eyes, Rachel Delacroix was blossoming, using her defeats as stepping-stones to maturity. And though he did not understand it, though it left him unable to sleep through the night, he would not resist. Which was why, when push came to shove, he was always there for her. Even when it came to allowing her to practice in the church.

It was her third day of rehearsal—standing in front of the empty chairs. With the help of some big-busted acting coach from an eighties sitcom and a speech therapist from Beverly Hills, his daughter was learning not only to overcome her fears but to maintain her grace and poise before a make-believe audience.

"Just pretend they're your best friends," the acting coach had instructed. "Or like you said, 'people in need of God's love.' Fill your mind so full of positive vibrations that there is no room for negative energy."

That was one of the exercises they ran—making her stand before the empty chairs and visualize her audience, sometimes up to an hour. And that was the exercise Delacroix interrupted when he left his accounting office for an extended lunch, picked up a couple of extra-large pizzas, and stopped by to see how things were going. It was a small gesture, but one he hoped would show his support, despite his disagreement.

"Oh, Daddy," Rachel called to him when he entered the room. "That is so sweet."

"*Sweet?*" His daughter never used that word, at least toward him. Was he already being patronized?

"But Iris here"—Rachel motioned to her acting coach—"she says I need to watch my weight."

"Watch your weight?" Delacroix looked from his daughter to the acting coach.

"That's right," Iris croaked, her voice smoke-cured by a two-pack-a-day cigarette habit. "The TV screen makes you look fifteen pounds heavier."

"TV?" Delacroix looked back at Rachel. "What are you talking about?"

Jude Miller smiled from across the room, where he'd been looking through fashion magazines with the Johnson girl. "We received a call from Seattle earlier this morning. GHN has asked your daughter to fly up and appear on their *God Is Good* show."

"You're not serious." Delacroix turned to Rachel. "You wouldn't go on that?"

"God's Holy Network has some of the highest ratings in the nation," Miller said.

"But . . . they're charlatans."

"Some of the most famous Christians in the country appear on it."

Delacroix scowled, trying to process the information.

"It's just one time, Daddy," Rachel said.

"Unless," Miller added, "you wound up in their good graces. Then they'd make you a recurring guest, a household name." He smiled. "You wouldn't mind that, would you?"

Delacroix did not wait for her answer. "No." He shook his head. "My daughter will not sell her soul to go on that program."

Looks were traded about the room.

"Nobody's selling their soul," Miller said.

Delacroix turned to him. "You've seen what they do. How they manipulate their audience." More pointedly, he added, "How they beg for money."

Miller was unfazed. "Yes, I have."

"And you agree with them?"

"No, not always."

"Then why—"

"I don't agree with the manufacturer of these chairs, either." Miller motioned to the metal folding chairs around the room. "I don't agree with how they exploit Third World laborers. But I sit on them just the same. And so do your people."

"That's entirely different."

"Is it? If you only associate with perfect people, you'd have to live in a cave by yourself."

"Those people use God to line their own coffers—buying their Mercedes, their fancy mansions, their private jets."

"Some would say that's proof of God's anointing."

"Some would say they're spiritual pickpockets!"

Sarah's baby began to fuss.

Delacroix continued, "But you're not opposed to fleecing God's sheep, are you?"

Rachel shifted, obviously wanting to speak. But she had the good sense to stay out of his line of fire.

Not Miller. His response was smooth and calm. "I am not opposed to using money from God's people to accomplish God's will."

"Jesus did not beg people for money!"

"Neither did He have to rent cafeterias, pay choirs, or lease lighting and sound equipment."

"Exactly. None of those are in the Bible."

"Nor is electricity. But you have no problem paying that bill with your congregation's money."

Delacroix strived for composure.

"Look, Reverend, I know we disagree on this. But if you're selling to today's audience, you have to use today's means."

"God is *not* a commodity to sell."

"Of course He isn't. But in today's market—"

"I know the people in this community. They can't afford next month's rent, but you had them believing that if they gave, they'd automatically receive."

"'Give and it will be given,'" Miller quoted, "'shaken together, pressed down, and overflowing.'"

"That's giving to God from your heart—not bribing Him for miracles."

"How can they expect *God's* best without giving Him *their* best?"

Delacroix felt his heart pounding. "God's best isn't always healing. Sometimes He uses sickness to accomplish His purposes."

"I couldn't agree more."

"I didn't hear that at your rally."

"Nor will you."

Delacroix simply stared.

"Actually, I can't think of anything more damaging to say— especially in a healing service. Can you imagine telling people that God may not want them healed? Not exactly a message of faith, is it?"

"Our faith is in God, not in receiving His gifts."

Unflustered, Miller again quoted, "Whatever you ask for *believing*, you'll receive."

"Satan quotes Scripture, too."

"Daddy!"

The baby started crying.

Delacroix turned to his daughter, saw the hurt on her face. "Don't you see what he's doing?"

She raised her chin. "I see . . ." But as their eyes connected she thought better of it and looked down.

"What?" Delacroix demanded. "What do you see?"

She remained staring at the floor.

"Rachel?"

But she would not answer, only shake her head.

Delacroix repeated his edict, "She will not go on that show."

There was no response.

"Do you hear me?"

The silence continued. No eyes looked at him. He had to get out of there before he said something he'd regret—as if he hadn't already. He turned and started for the doors. It seemed for every argument, Miller had an answer. Well, they weren't done yet. His smooth words and oily logic may have turned Rachel's head. But they weren't done.

He threw open the front doors and stepped into the bright sun. Hearing a commotion across the street, he squinted into the light. Three gangbangers in their late teens had gathered around a parked car, taunting its occupant.

"Quit hiding, man."

"Yeah, come out and play."

The third kid, six-pack abs showing through his open shirt, held a paper sack with one hand while sitting on the hood and banging the car with his other. "Soo-weee, piggy, piggy, piggy."

Delacroix's eyes adjusted and he saw a young white man trapped inside. It was the same car that had been parked down the block from his house the past several days and, more than once, near the church.

The first kid, white T-shirt, shaved head glistening in the heat, moved to the driver's side and shouted, "Come on out, Mr. Policeman, we'll be nice." He hit the window with his fist, then a second time, harder. They were obviously drunk or high or both. And if someone didn't bring them down, things would get ugly.

Delacroix started across the street to join them. "What you boys up to this fine autumn day?"

They looked over, then grinned.

"Hey, Rev." Six-Pack slid off the hood and tried hiding the bag behind his back. "How's it goin'?"

"It's going fine, son." Referring to the bag, he added, "A little early for that, isn't it?"

The kid produced the bag with a broader grin. "Never too early for a little fruit of the vine, Rev."

"What you making all this racket for?" Delacroix asked. "Scaring that poor white boy to death?"

"He ain't no boy," the bald guy said. "He's a pig." Turning to the driver, he grinned and slapped the window. "Ain't that right, piggy?"

The other kid, short and chunky, added, "He been stalkin' your daughter."

"And we don't like stalkers," the bald guy said. "Gives the neighborhood a bad rep."

"Soo-weee, piggy, piggy, piggy," Six-Pack repeated.

Delacroix knew the cop was showing uncommon restraint. But he also knew it wouldn't last forever. "Listen"—he shoved his hands into his pockets, appearing calm and casual—"why don't you boys head on out? I'll take it from here."

"That's okay, Rev," Six-Pack said with a grin. "We don't mind doin' our civic duty." He took a swig from the paper bag to underscore his machismo.

"That's right," the chunky kid said, "someone's gotta keep the *trash* off our streets."

"Yeah," the bald guy chuckled, "we're the local street sweepers."

"Ghet-to garbagemen." Chunky Kid reached over and bumped knuckles with Bald Guy.

"I see." Delacroix smiled. Then scratching his head, he said, "Well, I appreciate your civic-mindedness, I surely do. But that law enforcement officer and I, we've got some unfinished business to attend to. Kind of a private thing, if you know what I mean."

The kids exchanged looks.

Delacroix kept talking. "But thanks for keeping an eye out for me and the family. And if I run into any trouble, I'll give a holler."

"You sure?" Chunky Kid asked. "What if he pulls some cop crap on you?"

"I can handle him."

"Yeah?" the kid said

"He was a Marine, man," Bald Guy said. "Got them medals and everything."

"No way."

"Oh, yeah." Bald Guy turned to Delacroix. "How many ragheads you cap?"

"Thanks for your help," Delacroix repeated. He spread his arms, making it clear he was moving them on. "But I've got everything covered, trust me."

"Cool," Bald Guy said.

"Well, all right then." Chunky Kid glanced to his partners.

"He give you any trouble, just let us know," Six-Pack said.

Delacroix nodded. "I'll do that. I surely will."

Six-Pack returned the nod. He slipped off the car and pulled up his pants. "Cool." He flashed Delacroix a tilted peace sign, like they were old pals, then turned and started down the street. The other two followed.

"Just holler," Bald Guy called over his shoulder.

"Thanks, men," Delacroix said.

"No prob," Chunky Kid replied. And as they sauntered away, Delacroix heard him quietly ask, "He really pop someone?"

"Lots of 'em."

The conversation faded as they continued down the street.

When he was convinced they were gone, Delacroix strolled around the car and tapped on the passenger window. The locks clicked up and he reached down to open the door. Poking his head inside, he immediately recognized the young cop from the first visit to his home. "May I?" he asked.

"Sure," the cop said.

Delacroix entered the car and shut the door.

The young man motioned toward the boys. "Thanks."

Delacroix nodded as they disappeared down the street. "For that?"

"Yes, sir."

"You should have just got out and shot 'em. You know, show them who's in charge."

"That's not exactly my style."

"Come on," Delacroix goaded, "how else are you going to earn our respect?"

"I'm not here for respect, sir."

Delacroix scorned, "Of course you are. You all are."

The cop remained silent.

Realizing he was still a little hot from his encounter with Miller, Delacroix turned to the young man and sized him up. "You're the one who chased my daughter to the house a few weeks back."

"Yes, sir."

"The one she called up about her dream."

"Yes, sir. Both times."

The phrase caught him off guard. "*Both* times?"

"Yes, sir. The one about the flute player . . . and the other one, two nights ago."

Delacroix looked back outside. There was so much she wasn't telling him now. "She dreamed of another murder?"

"No. Nothing's happened. But she said it was like the others."

Delacroix closed his eyes a moment. "And that's why you're here. To keep an eye on her? In case she tries to kill again?"

The kid hesitated, then answered a bit more softly, "Yes, sir."

"Because you boys have already tried and found her guilty."

The kid swallowed. "Actually, we have no proof. Just the dreams. But . . . she's our only person of interest."

Delacroix turned back to him, amused at the candor. "You know, you don't always have to tell the truth. Sometimes you can lie. Comes in handy in your line of work."

"I never really got the knack of it, sir."

Delacroix took another moment to evaluate him. "Then maybe you're in the wrong profession."

The kid remained silent, and once again Delacroix wondered if he'd been too tough. There was something about this one. He was still young. Still idealistic. Well, give him time. He'd eventually turn out like the others. Delacroix gave a weary sigh. "So tell me, Officer, what exactly would it take to prove to you that my daughter is innocent?"

The kid said nothing.

"Other than telling her to stop dreaming, I mean."

More silence.

"Come on, Officer-Who-Never-Lies, there must be something."

The kid swallowed again, his Adam's apple bobbing.

"Go on," Delacroix said, "what?"

He cleared his throat. "What if you were to have—what if you were to allow one of our doctors to interview her?"

"My daughter has her own doctors. At least she did."

"Yes, sir, we know."

Delacroix gave him a look. Of course they did.

"What if one of our doctors ran some tests? If your daughter went in, of her own free will, and agreed to an examination, and if the findings were in her favor—"

"The findings *will* be in her favor."

"Then wouldn't that help eliminate the suspicion?"

"Considering your department's history of racism, I wouldn't hold my breath."

The kid looked back out the windshield.

Delacroix let a long moment pass before he asked, "So what do *you* think? About my daughter? You think she's some deranged serial killer?"

"I think"—the young man chose his words carefully—"I think she's a good, decent person, I really do. And from the few times we've talked, I believe she wants to do what's right."

"But?"

"But what if there's something wrong . . . inside her? Something even she doesn't know? What if the dreams are her way of crying out for help, of wanting to be stopped?"

"And what if Dr. Freud doesn't have all the answers?"

"Sir?"

"What if her dreams aren't some hidden, psychobabble thing? What if they really do come from God?"

The kid said nothing.

"It's certainly common enough in the Bible."

The officer fidgeted, looked back outside.

Delacroix noted the response. "I take it you're not a big fan of the Bible."

After a brief pause, he respectfully answered, "No, sir."

"Which part?"

"Part?"

"There are sixty-six books. Which ones don't you like?"

The officer frowned.

"What, you've never read them? You're not a fan of the Bible and you've never read it?"

"I guess . . . I just don't see a need for it, that's all."

"Really?"

"I mean with all of the beauty around us, with all of nature's marvels . . . I guess that's my Bible."

"I see," Delacroix said, trying to keep the amusement out of his voice.

"And the poets and artists, they're sort of my priests."

"Poets and artists."

"Yes, sir."

"They teach you that stuff at college?"

"I was an art history major."

Delacroix chuckled. "And now you're a cop."

The kid glanced away.

"My daughter loves art. But I guess you know that, too."

"Yes, sir."

Unable to leave the topic alone, Delacroix returned to it. "So you've got a college education and you've never read the Bible?"

The kid saw no need to repeat himself.

"Amazing," Delacroix said, shaking his head, "simply amazing." Another moment of silence. This time, longer. Finally, Delacroix reached for his door. "Well, let me thank you for the advice, Officer."

"Advice?"

"About seeing one of your doctors. I'll talk it over with my daughter."

He nodded.

Delacroix climbed out and turned back to him. "Oh, and son?" The officer looked at him and Delacroix motioned to the church. "You're welcome to wait inside if you want."

"I'm fine here, sir."

"You sure? I don't want to have to keep coming out here and rescuing you from us savages."

The kid remained silent.

"Seriously, we've got some warm pizza inside. And more than one of those silly old books you're not a fan of, which you're welcome to borrow just in case you ever want to know what you don't believe."

"I'm fine, sir. Thank you."

"Well, all right, then." Delacroix was about to close the door when the kid spoke a final time. "Reverend?"

He looked back inside.

"About our doctors?"

"Yes?"

"Maybe it would be a good idea if she had a lawyer with her, too."

"How so?"

"It's just good policy. To protect her rights, I mean. In case they find something." He hesitated, then repeated, "It's just good policy."

Delacroix searched the kid's face. He really was a strange one. Finally he answered, "Well, thank you, Officer-Who-Never-Lies, but they won't find anything. Of that I can assure you." Delacroix closed the door. He turned and started to cross the street. As he did, he heard the dull click of car door locks dropping back into place.

CHAPTER THIRTEEN

L OOK!" SARAH bounced her fussing baby while nodding at the news on the Town Car's TV. "There he is! There's Mr. Miller and your lawyer guy!"

Rachel raised her head from the back of the leather seat and opened her eyes. It was just past noon, and she was already exhausted. Now she understood what Mr. Miller meant when he insisted that a car and a driver would become necessities, not luxuries.

"You are God's anointed," he had said at one of the earlier rehearsals. "You need to treat yourself as such. Learn to rest and recharge so you're ready for any and all battles."

"Battles?" she asked.

"The devil won't give up ground without a fight," he said, then added with irony, "maybe you've noticed."

She certainly had.

"And if we're getting you out of school cafeterias and into The Arena by the end of the year, then it's imperative that you learn to—"

"I'm sorry," she interrupted. "The Arena?"

"That's the plan."

"The Riordan Memorial Arena?"

He smiled.

"But that's"—there was no hiding her discomfort—"that's . . ."

"Not for several months," he assured her. "Don't worry, I won't expose you to it until I'm sure you're ready. Not until you're thoroughly prepared, you have my word. But one of the ways to prepare is to know how to rest and recharge."

That's what she was trying to do now, rest and recharge. The latest battle had begun nearly four hours earlier, when they'd visited Dr. Fields's office.

First they had to push their way through a wall of reporters who had stationed themselves between the car and elevators. Someone had obviously leaked the information and Daddy, Mr. Hathaway, and Mr. Miller had to form a wedge in front of her just to shove their way into the elevator.

Once the doors shut, Daddy turned to her and asked, "You okay, child?"

She managed a nod and a faint smile. But of course they all knew better.

Then there was the doctor's waiting room. Rachel liked the giant O'Keeffe flower prints on each of the walls, and the glass furniture looked as if it was straight out of Los Angeles's Museum of Contemporary Art. But she was not crazy about the welcoming committee.

The first to greet her was the barrel-chested detective with the southern accent. "Hey there, Ms. Delacroix, thanks for comin'. You remember my partner, don't you?" He stepped aside to reveal the skinny, hawk-nosed man from her dream. The room shifted slightly and she clutched Daddy's arm a little tighter.

"Yeah." The detective smirked, reaching out to shake. "It looks like you do."

At first she could not take his hand, only look down at the blue veins and the thin, pale scar running across the back of his thumb. But he kept holding it out and grinning that awful grin until finally, under everyone's scrutiny, she found the strength and shook it. Even then, his palm felt cold and leathery, as if he were already dead.

She quickly scanned the room, hoping to see Officer Putnam. But he wasn't there. Which was too bad. If there was any reason she might have been looking forward to this meeting, it was to see him.

Dr. Fields was the last to greet her. After the formalities, she wasted little time in ushering Daddy, Mr. Hathaway, and Rachel into the safety of her office. But when Mr. Miller tried to follow, she suggested he stay in the waiting room. "The fewer people we have, the fewer the distractions." Mr. Miller wasn't crazy about being excluded. But making the best of the situation, he headed past the waiting room and downstairs to keep any remaining press members company.

The doctor's office had the same furnishings as the waiting room, but with the added bonus of a Hollywood Hills view from thirty floors up. The woman was as kind and thoughtful as Rachel remembered. After offering them juice, coffee, and some biscotti, she asked how they were faring with all the attention.

"Fine," Daddy answered stiffly, "couldn't be better." He wasn't rude, but he came pretty close.

Dr. Fields looked on sympathetically. She seemed to understand what he really meant. After a few more minutes of friendly chitchat, she finally got around to explaining the test. "There's nothing special about this," she said, passing the booklet over to Rachel. "It's the same exam you started to take at Parker Center. Doctors give it to thousands across the country. All you have to do is answer the questions as either true or false."

"And this will prove to the rest of the world that my daughter's not a serial killer?" Daddy asked.

Despite his tone, the doctor responded with gentle candor. "It will help us better understand what she's going through." She turned to Rachel. "It's been a trying time for you, and this will help us all get a better handle on what you're feeling."

Rachel nodded.

"Are you ready, then?"

Another nod.

"Good." Dr. Fields handed her a pencil. Rachel took it, opened the booklet, and began.

At first she thought the questions were kind of silly and use-less. Things like, "I would like to be a singer," "I like mechanics magazines," or "My hands and feet are usually warm enough." Others were more embarrassing: "My sex life is satisfactory," or "I have had no difficulty in starting or holding my bowel move-ment." But it was the ones about religion that Rachel found a bit unsettling: "A minister can cure disease by praying and putting his hand on your head." "Everything is turning out just like the prophets of the Bible said." She wondered that if she marked these true, the doctor would somehow think she was less stable.

In any case, the questions were easy. The fact that there were 567 of them began taking its toll. Even that wouldn't have been so bad if Mr. Hathaway didn't have to hear Dr. Fields read every question out loud before Rachel was permitted to mark her an-swer. It made the process long and tiresome, but it was the only way Mr. Hathaway, Mr. Miller, and Daddy would agree to let her take it. Originally Mr. Miller was opposed to the idea. In fact, just two nights earlier, over a dinner at Denny's, they had a long argu-ment about it.

"You're not serious?" Mr. Miller had looked up with concern from his salad. "You want to *help* the police?"

"If it will help clear her name," Daddy said.

"But it's completely contrary to our purposes."

"'Our purposes'?"

"As long as the community feels your daughter's being unfairly treated, they'll support her. Common enemy, common cause. It's the oldest trick in the book. Jesus had the Romans"—he gave his Caesar salad a poke—"we have the cops."

"I disagree," Daddy said. "The sooner we get them off our backs, the happier we'll be." He glanced over at Rachel, who was listening carefully.

Mr. Miller turned to Mr. Hathaway. "What do you think?"

The attorney chewed the ice from his iced tea for a moment before answering. "I think this good family has gone through enough controversy. And if meeting with the authorities again and taking that test will help reduce the family's hardship, I suggest we do so."

"Which, I'm sure, has nothing to do with your getting back into the limelight," Mr. Miller said.

Mr. Hathaway continued chewing his ice. "We all have a living to make, sir. Even you, with your little operation."

Of course that raised Miller's hackles, but once he settled down and they discussed the matter, he agreed that if Mr. Hathaway screened all the test questions first, he'd go along with the rest of the group.

Back in the office, nearly two hours had passed before Rachel finally finished the test. Afterward, as they relaxed over more refreshments, Dr. Fields asked if she could pose just a few more questions of her own.

"Long as I hear them first," Mr. Hathaway said, reaching for more biscotti. "It's fine with me if it's fine with her."

She turned back to Rachel. "There won't be many, I promise. And if they make you feel uncomfortable in any way, you don't have to answer. Do you feel up to that?"

"Is this really necessary?" Daddy asked.

"No. But it might help."

Rachel glanced at her father, who indicated the choice was hers. Of course, she preferred not to. The morning had been pretty stressful as it was. But since she was already there and since it would be only a few questions, she took a sip of juice and gave a nod.

"Good." Dr. Fields smiled. "Here's a tablet. I'll ask the question and if you don't feel like talking, just write down the answer."

Rachel took the paper and the questions began. Of course, they were the same ones she'd covered in the hospital: Yes, it was her candle that caught the curtains on fire. Yes, she was out of the house with Daddy when it happened. Yes, Momma had clearly forbidden having lit candles. And yes, Rachel felt totally responsible and would never forgive herself.

Dr. Fields listened intently, often nodding in understanding. All morning long Rachel had been drawn to the woman, sensing the same connection she'd felt that first time they'd met. She was definitely part of the pattern. An important part. One of the keys in helping to unlock the door for everything to make sense.

But then she stepped over the line. "Why is it, do you suppose, you always see yourself connected to the killer?"

Rachel frowned, unsure how to answer.

Dr. Fields explained. "In each of your dreams, you're not only present, but you always seem, at one point or another, to be a participant. Do you suppose that's because you could have actually—"

"And that's where we end it," Mr. Hathaway said.

"I'm sorry, I didn't mean to—"

"No, ma'am, the deed is done." The big man finished his coffee and prepared to rise. "Ms. Delacroix has already been extremely gracious in offering up so much of her time."

The doctor agreed, once again offering her apology, and Rachel nodded to make it clear she accepted. They gathered their things to leave and, as if paying penance, or at least to underline her sincerity, the doctor asked if anyone had spoken to them about a recently developed drug. "It's specifically targeted for areas of the brain involving some types of sociophobia."

"'Sociophobia'?" Mr. Hathaway asked.

"Fear of people. Particularly in groups."

Rachel and her father glanced at each other.

"Studies indicate it's quite effective in reducing anxiety for individuals struggling with those types of issues. I could write a prescription if you'd like."

"Is it safe?" Daddy asked.

"Absolutely."

Rachel's father appeared skeptical. "You're telling me there are no side effects? The last medicine they gave her, the stuff for her dreams, numbed her out, made her all cloudy-headed."

"No," Dr. Fields said. "This has nothing to do with sleep. Other than occasional reports of being overtalkative and some rare incidents of nausea, there have been no adverse side effects."

Again, Rachel traded looks with her father.

The woman rose and crossed to her desk. She picked up a prescription pad and began to scribble. "I'll give you the prescription and let you decide." When she finished, she tore off the sheet and handed it to Rachel. "And if you have any questions about it, I mean anything at all, call me." She reached for a business card in a holder on her desk. She flipped the card over and wrote on the back. "This is my direct line. Call me anytime, okay?" She gave it to Rachel. "Day or night."

Rachel took the card and managed to whisper a hoarse "Thank you."

The doctor smiled. "You're welcome."

They held each other's eyes a moment before Rachel finally glanced down. Yes, this woman was definitely part of the solution.

By the time the group reached the elevators, exhaustion had set in. More emotional than physical. But Mr. Miller, always looking out for her, had already anticipated it. Which is why he'd earlier called for the Town Car and driver. It's also why he'd ordered them to pick up Sarah Johnson to keep Rachel company on the way home. Daddy, of course, still refused to ride in the car and would be driving his own. While, with all the media presence, Mr. Hathaway and Mr. Miller felt obligated to hold yet another press conference.

Back in the Town Car Sarah pointed to the TV screen and giggled. "Look at them. It's like they're fighting over who gets to talk."

But Rachel was too tired to care. She closed her eyes and dropped her head back onto the seat. Mr. Miller was right. God's anointed did need to rest and pace themselves. Though it would have been a lot easier if Sarah's baby wasn't always fussing. She tried to be patient, knowing Sarah was doing her best. But still . . .

At last the baby quieted down and Rachel was just starting to drift off to sleep when Sarah's cell phone rang and the child started up all over again. Sarah moved the baby to her other side and pulled the phone out of her back pocket.

"Hello?" The child's cries grew louder. "I'm sorry, what?"

Rachel opened her eyes and watched as Sarah struggled with the baby. Reluctantly, she raised her arms to take him. Sarah mouthed the words "Thank you" and handed the child over to her. She pressed her finger to her ear and continued, "Who? I'm sorry?"

Despite Rachel's efforts, the baby's cries rose to screams. Rachel would definitely have to talk to her friend.

By now Sarah was practically shouting into the phone. "Timothy?" She covered the mouthpiece and whispered to Rachel: "The hottie from the PR company."

Rachel could only shake her head. Sarah thought any boy between eighteen and twenty-five was hot.

Straining to hear, Sarah shouted, "Yes? Does Mr. Miller know?" She looked at Rachel and grinned. "Uh-huh."

"What?" Rachel asked.

Sarah held up a hand for her to wait. "When? That's awfully soon."

"What is it?" Rachel repeated.

Sarah's grin broadened. "Sure, I'll tell her. No, thank *you*." Without another word, she clicked off the phone, looking like she'd just swallowed a canary.

"Sarah, what?"

"That was Timothy."

"And?"

"GHN just called."

"And?"

"And they've booked you on tomorrow night's show!"

Rachel gasped. "Tomorrow night?"

"Yes!" Sarah cried. "Tomorrow night!"

"But . . . that's so fast."

"That's what I said. And he said—"

"What?" Rachel asked. "What did he say?"

"He said, 'That's what they do with rising superstars!'"

Rachel stared in disbelief as Sarah grabbed her hands and began bouncing on the seat. "Isn't that incredible? Isn't that incredible?"

Rachel could only nod, dumbstruck . . . as the baby continued to scream.

Chapter Fourteen

I'M JUST saying what you always say." Rachel followed her father from the hallway into the living room. "'By your fruits you will know them.' Isn't that what you always say?"

He spun around. "I always say it because the Lord said it."

"Exactly. And I believe it's true." She held his eyes with her own. But he could see they were already growing moist—so honest and sincere, even in their fights. And full of such love that he was the one who had to look away. Because he could not give in. Not on this. On this there would be no compromise.

He continued into the kitchen.

She remained on his heels. "Look at all the people who watch their show. All the millions they reach. Compare that to . . ." she dropped off, but he knew exactly where she was going.

"Compare that to what?"

"Nothing."

"No, compare that to what? Our fifteen, twenty members?"

She glanced down, her silence speaking volumes.

"Well, let me tell you something, missy. Numbers are not an indication of success." He opened the refrigerator, looking for something to eat. It was nearly one in the morning. He wasn't hungry, but he needed something to do.

And still she held her ground. "Are you saying God doesn't care about the number of people we reach?"

He pushed aside the milk, searching. "I am responsible for the depth of my ministry. God is responsible for its width." He opened the vegetable bin. He hated vegetables. "The prophet Isaiah preached forty years, pleading with Judah to repent. And do you know how many converts he had? Did you know how many people followed him?"

She didn't.

"Zero. Not a one. Would you call him a failure?" He slammed the fridge door and headed for the cupboards.

"Daddy, nobody's calling you a failure."

"But you're calling those people on TV a success."

"I'm just not being so quick to judge them."

He opened the cupboard searching for chips, pretzels, anything. "Quality beats quantity. Every time. God would rather we touch a few lives deeply than a million superficially."

"Really?"

"Yes, really."

"'This is to my Father's glory, that you bear *much* fruit,'" she quoted.

He closed the cupboard and headed back into the living room.

She followed. "'Much fruit,' Daddy. That's what Jesus said. And that's what those people are doing on TV, bearing more fruit than you or I or our old-fashioned ways could ever bear. Not in a hundred years."

He slowed, then turned. "And this is what you want to do. Regardless of what I say, you've made up your mind."

She swallowed and raised her chin. It may have quivered slightly, he couldn't tell, but she managed her answer. "Yes."

He stood there, studying her, once again seeing her mother. Finally he spoke. "Then go." For a moment he was lost, unsure what to do, before turning and starting for the front door.

"I want you to come with me."

"No."

"Daddy."

"No." He turned to her a final time. "It's one thing to call me a failure. It's quite another to rub my nose in it." He scooped up the keys from the table near the door.

"Where are you going?"

"Mr. Emerson is sick. He may be going to the hospital."

"But you're hungry. I can make you something. Do you want me to—"

"I'll swing by Burger King."

"Will you be home before I leave?"

"Do you have a ride to the airport?"

She faltered, glanced down. "Mr. Miller's sending a car."

Of course. What did he expect? They stood another moment. But there was nothing more to be said. Nothing he could do to convince her. When she looked up, the moisture filling her eyes had spilled onto her face. But she'd made her decision. So had he.

He opened the door and stepped outside. "I'll be praying for you" was all he said.

"Daddy?"

Delacroix wavered the briefest second. He may have heard a sob, but it didn't matter. He had to go. He closed the door and started down the steps. He knew when he returned, she would not be there.

————

SEAN SHOULD HAVE been happy. This time he actually got five hours of sleep before they called.

"Hello," he mumbled. He'd moved the phone and charger to the nightstand, where it was more convenient to answer. More convenient, but less likely for him to be coherent.

"Picasso, get your butt out here to Burbank Airport, private terminal side." It was Killroy, sounding, if possible, even crustier than usual.

Sean rolled over and squinted at his radio alarm. It glowed a crimson 5:33. It may have been 5:33 A.M. or 5:33 P.M., he couldn't remember. Not that it made much difference. Not with his schedule. "It's five-thirty," he said.

"Which means you're gonna have to break a few traffic laws to get here in time. Quit bellyaching and get moving."

"Um—"

"And pack a toothbrush."

He scowled. "A tooth——"

The line went dead. Without hesitation, though plenty of muttering, he pressed 2 on his direct dial. Time to spread the love.

"Hello?" Traci sounded as out of it as he felt.

"It's me. I just got a call from—"

"Bring him over." His sister was getting used to the routine.

And so, after dragging Elliot out of bed (literally) and dropping him off at Traci's, Sean raced up I-5 to the private terminal section of Burbank Airport. Just outside, a white and gold Gulf Stream waited, quietly whining on the tarmac. Cowboy and Killroy were in front of it, grandstanding for Miller. Rachel and her girlfriend with the baby stood nearby.

"I'm telling you, son," Cowboy said to Miller, "you try to leave and we'll arrest her right here and now."

Miller bristled. "You can't arrest her. On what grounds?"

"Resisting arrest," Killroy said.

"You can't arrest her for resisting arrest."

"And she can't fly out of the country when she's a person of interest in a murder trial."

"Given her last dream, I figured you'd sleep better knowing she *wasn't* in the area."

"Is that a threat?" Killroy asked.

"Listen," Miller said, bringing it down a notch, "I told you, we're not flying out of the country."

"Right," Cowboy drawled. "Seattle. Which is like what, a hundred miles from the Canadian border?"

"One hundred and fifteen," Killroy corrected.

"We'll be home tomorrow," Miller said.

"Not if you go to jail today."

"This is absurd." Miller reached for his cell and started to dial.

"Son, if your lawyer weren't there a minute ago, he won't be there now."

"Who said I'm calling my lawyer? Sunday morning news always needs a little spicing up."

The detectives traded looks.

"So"—Killroy did his best to sound bored—"you're going to turn this into another circus by calling your media pals?"

"That's up to you."

"Actually," Cowboy said, "we'll have you packed up and out of here 'fore anyone shows."

"'Course, he'll still have his one call," Killroy said.

"Maybe he will, maybe he won't."

Miller held his ground. "Who's threatening whom, Detective?"

And so the standoff continued. No one paid particular interest to Sean's arrival except Rachel, who stole a couple of looks at him. The first was a nod of recognition. The second was a faint smile that moved something inside him. He'd heard the medication Dr. Fields had prescribed might relax her enough to talk a bit. Well, there was no time like the present to find out. But even as he started toward her he heard the alarms going off. Unwise, very unwise, particularly given his attraction to her. Still, he'd taken great pains to keep her at a distance. To build a professional wall. He could do this. He had to do this. It was part of the job.

As he approached Rachel and her friend, he wished them a "Good morning."

They returned the greeting, Rachel's eyes holding his a moment before looking at the ground.

"So, uh, you're going to Seattle?"

She nodded, then glanced over to his partners. "If they let me."

"They want her to go on TV," her friend said. "The *God Is Good* show." She shifted the baby to her other hip. "It's a super-big deal."

"Ah." Sean nodded. "Well, that's a good thing, then. Isn't it?"

"Yes," Rachel softly answered.

He smiled and she returned it, causing his heart to swell a little in his chest. "That's good, then," he repeated. "I'm happy for you."

"Thanks." She looked back to the tarmac.

He knew her friend was eyeing them, but he'd left no clues, done nothing to indicate his feelings. Meanwhile, Cowboy and Killroy continued their show.

"This is totally unacceptable," Miller complained.

"Actually, I think it's good police work." Cowboy turned to his partner. "Wouldn't you agree?"

"Absolutely," Killroy said.

Miller shook his head in disgust, obviously aware they were yanking his chain. He glanced over at Rachel, then at Sean.

"So what'll it be?" Killroy asked.

Miller watched Sean another moment before answering. "You gentlemen want to keep an eye on Ms. Delacroix, correct?"

"Very good," Killroy said.

Cowboy nodded. "I told you he wasn't completely deaf."

"You said he was dumb."

"No, I said he was stupid. You said he was dumb."

"Please," Miller said with a sigh, "can we get on with it? If you think she needs to be watched, why don't one of you accompany us to Seattle?"

Killroy turned to his partner. "You're right, he is stupid."

"No, listen," Miller said. "There'd be no expense involved. It's not like your department would have to buy a plane ticket. And it's only for twenty-four hours."

The detectives exchanged looks.

Miller continued, "We'll pick up the meals, the hotel, all expenses."

There was a brief pause as the detectives stopped to weigh the offer.

"Seattle's not in our jurisdiction," Cowboy said.

"She's not under arrest," Miller answered.

"Just twenty-four hours?"

"Twenty-four hours."

Cowboy turned to his partner. "What do you think?"

"Not me, man," Killroy answered. "I got a boatload of paperwork."

"Well, not me," Cowboy said. "I hate flying, you know that."

"You're the lead on this case," Killroy argued. "If anybody should—"

"I'm tellin' you, I'll be puking my guts out the entire flight."

Killroy shrugged and turned back to Miller. "Sorry. There's nobody we can spare."

Miller motioned over to Sean. "What about him?"

"Who?" Cowboy asked. "Picasso?"

"He's just a rookie," Killroy said.

"You have him parked outside her church and home doing surveillance."

"Well, yeah, but—"

"So just park him outside her hotel. What's the difference?"

The detectives frowned. It was an unusual request, but one that seemed to make sense. Sean continued to listen, his suspicions rising.

Finally Cowboy turned to him and called, "So what do you think, kid? You up to visiting Seattle for a day?"

Sean blinked, unsure how they wanted him to respond.

"Got a toothbrush?" Killroy asked.

Suddenly everything made sense. "Well, yeah, it's right in the—I've got one in the car."

"Really?" Cowboy said.

"That works out nicely," Killroy added.

"Fate," Cowboy agreed.

Killroy turned back to Sean and ordered, "Well, don't just stand there. Get a move on."

"Yes, sir." Sean turned and started back through the terminal to the parking lot.

"And don't dally," Cowboy called. "These people got important appointments to keep."

CHAPTER FIFTEEN

I LOVE YOU, son." Sean waited for a reply, but the boy had already hung up. Big surprise. The call had lasted less than a minute.

"So how's school?" he had asked.

"Fine."

"And the kids?"

"They're fine."

"What about homework?"

"Fine."

"How's Aunt Traci treating—"

"Fine. Dad, everything is fine."

Fine. The new f-word his son had started using to close him out of his life. A word Sean was beginning to find as odious as the original. He ended the call and, sitting on the expansive terrace overlooking Lake Washington, he breathed in the smell of the water and newly mowed grass. Any minute now they'd be picking up Rachel and her entourage (which he was apparently a part of) to take them to the studios of God's Holy Network. And if today's events were any indication of what tonight would hold, it would be another gaudy, gold-plated tour through *The Twilight Zone.* Though he doubted the gold would be plated.

The Gulf Stream had been more than impressive. Luxurious white carpet, calfskin seats, polished beryl-wood paneling and, yes, honest-to-goodness gold-plated faucets in the lavatory—along with green Italian marble and gilded mirrors. But most surprising, was the dog run. Not only had a trough been custom-built into the floor and filled with sand, but it had an automatic pooper-scooper. One push of the button and a bar would run its entire length, automatically removing any and all doggie doo-doo.

Jesus never had it so good.

Miller had seated Sean in the back of the plane, away from Rachel and her friend. He'd no doubt spotted the growing attraction. Certainly not on Sean's part. He'd taken every precaution to conceal the fact. But Rachel was another matter. With that open-book honesty of hers, along with her growing ease around him, her interests were becoming obvious. More than once he caught her glancing over her shoulder to check up on him. The plane had landed at Boeing Field, just south of Seattle, where they boarded a helicopter and were whisked off to the estate overlooking Lake Washington. The ride was as impressive as the private jet, although nothing compared to their greeting and subsequent tour.

"Welcome, welcome, welcome!" Stephie-Ann Jameson was practically jumping up and down as she joined them on the landing pad not far from the mansion. Handing off her two white shih tzus to an assistant, she threw her arms around Rachel as if they were old friends. "Praise God, I am so thrilled you could make it. Thrilled, thrilled, thrilled!" She pushed aside her ruby red coiffure, which blew in lacquered clumps from the rotor's downdraft.

Rachel returned the woman's greeting with only the slightest flinch. Sean could tell she still felt awkward, but he was proud to see the way she held her own. Introductions were made all around, Stephie-Ann greeting each with an enthusiastic hug and a blinding, bleach-toothed smile.

"And this is Sean Putnam," Miller finally said, "Rachel's . . . bodyguard."

"And that's some body he has." She laughed, giving him a wink.

It wasn't a come-on, not with Stephie-Ann. It was simply more of her unbridled excitement—her porcelain-tight face always smiling, the bracelets on her wrists always jangling.

"This is quite a spread you have here," Miller said, taking in the meticulously manicured grounds and two-story colonial mansion.

"Yes." Stephie-Ann beamed. "Our Lord is so good. Listen, we've got plenty of time before the broadcast. Let me show you around a little—unless you want to freshen up first."

"No, no," Miller said, "let's see how you've been blessed." Then with a smile to Rachel, he added, "So we'll know what to prepare for."

"Amen." Stephie-Ann laughed. "Make it so, Jesus, make it so." And after she ordered her assistant to call up another helper for the luggage, the tour began.

Sean brought up the rear as they passed a pair of tennis courts, then a swimming pool with a sandy beach entrance at one end and a large waterfall at the other. Just beyond that lay a corral for Michael and Gabriel, two miniature ponies no more than three feet high. And past that was Stephie-Ann's latest acquisition, a topiary where the bushes were not shaped and trimmed to look like animals, but like Bible scenes . . . Abraham with a knife poised in his raised hand standing before his son lying on the altar, Moses holding his staff over two long rows of rhododendrons manicured to look like the parting sea, Noah and the ark, complete with pairs of giraffes, anteaters, antelopes, and an elephant couple holding trunks. At the very top of the knoll stood the topiary's crowning glory: a life-size depiction of Jesus Christ hanging on the cross.

"Isn't that incredible?" Stephie-Ann asked, her voice thickening with emotion as she looked up to it.

No one answered, for reasons Sean could only imagine.

Eventually they turned and headed back down the hill to the mansion. Once inside, they were greeted by a bubbling three-tier fountain, a grand, sweeping stairway, and a magnificent Waterford crystal chandelier. The floor was made of white polished marble, and everywhere Sean looked he saw statues of angels—big ones, small ones, some in recessed alcoves, others in windows, others on tables. Each had a loving, serene face, their bodies so graceful and feminine you could almost smell the perfume. Sometimes Sean thought he could.

"They remind me of the angels protecting us," Stephie-Ann explained. She took Rachel's arm in hers as they started up the stairway. "Because people like you and me, we're always under attack. The devil, he's got this big, red bull's-eye painted right on our backs. But," she said with a sigh, "that's the cross we have to bear if we're serious about obeying God's call."

Rachel listened carefully, digesting every word.

"Oh, girl"—Stephie-Ann gave Rachel another squeeze and patted her hand—"there's so much you need to know about. So many things I've got to tell you." She looked over at Miller. "And you, too. There's lots of mean-spirited people out there, and plenty of land mines that Satan has laid for those of us called into this type of service."

Miller nodded. "I am sure there's much you can teach us. And Rachel appreciates every bit of wisdom you can share."

"Yes," Rachel agreed hoarsely. "Thank you, we really appreciate it."

"Oh, it's my pleasure, sweetie, my pleasure."

"By the way," Miller asked, "where is Mr. Jameson? Where is Samuel?"

"Oh, he doesn't stay here. He lives over at the other house."

"Ah." Miller nodded. "How many do you have? Houses, I mean?"

"In Washington? Just the two."

"And elsewhere?"

"Well, let's see. The ministry owns thirty-two in the United States. And another five overseas. Then, of course, there're the condos in Aspen and St. Thomas."

"That's a lot of homes."

"Yes, it is." She giggled. "God is so good. It's such a wonderful testimony of His faithfulness, isn't it?"

"Yes," Miller agreed, "it certainly is."

"And completely paid for. Our ministry is entirely debt-free."

"That's amazing."

"And not through any of our doing. No, sir. It's all because of our sweet little partners. I love them so much. Do you know some of them are living on only a few dollars a day? It's true. But they're always ready to do God's bidding. Such dear, dear souls. I love every one of them to pieces."

And Sean believed her. From the moment they'd stepped off the helicopter, he'd been suspicious, looking for signs of a con artist on the make. But try as he might, he could find no duplicity in her. Yes, she was overexuberant. But her love seemed genuine. She believed every word she said.

They reached the top of the stairway. The hall stretching before them had the same marble floor, several more angel statues, and a series of smaller fountains along the wall. He counted eight twelve-foot-tall doors, each apparently leading to a bedroom.

"Let's see." Stephie-Ann turned to Rachel's friend. "What's your name again, sweetheart?"

"Sarah, ma'am," the girl croaked. She'd been so tongue-tied that, unlike her baby, she'd barely made a sound since they arrived.

"Well, Sarah," Stephie-Ann said as they approached the first room, "I hope you'll like what I've chosen. You and that precious little child of yours can have"—she opened the doors—"the Balm of Gilead Suite."

Everyone took a moment to stare. The room was furnished in an elaborate, Old Testament motif—large water pots, a stone grinding wheel, a golden menorah the height of a person, and an entire wall of faux rock made to look like two giant tablets of the Ten Commandments. Outside the window, a picture postcard view of Lake Washington shimmered in the afternoon light.

Sarah stood speechless.

"Do you like it?" Stephie-Ann grinned.

"Yes . . ." Sarah answered breathlessly as she hoisted the baby to her other hip and stepped inside.

"Oh, good, good. The Lord said you would. Now remember, they'll be picking us up at four-fifteen, so don't be late." She kissed the baby on the forehead and said, "You take care of your momma now, you sweet little thing, you." Then turning, she headed back into the hallway.

"I think she likes it." Stephie-Ann giggled as they continued down the corridor. She turned to Rachel. "Do you think she likes it?"

Rachel nodded with a grin.

"And now, Mr. Miller." They stopped at another pair of doors. Stephie-Ann opened them to reveal an entirely different theme: cedar paneling; broadswords; bows and arrows; leather shields; and, for a table, something that looked like a stone altar. "You get the King Solomon room."

He stepped inside, taking it all in.

"There's a full bar over there." Stephie-Ann motioned to an ornate, gold-painted chariot with drawers built into its side. "And if you like wine, we have some labels you've probably heard of but have never been able to try."

He turned to her, obviously impressed. "Thank you. That's most gracious."

"Oh, don't thank me," she said, grinning. "It's all God. Everything you see is from God." Turning to Rachel, she squeezed her arm. "Isn't He good?"

Once again Rachel nodded.

"Remember now, four-fifteen."

"I'll be ready," he said.

They turned and continued down the hall to the next set of doors.

"And for you, my dear"—Stephie-Ann looked at Rachel, hesitated, then threw open the doors with a flourish—"the Queen Esther Suite!"

Instead of a biblical theme, the walls were covered with famous art prints. Sean guessed five, maybe six dozen of them—everything from the *Mona Lisa* to some Rembrandts, to Klimt, to Klee, Homer, Goya, and the list went on—each in a gaudy, ornate frame that, more often than not, detracted from the work instead of complemented it.

Rachel stood speechless.

"Do you like it?" Stephie-Ann asked, beaming.

Rachel turned to her, obviously moved. "Yes . . . thank you. Thank you so much."

"Oh, I just knew you would!" Stephie-Ann took her hand and pulled her into the room. "I just knew!"

Sean followed, taking a tentative step inside. As far as he could tell, the place was an eclectic explosion of bad taste, as if someone had taken all the great masterpieces of the world and just thrown them against the walls. Picassos beside Giottos beside Raphaels beside Warhols beside Whistlers—each competing with the other for attention, their collision of style so painful Sean barely noticed the dining room chairs with their high, gold backs and red velvet cushions, or the canopy bed draped in royal blue silk and gold braids.

Like an excited schoolgirl, Stephie-Ann took Rachel about the room, pointing out all the little details Rachel might have missed. Eventually she motioned to a bureau, a Louis XIV reproduction—at least Sean guessed it was a reproduction. "And here we have four different hairbrushes—we weren't sure which you preferred."

"Oh," Rachel said, "I brought my own."

"I'm sure you did, sweetheart. But this is for our telethon."

"Telethon?"

"So we can auction off your hair." Suddenly Stephie-Ann frowned. "I hope that's all right. I mean, it would be such a wonderful gift for our little supporters."

Rachel glanced at Sean, then answered, "I . . . if it will help . . . sure."

"Oh, it will, sweetie, believe me, it will. Little things like that mean so much to them."

Rachel nodded, obviously still trying to grasp the concept. Stephie-Ann turned for the door. "Well, you get yourself settled. I'll be up in a few minutes and we can have some nice girl-to-girl talk, okay? There's so much I want to tell you. So much, so much, so much."

"Yes." Rachel smiled. "I'd like that."

"It's not easy being God's elect. But I promise you, if He's put the call on you, there is nothing like it." Suddenly she raced back to Rachel and squeezed both of her hands. "Oh, I can tell we're going to be such good friends. Good, good friends." Then, before Rachel could respond, Stephie-Ann turned and motioned for Sean to step back out into the hallway, where she joined him. "Isn't she sweet? And the anointing. You can just feel it, can't you?"

Sean chose to remain silent as she escorted him down the hall to the next room.

"And finally for you, Mr. Bodyguard." She opened the doors to reveal another room whose interior decorating was equally over-the-top. It was part Roman, part Greek, complete with white marble furniture, a sunken bath near the windows, and an occasional Corinthian pillar. "I call it the Samson Room . . . as in Samson and Delilah." She gave another one of her winks.

"Well . . ." He knew she was waiting for a reply, and he did his best. "It's very . . . elaborate."

"When it comes to our guests, we spare no expense. Oh, and here"—she reached into her pocket and pulled out a key that she handed to him.

"What's this?"

She motioned to a door beside his bed. "It's for the Queen Esther Suite."

"I'm sorry, I—"

"I've seen the way she looks at you."

"I—"

"And the way you don't look at her."

He started to hand the key back. "I'm sorry, this is not what—"

She brushed past him and headed back into the hallway. "Every queen needs her king. With your looks, I'm certain you've learned that by now."

"But—"

"Every queen needs her king." Without turning to him, she continued down the hall, leaving Sean standing by himself, lost for words. Calling over her shoulder, she added, "The limos will pick us up at four-fifteen. Make sure you're not late."

KILLROY OPENED HIS apartment door, a bottle of Mexican beer in hand. "You guys are late."

"Had some refreshments to pick up," Cowboy said, motioning to the pretzels in Sharon Fields's hands and the six-pack in his own.

Killroy stepped aside as the couple entered. "Mine ain't good enough for you?" he asked.

"If I wanted to drink horse piss I'd move back to the farm," Cowboy said as they passed through the living room where Billings, McDoogle, and Wolfe sat watching TV. "Hey, guys."

They nodded, and welcomed Sharon, "Dr. Fields."

She returned the greeting. "Boys."

Cowboy felt a certain pride as more than one pair of eyes lingered on her backside. The couple followed Killroy into the kitchen. Sharon set the bag of pretzels on the counter as Cowboy pulled a couple of cans from the six-pack and opened the fridge. He slid the remaining cans next to some shriveled carrots and half a gallon of something that had been milk, now on its way to cottage cheese.

Fields motioned over to the TV. "We miss anything?"

"Nah." Killroy fished a dirty bowl out of the sink. "Just some warm-up acts. She'll be on in a minute."

Only when Cowboy shut the fridge did he notice the opened box on the counter—two feet long, six inches wide. "What's this?"

"Came in today's mail." Killroy opened the pretzels and dumped them into the bowl. "A gift from my admirer."

Cowboy pushed open the lid with his can. The first thing he saw was a child's umbrella. It rested on top of a brown-striped shirt. Beside it sat a comb and a white lace bonnet. He traded looks with Sharon, then glanced at Killroy, who pretended to be watching the TV.

"So where's the skirt?" Cowboy asked nonchalantly.

Without looking, Killroy answered, "Under the shirt."

Cowboy pushed down the lid to look for the return address. There was none. "You run this past the lab?"

"Just got it."

"But you will," Sharon said, as much question as statement.

Killroy shrugged. "Tomorrow, the next day, whatever."

"Hey, guys," Billings called, "you gotta see this. Unbelievable."

Killroy scooped up the bowl and started around the counter

to join the group until Cowboy reached out his beer and stopped him. "You *will* have it tested, right?"

"Yeah, I said I would."

Cowboy held his gaze.

"It's not that big of a deal."

"Hampton and Wilson would have said the same thing."

"I said I'll have it tested, all right?" Killroy shook his head, swearing as he moved past.

Cowboy remained, looking after him, then turned back to Sharon, who was carefully studying the package.

———————

WHEN SEAN WAS a kid, he occasionally attended tapings of sit-coms and talk shows—especially when out-of-town guests wanted more than the usual diet of Disneyland and Universal Studios. And sitting in the studio bleachers watching *God Is Good* was no different. Bright lights, cameras, scurrying floor crew, and a crane that swept back and forth over the audience: these guys were defi-nitely pros. The first hour of the two-hour show was just coming to an end and Rachel still had not been introduced. She'd been men-tioned plenty of times—"the powerful young prophet persecuted by the police"—but she was still backstage waiting her turn.

In the meantime, Sean had sat through the performance of a gifted trumpet player, a gospel quartet, and the teary-eyed Stephie-Ann reading praise reports from "my dear little prayer partners." She sat on a thronelike chair of gold and rich blue vel-vet. Her husband, Samuel Jameson, a robust sixty-year-old whose chocolate brown hair showed the telltale red of a dye job going bad, sat in an identical chair beside her. Above them hung chan-deliers similar to the one Sean had seen in the mansion. To their far left stood a gazebo covered in real flowers with a real stream of water flowing past it. To their right sat a white grand piano, and behind them rose a sweeping staircase with gold banisters and red velvet carpeting that led nowhere. During the last fifteen minutes of the hour, everyone was being "blessed out of their socks" by special guest preacher Brother Billy Buckley. He was a commanding man, well over six feet, with white, luminescent hair and a gray silk suit that glistened under the lights. With a worn Bible in his hand, he paced back and forth in front of the audience like the caged wolves Sean and Elliot had seen in the LA Zoo.

"Are you tired of praying for the same thing year after year with no breakthrough?" He closed his eyes and looked to the ceiling, speaking in mock falsetto. "O Lord, help me find favor at work. O Lord, help me with this month's rent. O Lord, help me win the lotto!" He took a peek at the audience. "Now, don't look at me all innocent like that. You telling me you never prayed the 'lotto prayer' before?"

The audience chuckled.

"I hear you," he said with a grin, "I hear you. And that's okay. There's nothing wrong with wanting to be rich and paying your bills. And you know something? God wants that, too. Yes, He does. He wants to give you His best. He wants to bless His children, so we can bless others."

There was a spattering of "amens."

"But the problem is, we keep blocking that blessing. Yes, we do. The problem doesn't lie with God, it lies with us. It's our fault. God's up there wanting to bless us, but we won't let Him." He shook his head, musing, then turned to one of the cameras. "When I started out, I was just like some of you. Couldn't rub two nickels together to save my hide. But I was praying. Yes, sir, every day. Every day I was praying for a bountiful harvest: 'O Lord, bless me, bless me, bless me.' And you know what I got? Nothing. And you want to know why?" He turned from the camera and back to the audience. "I said, do you want to know why?"

"Why?" several called back.

"Because I was eating the seed! That's right. Instead of sowing into my future, instead of trusting in my God, I was living in fear. I was eating the very seed He'd given me to plant!" The preacher held up his Bible. "Our little guidebook here, it says sowing and reaping, that's the natural order of things. But I wasn't sowing and reaping, I was hoarding and keeping! I didn't know then what I know now. Whatever you keep, that's all you'll ever harvest. I'll say it again. Whatever you keep is all you will harvest!"

There were some more amens.

"But—and this is where the blessings come—whatever you plant, *that's* where the harvest will be. Because God will take it, multiply it a thousandfold, and return it to you. You see, if you plant a little seed, you'll get a little harvest. But if you plant a lot of seed—hear me now, if you plant a lot of seed—your barns will not be able to hold it all."

The audience broke into applause.

"How do you expect God to invest in you if don't invest in Him?" He raised his voice. "I said, how do you expect God to invest in you if you don't invest in Him?"

More applause and amens.

Sean shifted in his seat and glanced around at the two-hundred-plus audience. They seemed to be normal, everyday people, the neighbors next door, a homogenous mix of all classes and races. Some wore suits and dresses, others were more casual. The only similarity he did notice was that all were middle-aged or older. There was not a single young person in the crowd.

"Now, I've heard rumors, we've all heard rumors, that this show is about to be taken off the air." The man looked over his shoulder to Stephie-Ann and her husband.

Both nodded sadly.

"And you know why? I'll tell you why. For lack of funds. That's right, for the simple lack of money. 'Oh,' but you say, 'pastor, look around you. Maybe they don't need this fancy set with all this fancy furniture.'" He cocked his head toward the audience. "Really? *Really?*" He started pacing again. "Tell me, have you ever watched any other shows on television? Have you? Have you seen the money they spend? And for what? I'll tell you for what. For spewing Satan's sewage across this great nation!"

There were more amens.

"That's right. Yes, it is. And you tell me, look me straight in the eyes and tell me if you don't think that the Lord God Almighty deserves something at least as nice as what the devil's messengers get."

More agreement. Louder.

"No!" He shouted back, jabbing his finger at a camera. "You're wrong! The God of the universe deserves something a thousand times better! A billion times better!"

Louder applause.

"That's right. That's right. So tell me, are we gonna lie down and let the devil take this show away from us?"

"No!" they called back.

"Are we?"

"NO!"

He resumed his pacing. "You bet we're not. And you know how we're going to stop him? We're going to work together. That's right. Together, you and me, we're going to give the devil a black eye. I want you to have the courage—no, I want you to have the *faith*—to join with me tonight and plant some seed."

More applause.

"'Oh, but I don't have any extra,' you say. Oh, but you do." He reached into his coat pocket and pulled out a credit card. "How many of you have this little tool of the devil's?"

The group chuckled.

"Because that's what it is, you know. His tool. How many of you are already ensnared by it, all tied up by the enemy with it?"

More agreement.

"Yes, sir." He nodded. "I hear you, I hear you. But tonight we're going to break his hold. Tonight we're going to break those chains and set you free. 'Cause tonight we're gonna take Satan's tool and shove it right back in his face. You wanna be free? You want to be debt-free and never be enslaved to this thing again?"

"Yes!" the crowd shouted.

"Then this is what you do. If you want to be free of this, I mean *really* free, then you take some seed from your card and you plant it. Hear what I'm saying? You want to be free of this, then you have the faith to boldly plant it. I don't care if it's fifty dollars, a hundred, a thousand, it all depends on what you want." He held up his card. "But you take this seed and you plant it. Shove it into the devil's face and give it to God. And then you know what you do? Nothing. You just sit back. That's right, you just sit back and watch the harvest come in." He raised his voice. "You sit back and watch how God Almighty, the creator of Heaven and Earth, will use your simple act of faith and miraculously wipe away all your debt. *More* than wipe it away. He'll give you an abundance! 'Shaken together, pressed down, and running over'!"

The audience clapped and cheered.

"Yes, He will!" he shouted over them. "Yes, He will! Now take out that card. You in the audience, take it out right now." He turned toward the cameras. "And you at home, take it out. Take it out and go to your phone. Plant your seed. The greater the seed, the greater the harvest. Do you want to be free? I said, do you want to be free?"

"Yes!" the audience shouted back.

"Then break those chains! Once and for all, break the chains, because whoever the Son sets free, shall be free indeed!"

The crowd cheered and applauded.

Sean watched as people all around him reached for their wallets and purses. Half a dozen ushers appeared with credit card machines and began working their way through the rows.

"Don't hesitate. The sooner you plant, the sooner you'll harvest! And don't be afraid. Plant a little seed, you get a little harvest. Plant a lot of seed, and I guarantee you, better yet, God Almighty guarantees you"—he raised his credit card in one hand, the Bible in the other—"God Almighty guarantees you that tonight you will be totally and completely delivered. Tonight the harvest begins. Because God is faithful. You hear what I'm saying?"

"Yes!"

"Do you hear what I'm saying?"

"YES!"

"There's no end to God's richness. He has the cattle on a thousand hills, and there's no end to His goodness. The fault is not His, but ours. Don't block the flow. Don't stop Him from blessing. Because God is good all the time! You hear what I'm saying?"

Once again the crowd clapped and cheered.

"Say it with me! 'God is good . . .'" He waited, letting them yell it on their own:

"All the time!"

"God is good . . ."

"All the time!"

"Amen!" he shouted over the applause. "Amen, amen, and amen!"

CHAPTER SIXTEEN

A ND HERE she is, the precious girl everyone is talking about." Stephie-Ann motioned offstage. "The miracle worker who was arrested for her faith in Jesus, and my newest and dearest best friend . . . Rachel Delacroix!"

The audience broke into applause. Rachel took a deep breath and stepped into the bright lights. The clapping grew louder; some even began to cheer. Fortunately she was able to squint through the bright glare to see their smiling faces. As she did, any residue of fear she'd been feeling quickly evaporated. They loved her. And she loved them. Nothing could destroy the warm, velvety peace she felt washing over her. Much of it was due to the hours of training with her acting coach, though she suspected even more came from Dr. Fields's medication—the two pills she'd been taking every six hours since yesterday, plus the additional two she'd taken when they arrived at the studio, just to be safe. And when the uneasiness started to resurface while she waited in the wings, the extra one she had swallowed just ten minutes ago. It was a lot, she knew that. But Stephie-Ann had warned her something very important was going to happen and she wanted to be prepared.

"There is such an anointing on you," the woman had said as

the two traveled alone in one of the two SUV limos that took the group to the studio. "I've never felt the presence of God so strong on anybody."

Of course Rachel's heart leaped at the words.

"You are God's prophet for this generation. Do you understand me?"

She looked down, embarrassed.

"No, I'm serious." Stephie-Ann lifted Rachel's chin. "I can feel it in my spirit. You are this generation's Elijah."

Rachel could only stare, blinking.

"But God is telling me something else." She took both of Rachel's hands into her own. "The Lord God wants you to stop hiding your light under a bushel." The phrase brought back memories of the arguments she'd already had with Daddy. But there was more. Stephie-Ann closed her eyes and raised her head toward Heaven. "'It is time, my daughter.' Thus saith the Lord, 'it is time to stop doubting Me. It is time to break the shackles of your past. Yea, it is time to throw away false humility and let Me raise you up to new heights. For yea, you are My chosen one, you are My selected instrument of glory.'"

Tears filled Rachel's eyes as she drank in every word—words she had sensed but never dared to trust.

Stephie-Ann looked back at her. "The Lord is telling me that tonight is going to be your night. Tonight, on my show, you're going to step into your holy office. Oh, girl," she said with a giggle, "I'm so excited! It's like little ol' me gets to be John the Baptist. I get to introduce you to the millions of precious souls watching as you enter into your season of bearing abundant fruit."

There was that phrase again: "bearing fruit." And it wasn't just quality, as Daddy had insisted. It was also "abundant."

"God will withhold nothing from you, child. Whatever you ask, you will receive. You're special, do you understand that? You are privileged." Then, with a smile, Stephie-Ann added, "I'm afraid you're just going to have to live with that. Where others can't, you can. Because you are God's hands to His people."

Rachel's heart leaped again. Weren't those the exact words Mr. Miller had been using? When she found her voice, Rachel croaked, "But . . . what am I supposed to do? What am I supposed to say?"

"Just go with the flow, honey. God will tell you what to do. I'll be there to help, but you gotta start trusting your heart. Just follow whatever that loving little heart of yours says. Your will is His will. You'll do just fine."

Those were the words that had gripped Rachel in the limo, that remained with her as she waited in the greenroom. She was "chosen." She was "anointed." Tonight she was going to "step into 'her' holy office." And now, as she joined Stephie-Ann onstage, as the cheering continued, and the last of the medication kicked in, she knew it was true. All of it was true.

Stephie-Ann took her hands and continued the introduction, saying many of the same things she had said in the limo. But this time Rachel was able to fight off the embarrassment. This time she kept her head raised and graciously received the words. And Stephie-Ann didn't end there. Soon she began recounting Rachel's past as the TV monitors showed photographs Mr. Miller had brought along . . . photos of the family, the devastating fire, the faithful teen taking care of her daddy, South Central's poverty and prejudice, and finally the ongoing police harassment.

Stephie-Ann reached for a tissue in her sleeve and wiped her eyes. "All because they refuse to believe in the gifts God has given our precious little saint." She turned to the audience. "But we're not going to refuse, are we?"

She was met with applause of agreement.

"And do you know why? Because we've got something they don't have. We've got faith! We've got belief!"

More applause.

"Amen," Stephie-Ann said. "Amen." Once again she took Rachel's hands, but this time she looked startled. "Gracious me, child. What's happening to your hands? They're on fire."

For the first time Rachel noticed. She nodded and whispered, "It's . . . God does that when He starts to move."

"Don't tell me, sweetheart." Stephie-Ann motioned to the audience. "Tell *them*."

Rachel took a breath and turned to the audience. "My hands, they do this whenever God, whenever He begins to move."

Excitement rippled through the crowd.

"You should feel them," Stephie-Ann said. She turned back to Rachel. "So what do we do?"

Rachel looked at her, eyes widening in uncertainty.

Stephie-Ann grinned. "Tell them what God wants, honey. You are God's hands now. You're His voice. Exercise your authority."

Rachel turned back to the audience. Everyone was smiling, waiting eagerly. "God wants"—she coughed and spoke louder—"if some of you are sick . . . I think God wants to help you."

Applause and amens.

She looked to Stephie-Ann, who nodded for her to continue. Rachel turned back to the audience and repeated more loudly, "If you're sick, God wants to heal you."

The clapping increased.

"So . . ." She glanced at Stephie-Ann, but the woman only smiled, making it clear it was Rachel's call. *You are God's anointed . . . just follow your heart.* Rachel turned back to the crowd. "If you're sick and want to be healed, would you come down here so I can put my hands on you?"

The audience members looked at one another.

"You heard the girl," Stephie-Ann called. "If you have a problem, get on down here and let God's anointed heal you!" Several people started to rise. "Ushers!" Stephie-Ann motioned to a group of men and women standing to the side. "Help us form a line, right down here in front. God's going to do some mighty things, I can just feel it. Isn't that right, Rachel?"

"Expect God's best!" Mr. Miller shouted from the wings.

"Yes." Rachel nodded. "That's right." She felt more boldness rushing through her. "If you're sick, God wants to heal you." More people came forward. Others rose to join them. "God wants you to expect His best."

"What did she say?" Stephie-Ann shouted.

"Expect God's best," a few replied.

"I can't hear you."

"Expect God's best!"

Suddenly the first person in line was standing before Rachel.

"Are you expecting God's best?" Stephie-Ann asked.

"Yes," the man said in a breathless whisper.

Feeling another surge of power, Rachel repeated Stephie-Ann's words. "I didn't hear you. Are you expecting God's best?"

"Yes," the man said loudly.

Rachel grinned and reached out to him. Her hands were on fire as she placed them on his shoulder. "Then receive God's best."

Immediately, the man slumped to the floor. The crowd cheered and applauded, shouting praises to God . . . as Rachel looked on, feeling freer and more loved than she had ever remembered.

———

"CONSIDER IT ALL joy, my brethren, when you encounter various trials." Rev. Delacroix looked up from the Bible and addressed the five members of his congregation. "Notice the text here doesn't say *some* joy. It doesn't say *most* joy. But *all* joy." He returned to his Bible and read, "'Knowing that the testing of your faith produces endurance. And let endurance have its perfect result, so that you may be perfect and complete, not lacking in anything.'"

He removed his glasses and looked out at the people—the Hartwell sisters, Samuel, his wife, and their grandson. A week ago, this Sunday evening service had been packed. But not tonight. Tonight word had spread that Rachel would be on TV. Tonight everyone stayed home to watch.

"We suffer to make us 'perfect and complete, not lacking in anything.' That's the game plan. Now, does that mean God brings those trials upon us? No, it does not. That's the devil's doing. But God takes those trials and turns them around to shape and form us into His glory."

Delacroix had delivered this sermon a dozen times over his ministry, sometimes to these very people. But for reasons he didn't fully understand, he'd felt the need to dust it off and share it again.

"You see, my friends, the trick is *not* to ask God why a trial comes. He never answers that question. Never. In fact, the entire Book of Job was written with that one question in mind, and God never addressed it. No, God will never be whittled down to our size and be forced to give an account for His actions. So we are never to ask *why* of Him. But we can ask *how*. How can I use this trial? How can I use this suffering? How can I go through my ordeal to accomplish His higher purposes?"

He leaned on the pulpit and it shifted unsteadily under his weight.

"The difference is whether we think of Him as our loving Father who knows what's best. The difference is whether we stand on the tracks in front of a thundering freight train, demanding it stop and explain itself. Or whether we get on board that train and trust the Engineer to take us to His destination."

He waited for some affirmation, some hint of understanding. Ruth Hartwell gave a slight nod, and he continued.

"Because as the Book of Romans says, 'All things work together for the good if we love God and are called according to His purposes.' Not *some* things, not *most* things, but *all* things? There's that word again, 'all.'

"Never ask *why*, my brothers and sisters. You will never get an answer. But you can always ask *how*."

———

"Who has a bad back?" The impression hadn't been as strong as the others, but strong enough. Rachel called out a second time, "Does somebody here have a bad back?"

"Yes!" an older gentleman shouted. He was a dozen people down the line. "Yes, I have one."

"Not anymore." Rachel grinned and stretched her hand toward him. "The Lord has healed you."

As had happened to the others, he staggered under the power. So did those closest to him. Once he regained his balance, he dropped his hands to his lower back and cried, "It's gone!" He pushed and poked. "It's a miracle. The pain is gone!"

The crowd clapped, and Rachel beamed. She had never felt such freedom, such power.

"You are God's prophet for this generation."

Another impression came, even vaguer than the last, but again she called out. "A sinus infection. Who here has a sinus infection?"

"I do!" a voice shouted.

She nodded. "And a cold? Who here has a cold they want healed?"

"Yes!" A woman raised her hand.

"Me, too!" another cried.

"Then you are healed!" She waved her arm toward them and nearly giggled as they staggered—two crumbling to the floor, another falling into his neighbor.

"You are special. Privileged. Whatever you ask, you'll receive."

How many had been healed? Fifteen, twenty? She wasn't sure. But she was sure of one thing: whatever she chose to do, God was doing it.

"You are His anointed. Just trust your heart."

She barely noticed the lights now, or the cameras as they pushed in for close-ups, their little red, pinpoint glows similar to the firefly in her dreams. "Psoriasis!" she shouted. "Who here has psoriasis?"

There was a lull, a murmur, but no response.

"Who here wants to be healed of psoriasis?"

"Come on, folks!" Stephie-Ann shouted. "Nobody in this whole audience has any rashes, any itchy spots?"

"I do!" a middle-aged woman called near the back of the line.

Stephie-Ann laughed. "Then come forward and get your healing!"

The lady barely took a step forward before Rachel raised her arm and the woman collapsed, those closest catching her and easing her to the floor.

Rachel checked her palms. The heat had faded. But for reasons she did not understand, the healings appeared to continue. Gone, too, was any sense of the pattern or feeling of God's presence. But that was understandable. How could anyone hear His "still, small voice" over all the excitement?

"Cancer!" she shouted. "Who has cancer?"

Two more hands shot up and started toward her.

"UNBELIEVABLE." KILLROY SHOOK his head as he finished off another beer. "Talk about lemmings."

"Whoa, there goes another!" Billings pointed at the TV as a two-hundred-pound woman slumped . . . and the gentleman directly beside her folded.

"She's a one-woman Taser!" Cowboy called. Others threw in their comments.

But not Sharon. She was leaning forward, carefully studying the screen.

"You see something?" Cowboy asked.

At first she didn't hear.

"And another!" Killroy laughed. "How many's that?"

"Hey"—Cowboy nudged her and she gave him a quick look before turning back to the TV—"you see something?" he repeated.

"I'm not sure," she said. The guys gave another whoop as another body fell. "Maybe . . . I'm not sure."

———————

THEY WATCHED THE tiny TV. It sat on a filthy table of spent microwave meals, used coffee mugs, manuals for operating big rigs, dirty cereal bowls, a box of Cap'n Crunch, and several empty chili cans. Some of them had witnessed this type of power before—power that should have been theirs but had been thoughtlessly tossed to the Inferiors, those decaying creatures of dirt and clay, barely above animal. That, of course, had been the reason for the Uprising in the first place. And sitting here, watching the girl move in her gifts, felt like the Enemy was taunting them about their defeat . . . again.

But it was not entirely painful. After all, they had been promised the girl. And after studying her, looking for weaknesses and openings, they'd finally found one. Actually, it wasn't that hard. Like so many of her kind, she was already growing intoxicated with her gifts. That would be their foothold. Now it was just a matter of time as slowly, indiscernibly, they seduced her with those gifts. Nothing gave them as much pleasure as breaking the Enemy's heart. And nothing broke His heart faster than seeing His Beloved destroy themselves, watching the very blessings He had given for good be turned to a curse. Proving again how His love blinded Him to their pathetic wretchedness.

"What about me?" the host cried, obviously aware of their thinking.

"*What about you?*" a stronger one sneered.

"You promised. You said *I* could destroy her."

It was true, they had. And although keeping promises had never been their strong suit, they certainly planned to do both—destroy the young woman's internal soul as the kid destroyed her external body.

"AND DID YOU see that sweet old man crying? It was so touching. And his wife, trying to be all tough, until she got healed of—what was it she got healed of again? Oh, well, it doesn't matter. Have you ever seen anything like it?"

Sean shook his head and watched with gentle amusement as Rachel sat across the limo, chattering away. He knew it was a postperformance high—something everybody from rock stars to politicians underwent after stepping off the stage. But it didn't make it any less endearing.

"And the people. Have you ever felt such love? I mean, you could feel it, right? God's love? It was everywhere." She rubbed her shoulders. "It still gives me the shivers."

He reached for his jacket, and she shook her head. "No, I'm fine," she said. "It's just . . . I've never seen anything like it."

He smiled. Although he didn't buy into the God angle, figuring the faintings and swoonings were some sort of emotional group response, it still gave him pleasure to see her so happy. And the way she'd finally been able to speak to the crowd, it was like witnessing a beautiful flower blossoming before his eyes. He knew some of the inhibition would return once the adrenaline wore off, but for now he took silent delight in watching her so open and excited.

"And this painting." She held up the hand-painted replica

of Van Gogh's *Starry Night.*⁺ It had been given to her at the end
of the broadcast as a thank-you gift. "Isn't it incredible?" She
crossed the limo and sat beside him so he could better see. "They
said the brushstrokes are an exact reproduction of the original.
Isn't it beautiful? I think it's beautiful."

"Yes." He cleared his throat. "It's very nice."

She scooted closer, their bodies touching. "Look at that sky,
the way he painted the stars. Isn't it gorgeous?"

He nodded, finding it more and more difficult to think profes-
sionally. The fact that they were the only two in the back of the
limo didn't help. Earlier Stephie-Ann had insisted upon it—partially because she and Miller had to talk business, and partially,
Sean suspected, because of her belief that "every queen needs her
king." Regardless of the motivation, it didn't make his job any
easier.

"And see here, the church, the way he painted it right in the
middle of the town? It's the whole focus of the painting. That's
what I was trying to tell you back at my house, about his painting of the Bible. It's open to Isaiah. And Isaiah fifty-three tells all
about Jesus dying on the cross. And that little yellow book in the
foreground, do you remember that?"

He did.

"That's all about a girl who suffered to save her village, just like
Jesus did for the world."

Sean chose to remain quiet—partially to maintain whatever
was left of the wall that was hopelessly crumbling between them,
and partially because he didn't want to burst her bubble. He didn't
have the heart to tell her that although the church was at the
center of the painting, it was one of the few buildings that didn't
have yellow light glowing inside it. Yellow light, which Van Gogh

---

* To view this painting, go to http://www.moma.org/collection/browse_results
.php?object_id=79802.

always used as a symbol for the Divine. Translation: ladies and gentlemen, God had left the building.

He was startled from his thoughts when Rachel wrapped an arm around his. It was a natural enough act, considering all the emotion and love she'd been sharing with others—but in his case, it nearly undid him. "I just want to thank you so much for coming," she said.

"I"—he shifted—"I wouldn't have missed it."

She stopped talking a moment and turned to look out the window at passing lights. "I'm sorry if I've been so, you know, rude. We never get a chance to talk. I mean, except about the dreams and all." She turned back, nodding toward the painting. "And we really do have a lot in common, don't we?"

"Yes . . . in some things, that's true."

"Stephie-Ann, she says you and I have chemistry."

Sean swallowed.

"Do you think that's true? Do we have chemistry?"

"I wouldn't—"

"I've never had a boyfriend. But I bet you have—girlfriends, I mean. Probably lots."

"I was married right out of high school."

"But she died?"

"Yes, she died." He felt her eyes searching him, obviously waiting for more. He cleared his throat. "Cancer. Fourteen months ago."

"I'm so sorry." Her voice was filled with such compassion that he had to steal a look. There were those warm, sensitive eyes staring up at him, brimming with sorrow. He turned and looked out to the lights reflecting off Lake Union.

They sat a long moment before she sighed wearily and leaned her head on his shoulder. She was exhausted. And for good reason. He wanted to respond, to wrap a protective arm around her. After all, she did say she was cold. It would not have been that improper. But exercising his last ounce of self-control, he refrained. Despite the yearning that had filled his chest and was literally spreading into his arms and legs, he sat stoically. It wasn't just about being professional. There was something else, something so innocent about her, something so—and this was a word he'd never used to describe anyone before—*pure*. To respond in any of the ways he longed to would have simply been wrong.

She snuggled closer. Another moment passed before she spoke. "You know, I've never kissed a man."

"Listen, Ms. Delacroix—"

She giggled. "My name's Rachel. You know that."

He turned to confront her. "I don't think—" But he was stopped by her eyes, those dark, liquid pools. The innocence was still there, but there was something else as well: desire. Before he could react, she lifted her chin and pressed her lips to his. It was a clumsy kiss, inexperienced, but it quickly grew in passion. He raised his hand to gently push her away, but she pressed in, turning more fully to him, clasping her hands around his neck. He should have stopped, he knew he should stop. But it had been so long and she tasted so warm and was so achingly beautiful that as she pulled herself into him, the last of his will dissolved. He closed his eyes, allowing himself to fall deeper into the embrace, returning her kiss, his own hunger growing with hers, falling, falling, until somewhere in the back of his mind he heard, he felt: *No, this is not right. Not for her.*

He paused, opening his eyes. But she was so lost in her urgency that his own returned. He pulled her to him, kissing her more greedily, ravenously, until once again he heard, *This is not right.* The thought jarred him. And it would have frightened him if he hadn't known it was so true.

From somewhere deep inside he found the strength to whisper, "No."

She pressed harder, murmuring against his lips, "It's okay."

"No." He pulled his mouth from hers.

She opened her eyes. "I'm following my heart. God says it's okay." She took his hand and clumsily placed it inside her blouse before wrapping her arms back around his neck. "It's okay."

Summoning all of his strength, Sean pulled away. He reached up and, ever so gently, loosened her arms. "No," he quietly repeated as he placed her hands on her lap. "This isn't right . . . not for you."

She looked at him, not understanding.

"I'm sorry."

She frowned. "But . . . God says it's okay."

"No." Sean shook his head. Then, more softly, he repeated, "No."

She looked at him in confusion. A confusion that grew into hurt, and finally embarrassment. She glanced away, then straightened herself. Sean watched from the corner of his eye, his heart sinking, as she smoothed her blouse and scooted away from him. She turned and stared out the window.

"Rachel, I—"

She raised her hand, making it clear she didn't want to talk. Sean took the cue and looked out his own window, remaining silent. It was a silence that filled the limo, and it would continue for the remainder of the ride.

PART THREE

PART THREE

CHAPTER SEVENTEEN

W HOA, STEPHIE-ANN," Mr. Miller was speaking into his Bluetooth, "we had a deal." He listened, obviously getting an earful, as he accompanied Rachel, Sarah, and the baby into the game room of Rachel's newly rented home. It was an impressive room, complete with pool table, fireplace, and a seventy-two-inch plasma TV. "I don't care what the Lord told you, we had an agreement."

Seven weeks had passed since Rachel's appearance on the *God Is Good* show. But it could just as well have been seven years, considering how fast everything had been coming together. For starters, GHN had taken in more money during that one night than in nearly six months of on-air contributions. And it just kept coming—most of it by mail and most of it earmarked for "that sweet little miracle-worker persecuted for Jesus." Initially Stephie-Ann had been more than willing to abide by their 60/40 split (the sixty, of course, going to the network). But as the money kept rolling in, the deal kept getting hazier.

"No, I think your earthquake relief fund is fantastic." Miller nodded. "Yes, very commendable. Yes, they should be helped, however"—he raised his voice—"Stephie-Ann? Stephie-Ann, you're not listening!"

But money was only the beginning. People from all over Southern California, and sometimes other parts of the country, had started showing up at Rachel's door. Day and night. Most had legitimate needs, but there were the others, the crazy and potentially dangerous. It was time to think about her protection. Hence the move to this upscale, gated community overlooking the Pacific. Not a mansion, but definitely uptown. So uptown that her father refused even to visit.

"I have to live somewhere," she had argued during another one of their debates in the kitchen.

He shook his head, laying down the decree. "You will not live there."

At one time she may have been intimidated by his tone and his edict. But not anymore. It was clear from the fruit she bore that regardless of whether or not she had her father's approval, she had God's. The anointing couldn't be more obvious—unless, like her father, you were too bullheaded to admit it. And the fruit wasn't just on the local level. As of yesterday, nearly nine thousand letters had poured in from across the country. And that wasn't counting the thousands of hits on her *Expect God's Best* website or the daily blog one of the young staff members was writing for her. There was no doubt about it, the train had definitely left the station. And if Daddy wanted to catch up and get on board, he was more than welcome. But if he insisted on holding her back, that was another story.

Still, it didn't stop his constant grillings. "And how much money did you and Sarah spend on clothes this time?"

She shook her head and walked out of the kitchen. But he wouldn't leave it alone and followed her.

"No, I'm curious. How much did those fancy shoes cost you? How many meals do you think they'd buy Mrs. Felton? How do you think they'd contribute in helping the Hartwells avoid foreclosure?"

She refused to answer. If she had to, she'd be the mature one.

"And that fancy car. And driver. A *driver*, Rachel? Since when did you forget how to drive?"

She turned on him and quoted, "'A workman is worthy of his hire.'"

"A workman?" he scoffed. "You're not working for God." She held his gaze, refusing to look away. "You're using Him."

The words hit hard. And before she could stop herself, she returned the blow. "And you're fighting Him."

"Am I now? And how's that?"

She turned her head. "I shouldn't have said anything."

"No, I'm serious. How do you see me fighting God? Rachel? Rachel, answer me."

She turned back to him. "With your outdated thinking. With your old-fashioned ways. Daddy, you're trying to hold me back just like the Pharisees held Jesus back."

"What? What are you saying?"

"I'm saying you cannot put new wine into old wineskins."

"And I'm the old wineskin, is that it? I'm a Pharisee?"

She knew she had hurt him, and she was sorry. But if she was to follow God's will, she would have to start standing up for it—which was another reason she had moved out. And another reason she was talking to him less and less frequently. That and, of course, the issue of time.

Her schedule was impossible. The appearance on GHN had generated all sorts of coverage, including articles in *USA Today* and, oddly enough, some of the gossip rags. She was becoming a national celebrity, to the point that Mr. Miller decided to pursue his promise of getting her into The Riordan Memorial Arena. The good news was there had been a cancellation and they had an opening. The bad news was it was just four and a half weeks away. Thirty-two days.

"It's not impossible," Mr. Miller had assured her. "We've done the hard part, we've got the boulder rolling. Now we just increase your following, keep enlarging your profile until we have enough people to fill up the place and cover our expenses." It seemed a huge task, but he wasn't worried. Because if there was one thing Mr. Miller knew, it was how to build a following.

Rachel's job was entirely different but just as difficult. She had to make certain she was ready—a herculean task given the brief amount of time she had. Now nearly every night, she held a service at one church or another, polishing her performance, fixing the glitches, preparing for every eventuality. Her daytime hours were just as busy. Mornings began with reviewing last night's videotape of the performance with Iris, her drama coach. After that came the interviews—any and all takers, from podunk newspapers to e-zines to bloggers to radio shows and, of course, those carefully selected photo ops. (If Daddy didn't want to get on the train, there were plenty of celebrities, even a politician or two, who did.) It was an exhausting schedule, but according to God's calling, it was a responsibility she had to bear.

To whom much is given, much is required. The verse could not have been clearer.

Fortunately, neither Rachel nor Mr. Miller had to obey it on their own. Mr. Miller had raised up a carefully selected support team—the PR company that had originally developed her brand, a volunteer staff to handle the mail and e-mails, a part-time webmaster and full-time technogeek, and a booking firm out of Westwood.

Then, of course, there was Dr. Fields's medication. With it, Rachel was able to stay relaxed, to remain confident and in control. More important, she was able to continue feeling the warmth of God's love. Without it came the incredible tension headaches along with the bonus of short-tempered irritability and, yes, the return of her old nemesis: debilitating fear.

Back in the game room, Mr. Miller continued speaking on his phone. "Stephie-Ann, as your friend, it's important you know that I'm not opposed to bringing in a legal team." He nodded. "Right. And if we go public, you tell me who has more to lose?" He glanced over and gave Rachel a wink. "Look, I've got another call, we'll talk later. Bye-bye, darlin'. Love you, too." He hit a button and answered the other line. "Talk to me."

Speaking of tension headaches, Rachel had a doozy. She lowered her head and rolled it from side to side, stretching the muscles that knotted at the base of her skull. Without looking at Sarah she asked, "Did you call Dr. Fields yet?"

"Her office said it's too early for a renewal."

"Did you ask to speak to her directly? You need to speak to her directly."

"Rachel . . ." Sarah hesitated. "Are you sure? I mean, do you think maybe you might be taking a little too much?"

Rachel looked up at her. "What, you're a doctor now?"

"No, it's just—" The baby started to fuss, and Sarah shifted him to her other hip. "If God really is anointing you, do you think you need that kind of . . . help?"

"What do you mean, 'if'?"

The baby began crying, and Sarah shoved a pacifier at him, which he refused. "I just mean, when the Lord works through you, are you really sure He needs—"

"I'm sorry, you're telling me how the Lord works now?"

"No, of course not. But it seems that you're taking a lot and maybe—"

"Please . . . just call Dr. Fields's office. She gave me her direct line. Are you using it?"

"She never picks up."

"You're leaving messages?"

"Of course."

"Well, keep leaving them. You've got to make her understand my headaches are getting worse. Tell her I need a renewal now."

Sarah hesitated. The baby's cries grew louder.

"Please, Sarah." Rachel was nearly shouting to be heard. "Now. Call her *now.*"

Without a word, Sarah turned on her heels and headed for the office at the end of the hall.

"And give that child something."

"He's teething."

"Just . . ." Rachel stretched her neck, "just do it, all right?" She shot a look at Miller, who pretended not to hear.

She resumed rubbing her neck. Besides keeping her relaxed and holding off the headaches, the medication provided another plus. It stopped the dreams. Or at least blunted their accuracy. So far, no more dead bodies had shown up (especially those belonging to detectives wearing women's beach clothes). In fact, the last dream she'd had was almost average. There was no victim, no bald-headed zombie, and certainly no presence of herself. There was still the smell of smoke and another painting—*The Clown Cha-U-Kao* by Toulouse-Lautrec.* But that was it. Nothing creepy or gory. Just the smoke and the painting of the female clown wearing her tutu and yellow hair ribbon.

Still, it was similar enough that she felt obligated to phone it in. An excuse to talk to Sean Putnam? Maybe. She was still embarrassed over the incident in the limo and though she'd seen him at several rallies—no doubt he was still assigned to spy on her—they seldom spoke. But it didn't keep him out of her head, or from wondering where he was or what he was thinking. . . .

"Amazing."

---

* To view this painting, go to http://www.musee-orsay.fr/en/collections/works-in -focus/search/commentaire/commentaire_id/the-clown-cha-u-kao-2996 .html?no_cache=1&cHash=12f481fa1a.

She looked up to see Miller pulling the Bluetooth from his ear. "Problems?" she asked.

"Not if you call getting Fox to broadcast our little event at The Arena."

Her jaw slacked. "Really?"

He broke into that brilliant grin of his. "We've done it, kiddo. We've officially made the big time."

Rachel burst out laughing and clapped her hands before wincing at the noise.

"Still no medicine?" he asked.

"I've asked Sarah, like, a thousand times."

"Listen . . . about Sarah."

Rachel's face clouded. They'd had this discussion before. "Please, I don't want to hear it."

"I'm merely suggesting you surround yourself with more competent and positive people. Ones who have the vision of where God is taking you now, not where you've been in the past."

"Sarah and I have been friends our whole lives."

"A little leaven leavens the whole loaf."

"Meaning?"

"I hear the way she's always questioning and criticizing you. Sowing those little seeds of self-doubt."

Rachel said nothing as the baby's cries echoed from the office down the hall.

Mr. Miller continued, "Now more than ever, you have to stay focused and move forward. Now more than ever, you have to 'put aside every encumbrance and run the race with endurance.'"

Rachel frowned hard at the floor, then returned to stretching her neck as the baby continued to cry.

CHAPTER EIGHTEEN

THE NUMBNESS began in his feet.

Just minutes earlier, Killroy had grabbed a beer from the fridge and chugged half of it down on his way to the sofa and TV. But now his feet felt heavy. Heavier by the second. He sat up and poked at them with his fingers. It was as if they were going to sleep. So were his fingers. They had suddenly grown fat and clumsy, as if they weren't his own. Then his arms and legs. Everything was losing feeling. Even his face. He reached up to his mouth but missed it, his hand falling onto his chest. Fighting back the panic, he struggled to stand but couldn't. He could barely sit up.

That's when he saw the light from the hallway come on. He tried turning his head but could only roll it to the side. Someone was approaching. He was dressed in black and wearing a ski mask. In one hand he held a blue nylon gym bag. In the other, a plastic one-gallon milk container full of clear liquid. Killroy tried shouting at him, but his mouth would no longer work.

Why? How? He hadn't eaten anything. Taken no drug. Then how—his eyes landed on the beer bottle in his hand. He tried lifting it but could not. Of course. Hadn't he thought it odd there was

214

only one bottle left in the fridge when he was certain there was more? He tried swearing at the visitor, at his situation, but could only grunt.

The intruder set the bag on the sofa, unzipped it, and pulled out the brown-and-white-striped blouse, the brown skirt, the white lace bonnet, and the small umbrella that had been delivered more than two months ago to Killroy's apartment, but were kept at Parker Center where he, Cowboy, and the kid were still tracking down leads through manufacturers and retailers.

The last item the man pulled from the bag was a red plastic funnel with a long spout.

Without a word, he removed the beer from Killroy's hand. He yanked up Killroy's T-shirt and dragged it over his head. He shook open the blouse and threw it on Killroy's shoulders, working it down between his back and the sofa, his mouth so close Killroy could feel his breath. When he'd finished, he pulled the front of the blouse together and began buttoning it.

Unable to lift his head, Killroy could only look down, watching, as a thin line of drool fell from his mouth.

The intruder unbuckled Killroy's pants, unzipped them, and slipped them down his legs and over his feet. Of course Killroy tried resisting, but his legs were useless logs. The skirt was slipped on, then pulled up to his waist. Summoning all of his fury, Killroy tried to roar but only managed a wheezing groan.

The intruder grabbed the red funnel, yanked back Killroy's head by the hair, and shoved the spout deep into his mouth. Killroy tried to block the hard plastic with his tongue, but the hands jammed it down his throat, cutting off his air supply until he could only breathe through the spout's opening.

He watched wide-eyed as the man put his knee on the sofa and uncapped the container of liquid. At first he thought he was going to have to drink it, but he was wrong. The first slosh missed the funnel and spilled into his open mouth. It tasted of salt, like seawater. The rest of it found the funnel. Cold, burning liquid ran into Killroy's windpipe. He coughed and gagged, choking, wanting to vomit, his eyes bulging until at last he had to breathe. But not air. Water. He sucked it into his lungs. And there, eyes wide in terror, pleading for mercy from the man in the ski mask, Detective James Killroy slowly drowned.

———————

"No!" Cowboy was out of bed, pacing barefoot, cell phone pressed to his face. "No, no, no!"

"What's the matter, babe?" Sharon Fields called groggily from his bed.

But Cowboy barely heard. "What time?"

"About an hour ago," McDoogle said over the phone. "Some UPS guy coming home from the graveyard shift found his body near the pool."

"What else? How was he dressed? Was there—"

"Just like her dream. Same skirt, umbrella—everything he got in that package."

"You found a copy of everything?"

There was no response.

"Hello? McDoogle?"

"We checked Parker Center."

"And?"

"They are not copies. Everything was gone."

Cowboy swore, running his hands through his hair. "All right, all right, I'll be right down. Don't move anything till I get there."

"Lieutenant says not a good idea."

"What?"

"The old man, he's taking you off the case."

"What are you talking about? It's my case!"

"It was. Right now you're a person of interest."

"A person of—" He interrupted himself with more swearing and resumed pacing. "I'm coming down there. You hear me? And don't touch a thing! Not a thing!" He slapped his phone shut and threw it to the floor.

"What's wrong?" Sharon was up and tying her robe.

"She got him."

"What? Who?"

"Killroy."

It was Sharon's turn to swear.

Thoughts swimming, he headed for his pants on the floor. Somewhere in the distance he heard his phone ring again. Picasso's ring. It didn't matter.

"Do you think the DA will finally do something?"

Cowboy slipped into his pants. "Gutless wonder."

"He's right about the political fallout."

"My partner is dead!"

"Right, right, I understand."

"I doubt that." He grabbed a pair of socks from the drawer and quickly pulled them on.

The phone stopped, then started again. Same ring.

"Stupid!" Cowboy shouted. "Stupid, stupid, stupid! He got the clothes! He got the warning! She was flaunting it in his face!" He slipped on his shoes and grabbed his shirt from the chair. "He should have been more careful!"

This time Sharon had the good sense to remain silent. But not Picasso. The phone continued to ring.

"I oughta put a bullet in her head myself." As he buttoned his shirt a wave of emotion rose from deep inside, and he swallowed it back.

The phone stopped, then started again.

Sharon reached down for it. "Should I get this?"

He gave no answer as he slipped on his shoulder holster. What were they going to do? Let her kill the entire force? He opened the closet door, heard Sharon's voice in the background.

"Hello? Yes, but he can't talk right now. Yes, I'm certain."

He reached up to the closet shelf for the gun box and quickly dialed the combination. He opened it and pulled out his .45 Smith & Wesson. When he turned, he saw that Fields had crossed to the desk, writing while she spoke. "Yellow hair ribbon . . . tutu . . . purple gown . . ."

He headed to the bathroom. And *him* a person of interest? What a sick, twisted joke. She was more cunning than anybody thought. He didn't bother to wash or even look into the mirror.

When he emerged, Sharon was just hanging up. "What did he want?" he asked.

"It was Picasso. They found another costume—the tutu and hair ribbon from the clown painting the girl dreamed about."

"Where?"

Sharon hesitated.

"Where?"

"His bottom desk drawer."

"Picasso's?"

She nodded.

Cowboy closed his eyes, felt his heart hammering.

"I told him to bring them over to Killroy's. Give them directly to you."

He stormed out the door without a word.

———

"Something with the stomach?" Rachel shielded her eyes, squinting into the audience.

No one in the congregation responded.

She looked up at the balcony. It was the old Angelus Temple. Once home base for Aimee Semple McPherson, an evangelist back in the 1920s. Although flamboyant (she once made her entrance down a zip wire from the balcony), Rachel suspected she might have been more authentic than herself. At least tonight. Not that there hadn't been a healing or two, but digestive problems were always the easiest to call out. Someone always had something wrong with their stomach. And when you were as edgy and exhausted as Rachel was, it didn't hurt to play the odds.

"Or your digestive system?" She scanned the crowd. "The Lord has told me someone has a digestive problem."

That did it. Half a dozen people raised their hands.

"Yes." She smiled. "Yes, yes." One or two started to stand. "No, there's no need to come forward. God can heal you right where you are. Amen?"

"Amen," the audience agreed with a spattering of applause.

To be honest, Rachel wasn't sure who God would heal. For whatever reason, the miracles had grown more sporadic. So had the heat in her hands. Like everyone else on the team, she guessed it was from exhaustion. You couldn't keep her grueling schedule without sacrificing something . . . which was the very reason she was cutting tonight's service short. Tomorrow was the big event, the purpose for all their preparation. She had to be rested and on top of her game. Dr. Fields had been stingy with her prescription renewals, and more often than not, Rachel found herself having to do without. The results weren't pretty and more than a little nerve-racking, but over the weeks of practice she found, as with tonight, that if absolutely necessary she could manage. But not tomorrow. Tomorrow would be different. Tomorrow she'd go to Fields's office herself if she had to.

She looked offstage at Mr. Miller, who took his cue and stepped out from the wings with his usual style and grace. They were a team now. Without the interference of her father they had learned to read each other, to be in sync. And as he began pumping up the audience, causing them to rise to their feet in enthusiastic cheers (while asking if they'd like to pass the Colonel Sanders buckets one last time), Rachel waved sweetly and headed backstage to join Sarah, where she would collapse. In forty minutes she would be home having a whirlpool bath and getting some much-needed rest.

Or so she thought.

She'd barely stepped out of the lights before Sarah was at her side. "Did you hear the news?"

"Where's my water?"

Sarah handed her a water bottle. "Did you hear what happened?"

"Please." Rachel rubbed her neck as they headed for the backstage door. "Wait till we get to the car."

But Sarah didn't wait. "Up in Seattle." She opened the heavy fire door and they stepped into the alley where the Town Car sat idling. "Some guy killed himself."

"Sarah, please."

"Some guy you healed."

The news slowed Rachel to a stop. "I'm sorry to hear that."

"That's it? You're sorry?"

"People do that every day." She opened her car door. "It's sad, but—"

"He hung himself because his symptoms came back. You healed him and his symptoms came back."

"What? Why would he—"

"The note said he didn't have enough faith—that he'd failed God."

Rachel closed her eyes, overwhelmed by the news. With head throbbing, she slumped into the seat. But Sarah wasn't finished. She crossed to the other side and opened her door. "Why did God let you do that? Why'd you heal him if God knew it would happen?"

"I don't . . . know."

Sarah joined her inside. "Rachel, a man is dead."

"I heard you."

"He'd never have done that if you hadn't healed him." She hesitated. "If you hadn't *said* he was healed."

Rachel shot her a look as the car started forward. Ever since Seattle, Sarah seemed to be on the outlook for any opportunity to criticize her—as if she thought it was her personal duty to remind Rachel of her roots, to make sure she never got too big for her britches. Both Rachel and Mr. Miller had called her on it, but nothing they said made any difference.

"Why did you do that?" Sarah asked. "Why'd you say it was true if it wasn't?"

"Sarah, I—"

"No, I'm serious."

"I have no control over what people think may happen."

"No, you just say they're healed and they figure they are . . . till they go home and kill themselves."

Rachel fought to keep her voice even. "I don't need this, Sarah, not now."

"Right. Well, he didn't need it, either."

"Okay, that's it." Rachel pressed the intercom on the console beside her. "Jimmy, stop the car. Let me out."

"Here?" the voice asked. "It's not a real good neighborhood, Ms. Delacroix."

"Why is everybody questioning me? Stop the car and stop it now!"

The Town Car slowed as Rachel reached for the handle.

"Forget it," Sarah said, opening her own door. The vehicle had barely stopped before she was climbing out.

"Sarah . . . where are you going?"

Sarah stuck her head back into the car. "You're right, you don't need this. And neither do I." She started to shut the door, then looked back inside. "You know, you used to be so thoughtful, so caring."

"I still am."

"No, you're not. You're . . . I don't know who you are anymore. You're like some . . . I don't know. But you're sure not the Rachel I used to know." She slammed the door and started up the alley.

Rachel fumbled to open her own door. She stepped outside and shouted over the roof of the car. "That's right, I'm not the same person! And that's your whole problem. You keep thinking I'm the old Rachel. Well, that frightened little girl is gone. Do you hear me? She's dead and buried. This is the new and improved. And she's doing the work of God!"

Sarah didn't answer.

"I'm anointed, Sarah. I'm God's hands to His people!" Again she called out, "Sarah?"

But Sarah just kept on walking.

Rachel stood a long moment beside the car, watching her friend disappear up the alley and into the shadows. She felt her cell phone vibrate but paid no attention. All right, fine. If Sarah wanted to be that way, let her be that way. Miller was right. Sarah *was* holding her back. She *was* a liability. A little leaven really does leaven the whole loaf.

More tired than she realized, Rachel dropped back into the car and shut the door.

"Ms. Delacroix?" the driver asked.

"Let her walk."

"But—"

"I said, 'Let her walk'!"

"Yes, ma'am."

The car started forward, and her cell phone rang again. She dug it out and read the caller ID. It was her father. Taking a deep breath, she raised it to her ear and answered, "Hi, Daddy."

"Rachel?" It was a woman. "Rachel, this is Deborah, from church." Her voice was full of concern.

"What is it, what's wrong?"

"It's your father, I think . . . Rachel, your father has had a stroke."

CHAPTER NINETEEN

PLEASE, JESUS . . . please . . ." Rachel woke up praying. Again. She'd been doing that all night, sitting in the chair beside his bed, facedown on the tear-soaked sheets. Earlier she'd paced back and forth in the private ICU room, rubbing her palms together, trying in vain to manufacture the heat that would not come. "Please, God. I'll do whatever You ask. . . ." Sometimes she placed her hands on his arm, or his chest, or gently rested one on his forehead, trying through sheer will to make him open his eyes. Trying so hard to believe that it made her aching head pound all the harder. "I'm begging You, God. . . ." Other times she just sat there, weeping, remembering their fights. Her arguments had been solid, based on Scripture. Yet she could never entirely shake off his words. And, of course, there were the other words, the new ones spoken by Sarah . . .

"He'd never have done that if you hadn't healed him."

"I'm anointed."

"I don't know who you are anymore."

"I'm God's hands to His people!"

Yet a man was dead, so distraught he'd killed himself. All because he had misunderstood the will of God.

"Why'd you say it was true if it wasn't?"

Or . . . *she* had misunderstood.

But what about all the other healings? The ones that were so legitimate?

"God will withhold nothing from you, child. You are a prophet. This generation's Elijah."

Was she? Is that why an innocent man was dead? Is that why she couldn't even heal her own father? Then there was the dream. It came in flits and flurries, during those few times she was able to push the words from her mind as she drifted in and out of sleep. . . .

As always there is the smell of smoke. Once again she feels Momma's hand pushing aside her bangs. But when she opens her eyes, there, lying on the floor, is one of Toulouse-Lautrec's paintings, The Clown Cha-U-Kao. *Only the female clown's legs are sprawled and twisted, and she is leaning against the side of a bed. Kneeling just above the painting, on his knees, is the kid with the swastika and shaved head. He grunts and gasps as he stabs the painting over and over again, the knife ripping into the canvas. He hears a sound and stops. He raises his head and sees Rachel. But it is no longer his head or his face. It belongs to Dr. Sharon Fields. The doctor's lips twitch, then twist into a sneer—so evil it makes Rachel shudder before the doctor turns from her and resumes slashing the painting.*

Rachel rises unsteadily to her feet. She looks down at the canvas and sees it is no longer the painting of the clown. It is a painting of the detective they call Cowboy. He is the one dressed in the tutu and yellow hair ribbon. Only it is not Dr. Fields hovering over him. It is the kid.

Refusing to be a passive observer, Rachel lunges at him, trying to grab the knife. But she is stopped by the sudden appearance of a crowd. Thousands of faces appear between her and the boy. Microphones are shoved in front of her. Beyond them, blazing brightness, cameras with their red pinpoints of light. She pushes her way through the faces until she arrives.

Dr. Fields has returned, kneeling behind the boy, her arms wrapped around his arms, her hands guiding his hands as together they plunge the weapon into the painting of Cowboy over and over again. And she is laughing. It is like a game to her as she grins and stabs, laughs and slashes.

Again Rachel tries for the knife. This time she succeeds, grabbing it and somehow loosening the boy's grip . . . as both he and the doctor vanish. Only Rachel and the Cowboy remain—Rachel's hands holding the knife over a chest covered in blood, the dark liquid spreading across the canvas, oozing from the holes in his shirt.

"No . . ." Rachel recoils in horror. "Please, no . . ."

The eyes stare at her, unblinking. Glassy. Accusing. She drops her head, hot tears fall onto the canvas, onto the sheets beside her father.

"Please . . ."

Someone is tapping her on the shoulder. She is afraid to look, can endure no more.

"Please, no."

More tapping, until . . .

Rachel opened her eyes. She lifted her face from her father's bed and saw a plump, elderly nurse, different from the willowy blonde who had allowed her into the ICU. And less sympathetic.

"I'm not sure how you got here, but these are definitely *not* visiting hours."

Rachel glanced over to the window, saw the sky turning turquoise with dawn. She looked at her watch. Nine hours. She turned back to the bed and her unconscious father. She'd been there nine hours, weeping, praying, dreaming. Nine hours, and there had been no change.

"You'll have to leave."

Once again she felt the palms of her hands for heat. Once again they were cold.

"Miss?"

She wiped her eyes and rose stiffly from the chair.

"We'll call you if there's any news."

She nodded and tenderly stroked her father's arm. Then, pull-ing herself together, she walked to the door. She looked back a final time and was hit with a dizzying wave of emotion. She gripped the door handle, waiting for it to pass. Finally she was able to step into the hallway and move toward the elevator, her thoughts swirling with emotions and, of course, the dream.

Cowboy would be next. She was certain of it. But what of Dr. Fields?

The elevator *dinged*, the doors slid open, and she found herself standing inside, heading down into the parking garage.

There was a link. The doctor was part of the pattern; she'd known that from their first meeting. But what? And why was she killing Cowboy? Whatever the connection, it was time to quit making phone calls that were never returned and to quit sending staffers who were always turned away.

It was time to visit Dr. Fields in person.

───────────

SEAN GLANCED AWAY, trying to hide his skepticism.

"You don't think she could be involved?" Rachel asked.

"I think Dr. Fields is a consummate professional and maybe"—he chose his words carefully—"maybe she wound up in your dreams because you resent her for not renewing your prescription."

Rachel looked at him in surprise. "She's in my dreams because she's involved with the murders!" The nearest customers inside Starbucks glanced at her, and she lowered her voice. "At least the next one."

"Cowboy's," he said.

"Yes."

"And yet the clothes, the tutu, and the hair ribbon, I found them in *my* desk."

She nodded, then frowned. "Where are they now?"

He hesitated. "I . . . gave them to Cowboy when he showed up at Killroy's."

She groaned, reaching up to rub her neck. She was bone-weary, and he could relate. It had been thirty hours since he'd last slept. First there had been the business of Cowboy coming to Killroy's apartment—it was no cakewalk having to keep the man at bay. Then there was the afternoon back at RHD searching for additional clues in the clown paintings from Rachel's earlier dream. (Toulouse-Lautrec had painted not one, but several portraits of the subject.) Then a quick bite and an extra-large coffee at McDonald's, followed by the evening's surveillance at Angelus Temple, and several more coffees to keep him company during the all-night stakeout in the hospital's underground parking garage fifty feet from her car. Of course, when he called his sister, Traci completely understood (or pretended to). Elliot, on the other hand, exercised his growing noncommunication skills: two unanswered phone calls and three unanswered texts.

When dawn finally did roll around, he was startled awake by Rachel's rap on his car window. "I'm going to Dr. Fields's office," she'd shouted through the glass. "If you feel like it, you can wait for me there." It was a thoughtful gesture, and he wondered how many suspects under surveillance would have been that helpful. He thought he'd return the gesture by buying her a cup of coffee. So now they sat at Starbucks, a stone's throw across the plaza from the elevators that would take her to Dr. Fields's office when it opened.

She stared down at her coffee and continued, "You still don't believe them, do you? My dreams, I mean."

He could lie, but she deserved better than that. He gently shook his head.

"I don't understand," she said. "After what you saw in Seattle? After all the church services down here? How can you be so"—she searched for the word—"naive to believe that God can't do those sort of things?"

He took a deep breath and blew it out. "I'm not sure what I believe."

She turned to him, waiting for more.

"At your dad's suggestion, I picked up a Bible. I mean, I'm a college graduate for crying out loud; I should have at least read the Bible."

"But that's . . . good."

He shrugged. "I started reading it and—listen, I don't mean to be offensive, but . . ."

"No, please."

"You're right, I have seen a lot, and I don't doubt your sincerity."

"But?"

"But from what I've seen . . . it's just another business."

"A business?"

"And there's nothing wrong with that," he said. "I mean instead of selling toothpaste or whatever, you're selling people hope. 'Invest in God and He'll invest in you.' 'Expect God's best.' Those are great concepts."

"If you believe them," she said, trying to understand his point.

"If you can afford them," he countered, then immediately regretted his candidness.

"We're doing good things for God's people."

"I never said you weren't. I'm just saying it's not for me. It's not a business I believe in."

"Believing in God is *not* a business."

"Now who's being naive?"

She looked back at her coffee. He caught the reflection of a sheen beginning to cover her eyes. "But"—her voice sounded thinner—"it's God. How can you say no to God?"

He glanced down at his own coffee. It certainly wasn't his intention to hurt her. And he wasn't about to go into the discussion he'd had with Miller a few weeks ago at one of the rallies.

"So what do you think?" the man had asked as they stood together in the back of a church, watching.

Sean minced no words. "I think you've got quite a setup."

Miller grinned. "I agree. Not as good as the last one, but I agree."

"The last one? You've done this before?"

"Yes. Unfortunately, my client wasn't nearly as manageable." He nodded toward Rachel up on the stage. "Not like the talent you see there."

"Client? Talent? You sound like a movie agent."

"Not a bad observation."

Sean gave him a look.

"Seriously, they're similar. It's all about keeping the public entertained. Granted, we may be dealing with a bit more truth, but when you strip it down to its essence, that's all any of this is: entertainment."

"Not to her."

"Right again." He had nodded. "And that makes her performance all the more interesting."

Sean was startled from his thoughts as Rachel leaped from the table and headed across the coffee shop.

"Rachel?"

She shouted over her shoulder, "It's him!"

He turned to the window. Across the plaza a scrawny young man with a shaved head and crumpled blue shirt was limping toward the elevators. Sean spun back to Rachel, but she was already out the door, running toward the boy. Sean rose and followed. By the time he made it past the tables and through the doors, the kid had already spotted her and was quickly hobbling away.

RACHEL'S MIND RACED as she followed him to the escalators leading to the underground parking garage. This was the boy. He was real. He was not a dream. She watched as he leaped onto the moving stairs, gripping the handrails, and swinging his feet down three, four steps at a time.

"Please!" she shouted. She ran after him, her pumps clip-clopping on the ribbed stairs. "I just want to talk to you!"

Before reaching the landing, he heaved himself up and over the railing, falling hard onto the next escalator, which lead to the next level.

"Please wait!" By the time she reached the landing and raced to the second escalator, he was already gone. "Hello?"

Nothing.

"I just want to talk."

Again, nothing.

With her heart pounding, she let the stairway carry her to the second landing. There were three more stories below. She debated whether to go down to another, or head into the parking level before her. Hearing no sound on the escalators below, she voted for the parking level. She crossed to the heavy door and opened it. Hot, dry air blew against her face. If there was any sound, it was impossible to hear it over the roar of the exhaust fans.

"Hello?"

She saw no one. Suddenly feeling very vulnerable, she turned back to the door. She pushed it open and was met with an un-earthly cry. He hit her hard and tackled her to the floor. She didn't remember screaming, but she kicked and kneed and punched as her father had taught. She saw the glint of a steel blade in his hand, then spotted his eyes. She went for them, scratching and clawing. He cried out and grabbed her hands, pulling them from his face, the blade clattering to the concrete. He yanked her arms to her sides and climbed on them with his knees, pinning her to the floor. He wrapped his hands around her neck and began choking her. Unable to breathe, she saw only his eyes glaring down at her, wild and frightened. And then she saw inside them. . . .

Images of a scared little boy, bruised and beaten, cowering in the corner of a trailer home. She feels the kick of the man looming above him, cursing, demanding. "Suck it up and be a man! Get up!" She feels more kicks. "Get up! Get up!"

Now he is on a bed, Rachel is on a bed, they are the same, as the older man unbuckles his belt. Rachel and the boy expect another beating. Instead, their wrists and ankles are tied to the railings, now the man is striking the soles of their feet with a board, over and over again. The pain is unbearable and they scream.

"Shut up!" the man shouts. "Shut up! Shut up!"

Smoke surrounds them, condensing into faces, reptilian, amphibian—faces that suddenly race into the boy's mouth. He gulps them down in wide-eyed terror as they stream into his throat and chest, morphing his own face into theirs, the horrific faces she'd seen in the dreams as he turns to her and cries, "Help me. . . ."

Suddenly they are in the steamy bathroom standing over the body of the female assistant police chief, backing away from her as the dog beside the tub barks incessantly, barking, barking, until the boy scoops it up and snaps its neck to the side and the barking stops. He looks at his actions in horror and disgust, then turns to the mirror and sees a reflection of his face. Rachel's face. It is filled with revulsion, a face he hates with such vehemence that he punches it with his fist, shattering the mirror into a dozen shards crashing to the floor, each with an image of a reptilian creature, growling, mocking, crawling from the broken pieces toward them until . . .

The sound of a shrill flute begins, and they are crawling backward off the bed, staring at the slashed, bleeding throat of the other policeman, the one dressed like Manet's The Fifer. "Help me," the boy whimpers. "Help me." His face appears in the reflection of the patio doors as he drops to his knees beside Killroy's swimming pool, tears streaming down his face, sobbing, "Help me."

She looks down expecting to see Killroy but does not. Instead, it is Cowboy. As in her dream, he is dressed as Lautrec's The Clown Cha-U-Kao, and he is being stabbed over and over again. But unlike the dream, these colors are intensely real, beyond vivid. She is filled with a desperate urgency, knowing Cowboy is next, that he will be . . .

The kid's eyes blinked, spotting something to the side. Whatever vision Rachel had seen evaporated. But his hands remained tight around her throat, cutting off her air, her blood. Light was fading. She was on the verge of losing consciousness when his eyes returned to hers and she saw . . .

Sean racing toward her through the fog and smoke. She hears a gunshot and sees his face fill with surprise. He grabs his chest while two more shots fling him backward, tumbling onto a flight of concrete stairs.

"No!" she screams. Before she can help, a red light flares into her eyes. She shields them to see an ocean of empty seats, thousands of them. She is all alone on a stage as the tiny firefly flits about her hand, then moves to her chest, darting toward her throat. She hears a single shot fired, whoomp, feels her head thrown back. There is no pain, only encroaching darkness as she looks up and sees a giant video image of her face staring down at her, pieces missing from it like a jigsaw, until she collapses and falls to the stage, falling away from the image, falling into light. . . .

"Rachel?"

She tried opening her eyes, but they were too heavy.

"Rachel?"

She tried again and with determination finally forced them open to see Sean staring down at her.

"Are you all right?"

"Ye—" She was stopped by the pain in her throat. She could still feel where his hands had been. She could only nod.

"Are you sure?"

She forced out the word. "Yes." Only then did she see the handful of people staring down at her. Embarrassed, she tried to sit up.

"No," Sean said, gently holding her down. "Just stay there. I've called nine-one-one. Stay there till they check you out."

"Cowboy," she croaked.

"What?"

"He's going . . . after Cowboy. Now."

Alarm filled Sean's face. "Now? Are you sure?"

She nodded. "Yes, and—"

He turned toward the escalator, hesitating, trying to decide.

"I'll watch her," a heavyset woman in a business suit said. "You go ahead."

Sean rose, looking up the escalator.

Rachel tried to grab him, to warn him. "Not just—"

"You'll look after her?" he repeated to the woman. "Stay here until the EMS arrives?"

"Yes."

Rachel tried again. "Not just him—"

"It's okay." He kneeled next to her again. "She'll stay with you."

Rachel shook her head. But he was already rising and heading toward the escalators.

"No," she cried, then broke into coughing. "Sean—"

"Easy," the woman said. She stooped down, trying to calm her. "Just take it—"

Rachel struggled to sit up. "Sean!"

But he was already sprinting up the steps, disappearing from her sight.

THE KID ENTERED the security code she had provided for Cowboy's apartment building. The lock gave a dull *buzz-click*, and he pulled open the glass door. Before stepping inside the lobby, he slipped the mask over his face. It was a cardboard cutout he'd made of some famous painter. Another one of her games. She liked games. She lived for games. And although the cluster hated sharing control of him, they still enjoyed playing. Besides, the mask actually served a purpose, keeping his identity hidden from the video camera up in the corner.

He turned right and limped up the stairs.

It was earlier than she had ordered. They weren't supposed to come until after they visited the office. But the girl had appeared and messed up their plans—she always messed up their plans. So they improvised and postponed their visit to the office. Instead of receiving any last-minute instructions for the big night, they came directly to the apartment building.

Of course the host voiced his usual complaints. "When do I kill the girl?"

"In time."

"You always say that!"

"Do you or do you not wish for glory?"

"Well, yeah, but—"

"Then be patient."

They arrived at the top of the stairs, and his mind shifted gears. "What if we're too early? What if she's still in the apartment? What if she hasn't given him the drug? What if—"

"Silence!"

Moments later they arrived at the door. It was unlocked, just as she had promised. He slowly pushed it open. Morning sun filtered through the shutters, throwing stripes of light and shadow across the beige Berber carpet. It was a man's apartment—leather couch, big-screen TV, a bar. On the nearby end table a lamp had been tipped over. He turned and headed down the hallway, stepping over a glass tumbler whose brown contents had spattered the wall and spilled across the carpet. He could still smell the alcohol. Near the bedroom, a picture had been pulled off the wall, its glass frame shattered.

Inside the bedroom, the fat detective was passed out on the bed in his Jockey shorts. Beside him, on the nightstand, lay the body stocking, tutu, and hair ribbon . . . exactly as she had promised.

The detective stirred, then spoke. His voice was slow and slurred, barely a mumble. "Shaawon?" Good. He was ready.

They could feel the kid's heart racing the way it always did before a kill. *"Easy,"* they cautioned.

"I know what I'm doing!"

"Patience and obedience."

"I know, I know."

"They are your paths to glory."

CHAPTER TWENTY

COWBOY?" SEAN knocked on the apartment door. "It's Sean. Picasso."

He tried the door. It was unlocked. Immediately suspicious, he pulled his Glock from the holster, nudged open the door, and stepped inside. There was a lamp overturned on the end table. He moved past it, around a leather sofa, and checked behind the bar. He took a quick peek into the kitchen, then headed down the hallway—all the time keeping his gun raised toward the ceiling, straining to hear any movement. Up ahead he spotted a glass that had been dropped, its amber liquid staining the carpet. He continued toward the closest doorway, which he guessed was the bathroom. He pressed himself against the wall, then spun into the doorway, gun aimed.

It was empty. A green hand towel was left crumpled beside the sink, and there was the faint smell of aftershave. A grimy film had accumulated around the base of the faucet, and the mirror had a month's worth of water spots. The glass door on the shower was no better. But nobody was present.

He stepped back into the hallway. At the end, near the bedroom, a framed poster of a cowboy riding a bucking bronco had fallen to the floor. The glass was broken, with large pieces still clinging to the frame. That's when he heard it—movement, grunting. With every nerve on edge, he eased toward the bedroom. He'd practiced this a dozen times at the academy but never with live ammunition and never without a partner. Again he pressed against the wall, pausing a moment to catch his breath. There was a dull thud followed by a loud grunt and a groan.

He spun into the doorway, gun poised. Cowboy and the kid with the shaved head had fallen off the bed and were grappling— though Cowboy was more asleep than awake. He was dressed in a body stocking, tutu, and hair ribbon.

"Police!" Sean shouted.

The kid looked up, startled, then lunged for the Smith & Wesson on the nightstand. Cowboy's position made it impossible for Sean to get a clean shot, so he holstered his weapon and leaped at them. The impact seemed to wake the detective, but only for a moment. He was no help as Sean pulled the kid off him and the two rolled across the floor. The boy had managed to get the gun, but only by the barrel. He was no fighter, but his strength was superhuman. Sean kneed him in the gut, once, twice, but it barely registered. They rolled the opposite direction, and Sean tried to choke him out, but was stopped as the kid smashed the butt of the gun into his face. Seeing stars, Sean fought to keep conscious. He found the hand holding the gun and grabbed it. He slammed it against the ground once, twice, three times until he broke the kid's grip and the weapon clattered across the floor toward Cowboy. Sean started for it, and that was his mistake. The kid threw a headlock on him and began punching Sean's skull over and over again. The blows should have broken his hand, maybe they did, which may explain why he released Sean, pushed away, and made a run for it.

By the time Sean had rolled onto his hands and knees, shaking consciousness back into his head, the kid was gone. But not Cowboy. Sean heard a gun chambering a round and the detective's slurred voice. "So izz you."

He looked up and saw Cowboy, head propped against the bed, half asleep or, Sean suspected, half drugged. Still, the man was coherent enough to be aiming the gun at him.

"Are you okay?" Sean asked.

"Pu yer gun there." Cowboy squeezed his eyes shut, then opened them wide, trying to focus. "On the dresser."

"What?"

"You're unner arres."

Sean started toward him. "What are you—"

Cowboy stiffened, ready to fire.

Sean froze and motioned toward the door. "He's getting away."

Cowboy shook his head, then discovered his tutu and body stocking. He glared back at Sean and swore.

"No," Sean said. "You don't think I—"

"She sayz it waz you."

"Who said?" Sean started toward him.

"Stay back. She sayz you fi the profile."

"Who said? What profile?" Sean continued toward him. "Listen, I don't know—"

The room roared with the explosion of Cowboy's gun. The .45-caliber hollow-point smashed into Sean's upper arm with such force that it spun him backward. The blazing hot pain came a moment later.

"He waz my partner!" Cowboy shouted. "Eleven yearz!" He swore and took aim.

This time Sean had the good sense to roll to his left as a second round splintered the wood of the dresser directly behind his head. The concussion of the gun had given Cowboy greater clarity. Or at least better aim.

Sean scrambled to his feet, saw the gun following him, and leaped behind the bed, dodging a third round.

"It wasn't me!" he shouted.

Cowboy continued swearing.

Sean looked up at the door and bolted for it. Cowboy fired again, shattering the door frame just above his head as Sean stumbled over the fallen rodeo poster and raced down the hall. But even as he ran he understood Cowboy's reasoning. People had always thought the murderer could be internal. Killroy's death only confirmed it. But it wasn't Cowboy doing the killing. Cowboy was wearing the clothes of the next victim . . . the very clothes *Sean* had given him. No, there was little doubt who Cowboy or the rest of the department would now suspect.

"She says you fit the profile."

RACHEL GATHERED THE papers from the floor of her father's cubbyhole office. This was where they found him. No surprise. He often came here in the middle of the night to read, study, and, more important, to pray over his flock. Sometimes early Sunday mornings she'd catch him kneeling in the sanctuary before a specific chair, laying hands on it, praying for the same person who sat there week in and week out. Today she'd come here to search for his Bible. It wasn't at the hospital, and she couldn't imagine him being without it. Setting the papers on his desk, she rose, stiff and sore from the morning's encounter in the parking garage. At Sean's request she'd let the EMS team check her out. Other than a few scrapes and bruises, they gave her a clean bill of health.

She bent back down to pick up his fallen chair and found the Bible crushed underneath it, facedown. She scooped it up, ever so tenderly, and began straightening the pages, smoothing the cover . . . until emotions rose up so strong that she had to lean against the desk just to stand.

Her father had not yet regained consciousness.

But there was more.

She'd tried calling Sean a dozen times to warn him, but he was not picking up. Maybe he was already dead. She'd seen the shots clearly enough, saw him tumbling backward on the steps. And she'd seen something else as well. When she looked into that boy's eyes she saw her own head flying back, her own body falling onto the stage. From that instant on she knew Sean Putnam would not be the only casualty.

And yet just twenty minutes earlier she'd received a call from Cowboy. Despite her dream, despite her vision, the detective was alive. Alive and searching for Sean.

"You hear from him, you call me immediately, got it?"

"Is he okay?" she'd asked. "Is he in trouble?"

"If you only knew, sweetheart. If you only knew."

"Listen, I had another dre——"

But the line went dead. He'd hung up. She thought of calling him back, of telling him what she knew, but she doubted it would help. Since the beginning, the more information she provided, the worse things got. So at least for now, she would wait. And she would pray.

She straightened herself up and, clutching the Bible, stepped into the small, bare room they called the sanctuary. She drifted through it, running her hands over the backs of the folding chairs, losing herself to memories. This was her second home. She'd played here with her sister as a child. Ricky Turner had asked her to the prom by the front door. And when she'd returned from the psychiatric hospital, she often came here to find peace and solace within its silence. Not only peace and solace, but sometimes, if she was very still, the patterns. Something she'd give anything to experience now.

"You are God's hands to His people."

"From what I've seen it's just another business."

"You're not working for God, you're using Him."

"I don't know who you are anymore."

So many voices. So much input. And now the boy with the shaved head. Why did she keep seeing herself in his place? Why did she keep feeling his guilt and his pain? How did that fit with the other missing pieces of the puzzle? A puzzle as fragmented as her own face in that vision before she'd collapsed onto the stage. They were all related. There *was* a pattern. But it was just out of reach, just beyond her understanding.

"Rachel?"

She turned to see Mr. Miller silhouetted in the midday sun that poured through the doorway.

"How do you feel?"

She'd not told him about the attack in Century City, or the vision of Sean's death. Or hers. She wasn't sure why. She suspected it was because she didn't need to hear any more voices and certainly no more opinions. "Your headache," he said. "How do you feel?"

She stretched her neck, surprised that the pain was fading. "How odd." She rolled her head in both directions. "It's almost gone."

"That's terrific. So you'll be able to perform tonight without the medicine."

Perform. He'd used that word for weeks, but this was the first time she really heard it. And it made her uncomfortable.

"Snake-oil sellers and con artists."

"Rachel?"

She turned to her father's makeshift podium and frowned.

Mr. Miller stepped quietly into the room. "Is there a problem?"

"I don't . . . know." She turned back to him. "Something's not . . . I don't know if I'm ready."

"Oh, you're ready," he said with a chuckle. "After all the time we've been rehearsing, you're more than ready."

Rehearsing. The word struck her as strongly as the other.

She shook her head. "No, I don't mean that, I mean . . . I don't know . . . I don't know if it's really for me."

Mr. Miller shifted, letting the silence grow.

"Maybe Daddy's right. Maybe we really are only supposed to focus on the depth of our ministry. Maybe God is the one responsible for its width."

"'This is to my Father's glory, that you bear *much* fruit and so prove to be—'"

"I know the verses, Mr. Miller. You've quoted them a dozen times." More softly she added, "And so have I."

"That doesn't make them any less true."

She nodded and looked about the room. "We used to be so excited when someone came to Jesus. Momma, she'd invite them over to the house or sometimes we'd have big potlucks, right here, right in this room." She quietly mused. "The Bible says the angels rejoice when just one sinner comes to know Jesus. Daddy said if it was good enough for the angels to throw a party, it was good enough for us." Her voice grew even softer. "Right then, they were the most important people in the world."

"That's a wonderful outlook, and from your father's perspective, absolutely correct."

She turned to him.

"Considering the size of the church, a single new member would increase the congregation by up to five percent."

She shook her head. "You never stop, do you?"

"'The fields are ripe for harvest,' Rachel. 'To whom much is given, much is required.'"

"And Daddy? Was his work here just a joke?"

"Your father's a good, decent man. And there's far more you two agree on than disagree."

"But we both know what he feels about my work. We both know what he'd have me do."

Miller shook his head. "I don't think so."

She looked at him.

"Your father trusts you. Despite his temper, despite the arguments, he's always known you would obey your calling."

She nodded, slowly repeating the concept, "My calling."

"No one can tell you what the Lord wants you to do, Rachel. No one except the Lord."

She gave another nod and took a deep breath. "Then, I think . . . I need more time."

"Fine. After tonight we'll take a break and—"

"No. Before tonight."

"What?"

She did not respond.

"Rachel, what are you saying?"

She closed her eyes, struggling to see the pattern. A clue. Anything.

He continued, "You would have me cancel tonight? After all our preparation? After all our hard work?"

"I need more time."

"Okay. After the—"

"Now. I need more time now."

He stood a long moment. She knew he was trying to stay calm. At last he answered. "All right, I understand. But would you at least do this?" He glanced at his watch. "We still have a few hours before the tech rehearsal. Will you spend that time praying and make sure it's really what God wants you to do?"

She hesitated a moment, then slowly nodded.

"Okay then. Rehearsal is at three-thirty. If I see you there, we'll continue. If not . . ."

She answered quietly, her voice thicker than she expected. "Thank you."

He nodded, hesitated another moment, then turned and stepped from the church into the bright sunlight.

Rachel stood alone in the quiet. At last she turned and eased down into the nearest chair, not far from her father's pulpit. She breathed in the silence, trying to calm her mind. If she could just be still enough to let the patterns emerge, to take shape. If she could just be still enough to know.

DR. FIELDS DID not bother to hide her contempt. "So you came here because your lady friend had another dream?"

But Sean would not be put off. "You didn't answer my question. How do you know him? Is he one of your patients?"

"Of course he's one of my patients. Willy Arden. I've been treating him for months."

"And you never thought to mention it?"

"I never saw the need."

Sean repositioned himself in the chair, trying to block the pain in his upper arm. The wound had turned from a searing fire into something even less bearable. Hollow-points do vicious damage—not so much going in as coming out. He'd shoved paper towels soaked with alcohol into and around the torn flesh, keeping everything in place with tightly wrapped duct tape, all courtesy of the nearest Target. But he knew infection was setting in. He also knew that dropping by an ER would mean certain arrest—not the brightest move given his current lack of favor with Cowboy and the rest of RHD.

She saw him wince and said, "You really should have that looked at."

"I'm all right."

"Are you sure? At least let me give you something for the pain."

It was Sean's turn for contempt. He was in pain, not stupid. "No, thank you." She smiled and he pressed in. "What's his connection with the girl? With Rachel?"

"Oh, he doesn't like her, I can tell you that much. His personalities keep claiming she's spying on them."

"Personalities?"

"Dissociative identity disorder."

Sean frowned.

"Multiple personalities. Textbook. Though in his case, every one of them has a nasty disposition. Strange." She took a moment and quietly sighed. "Regardless, she's played a great game . . . which is why she'll be the ultimate prize."

"Game? Prize?"

"Don't tell me you forgot what I'd said about sociopaths—the game is all that matters. Winning is the only joy."

"So he's a sociopath?"

She broke into a laugh, shaking her head. "And I thought you were the bright one." With another sigh, she reached for the phone on her desk.

Sean's pulse quickened. "You said a prize. How will she be a prize?"

"He's been very patient and played along—always with the promise that he could take her out with a bang, a real blaze of glory." She chuckled as she began to dial. "And it doesn't get any more glorious than an audience of thousands on national television."

"You're talking about tonight? The Arena?"

She finished dialing and tossed back her hair, ignoring his question.

Sean tried another approach. "He's the one she keeps seeing in her dreams?"

"Apparently. After the assistant chief's death, her dreams made her a player. It wasn't planned, but it definitely heightened the excitement." She sat back in her chair, waiting for someone to pick up.

"Assistant Chief of Police Hampton?"

"Yes, a closet lesbian with some definite luggage."

"She was a patient of yours?"

"Until I started making house calls."

Sean's mind raced, trying to make sense. "You were her lover? That's how he got access to her house?" Fields remained silent and he ventured, "What about Deputy Police Chief Wilson?"

"Not much in the sack, but he made a nice trophy."

Sean swallowed. "The clothes delivered to Killroy . . . they were taken right from Parker Center. And the Lautrec clown outfit, it was in my desk drawer. You have access to the division, don't you?"

Fields's face brightened, and she spoke into the phone. "Hey, babe. When you're right, you're right." She nodded and looked at Sean. "Yes, right here in front of me."

Sean tensed.

"Actually, I'm not sure how I can do that. He has a gun pointed at me." She looked at Sean. "I can't talk you into staying, can I?"

Sean rose from his seat.

She returned to the phone. "Nope, don't think so. If I were you, I'd hurry though. He seems a bit antsy. Right. See you soon." She hung up but Sean was already heading for the door. "Sure you can't stay? Your buddies from RHD should be here any minute."

He rushed into the waiting room and threw open the door to the hallway. He barely heard her parting words.

"Be careful out there, the world's full of crazies."

RACHEL HAD RETURNED to the hospital to bring her father's Bible and to sit with him. Though the empty church had been full of memories, she had found little guidance on what to do. Maybe here, in this silence, she could better hear direction. But she'd barely pulled the chair up to her father's bed before the door to his room opened and some pudgy businessman with buttery jowls entered.

"I'm sorry, I don't mean to interrupt, it's just . . . well, it's my daughter. We've been waiting for you all morning. I was wondering if you would, you know, maybe pray for her."

Rachel closed her eyes. The intrusions were happening more and more often. She didn't begrudge the people for asking; how could she? But if the anointing wasn't there, it wasn't there.

"I'm sorry," she said, trying her best to sound pleasant. "I'd like to, but it only happens when God's power is here. When I feel His presence." She spread out her palms. "And right now I don't—"

"Right, right, I understand," he said, fumbling for something inside his suit jacket. "So just tell me the amount."

"I'm sorry?"

He pulled out a checkbook and opened it. "Five hundred, a thousand—just tell me the amount to make this out for."

Rachel was stunned. "What are you saying?"

"For the healing. Just tell me how much will it cost for—"

"God's healings are not for sale."

"Right. No, I understand that. But . . ." He pulled out a pen and clicked it. "The amount, I just need to know the amount."

Her indignation grew. Was it possible? Was he actually trying to bribe God into healing his daughter? "You're not serious." Her voice grew unsteady, the way it always did when she was upset. "You want to buy God? You're trying to pay for His favor?"

He frowned. "Well, no, not that. But I mean—"

"This is a joke, right?" Another thought surfaced, Stephie-Ann's warning about the world's treachery. "Are you with the press?"

"No, ma'am. I'm an insurance agent. I'm sorry. I'm not trying to bribe God, but . . ." He dropped off, looking confused. Rachel studied his face. He appeared sincere. "On TV, at the rallies, they said, *you* said to expect God's best. You said that if we give to God, He'll give to us."

The words brought her up short. He *was* sincere. She could tell by the urgency in his eyes, the desperation in his voice. And the fact struck her like a blow to the gut. He was right. That's exactly what they'd said. What *she'd* said. The man wasn't at fault. He was simply taking her up on her word. A distraught father trying to find God's favor. A businessman trying to buy God's blessing like it was merchandise from Wal-Mart. How could she be angry at him? Wasn't he merely doing what he'd been told?

She felt the pattern begin to reemerge. Was this what was happening? Was this what they had reduced God to? A commodity, a service? And if that was the case, how did that make her anything but . . . His salesman?

"*Believing in God is not a business.*"

"*Now who's being naive?*"

With that understanding other pieces of the pattern appeared. Other realizations. Big business had to be efficient.

"*Sarah and I have been friends our whole lives.*"

"*I'm merely suggesting you surround yourself with more competent people.*"

And what business didn't have its perks for upper management?

"*We own thirty-two homes in the United States. And another five overseas. God is so good.*"

Rachel closed her eyes. No! God was not a business. He was not a product to be promoted and sold. Not through carefully rehearsed performances, not through expensive television shows, and not through sold-out arenas. The Creator of the universe was not to be handled like mass merchandise!

Finally she had her answer. The one she'd been struggling with all last night and throughout the day. Maybe since the very beginning. It was clear now. She would not go on. At least not tonight. Perhaps never again.

"Please, miss . . ."

Nor would she sell God to this . . . *customer*.

"You're our last hope." The catch in his voice drew her eyes back to his. There was so much desperation. So much need. "I didn't mean, I wasn't trying to be offensive. I just thought . . ."

As he stumbled over his words, Rachel began feeling the heat. She looked down at her hands. It had been weeks since she'd felt anything. But now . . . she touched them with her fingers, rubbed them together. It was happening. But why here, why now? If she was right about refusing to sell God, then why was He starting to move?

And the pattern . . . yes, it had started coming together, but the pieces still didn't fit. Not exactly.

"Please," he pleaded, "just pray with her. She's out in the hall. Just step outside with her for a minute."

Rachel was still angry and upset. But now even more confused.

The man opened the door, holding it for her. "Please."

She looked at him, then down at her palms. And almost against her will, she followed him into the hallway. There, in a wheelchair, her hands gnarled into claws, her face drooping with a trickle of saliva hanging from her mouth, sat his little girl. Six or seven. Rachel's anger immediately drained away. Whatever outrage, whatever confusion she had felt was overcome with compassion. She watched the man kneel before his daughter.

"Brandie, this is Ms. Delacroix. The lady we saw on TV."

Brandie looked up and gave her a twisted, sagging grin. It was grotesque, and Rachel's heart swelled until she thought it would burst.

She kneeled down to the girl. "Hi there," she said.

The child slurped back her drool and nodded an enthusiastic greeting.

Rachel smiled and looked down at her palms. They were as hot as they'd ever been. She looked back to the girl. "Can I hold your hand?"

Brandie did her best to stretch out her arm, and Rachel gently took the deformed fingers into her own. At once the girl looked up, startled.

"I know," Rachel said with a smile. "They're hot, huh?"

Brandie nodded.

"That happens sometimes. Whenever God is going to do something important. Is that okay with you? If God does something?"

Again the little girl nodded.

"Good." Rachel patted her hand. "It's okay with me, too." She smiled again, then closed her eyes and began to pray silently. The heat increased and for the first time in a very long while, Rachel Delacroix felt that indefinable peace that came only with the presence of her God.

The child flinched but did not pull away. And a moment later, the father gasped, "Praise God." Then louder, "Praise the Lord!"

But Rachel kept her eyes closed, feeling the heat and the movement under her hands—tendons popping, muscles growing, bones straightening and shifting.

"Thank You, Jesus, thank You!" The father had begun to weep. "Thank You."

And as she continued praying, as God continued moving, more of the pattern came into place. She'd made a mistake. God wasn't telling her she shouldn't go to The Arena. He hadn't said He had a problem with her ministry being run as a business, that there was too much money, that He didn't want His truth proclaimed to the masses.

No. Size and money and marketing did not matter. Not to Him. He was greater than that. His servants, His Stephie-Anns, His Jude Millers . . . or His Rachel Delacroixes may not understand, they may treat Him as a commodity, but it didn't make Him one. He was still God. His children were still His children. Whether rich like this father, or poor like Sarah with her baby, whether the crowds would be big like tonight, or small as in Daddy's church: Christ paid for each of them with His life. Each and every one. They were not crowds to Him. They were never a mass of people. Only individuals. And that was the key: the individual.

It made little difference how they marketed God or tried to exploit Him. All that mattered, all that God desired, was for each person to be treated with love and compassion—as if they were the only ones He cared for. Because for an infinite God with infinite love, it was true. Each person was unique, a precious, individual soul, the only one He lived for and died for. God was not interested in changing a world of people, He was interested in changing each person's world. That's what ministry was to Him. And if she was His representative, "His hands to His people," that's what ministry must be to her.

"*Such sweet, dear, dear people. I love every one of them to pieces.*"

Stephie-Ann was right. In all her mixed-up, corporate thinking, she was still right. She saw them as God saw them. And all the arguments about style and extravagance and money made no difference. If His individual children were in need, then He would individually touch them, individually hold them, and individually forgive them . . . because when He chose to die on the cross, *each* of them had been more important than His own life.

The girl's father had thrown his arms around his daughter and was sobbing like a child. And for good reason. When Rachel opened her eyes, she saw the girl was healed. Completely. Whole. Bright-eyed and healthy. They were so excited that neither of them acknowledged Rachel's presence. And that was fine with her. She rose and silently headed back to her father's room. She understood now. She would go to The Arena. But she would not be speaking to a crowd. She would be speaking to individuals. She wasn't sure which ones. That wasn't her concern. All she knew was that He was not the God of crowds. That's not who He had given up His life for. And that's not who she'd give up her life for.

Because, as she had suspected, she would give it up. Tonight. She understood the pattern now. The dreams, her vision, the dancing dot on her hand. It all made sense, and it was okay. If that's what He'd called her to do, she'd do it. But for the individuals.

She entered her father's room and approached his bed when her cell phone rang. She pulled it from her pocket and answered, "Hello?"

"Rachel, thank God I caught you."

Her heart leaped at the sound of Sean's voice. "Where have you been?" she asked. "I've been trying all afternoon to call you, but—"

"I had to get rid of the phone; they could trace it. Rachel, they think I'm the killer."

"I know." She took a breath and continued, "And they're going to kill you, Sean. I saw it. Somebody's going to shoot you and—"

"It's already happened."

"What?"

"Yeah, they tried but I'm okay."

Relief washed over her.

"You were right about Dr. Fields. She's the one pulling the strings."

Rachel closed her eyes and nodded. "Yes."

"And that kid. He's going to try to take you out tonight. I don't know how, but some way he's going to—"

"I know."

"You know? You saw that, too?"

"Yes."

"Then . . . you're not going. Because he's going to try to do it there. Somehow he's going to—"

"It's okay, Sean. Everything's all right."

"But . . . not if you're going."

"It's all right." She looked over at her father.

"Rachel, you don't understand."

"Yes, I do."

"But—"

"I've got to go. Thank you for everything." Her voice grew husky and she took a moment to swallow. "You're a very special friend, Sean. Thank you for all you've done."

"Rachel, wait—"

She disconnected before her emotions could stop her. A moment later he called back. But instead of answering, she turned off the phone and eased into the chair beside her father. Here she would sit, praying for God's strength and wisdom until it was time to go. And then she would rise, gently kiss her father on the forehead, and say good-bye.

CHAPTER TWENTY-ONE

I T TOOK all of Sean's training to keep his panic in check as he scanned the crowd outside The Riordan Memorial Arena. The kid was here somewhere. And if Dr. Fields was to be trusted, he was here to kill Rachel. That was the only reason Sean had come. It infuriated him that despite his warning, despite her very dreams, Rachel insisted upon attending. It was as if she'd already given up, as if she saw no reason to put up a fight and defend herself.

Well, if she wouldn't, he would.

His efforts might have been easier if his name and photo hadn't already been leaked to the press. The LAPD had little patience for rogue cops who killed their own. Not that he blamed them. Fields had done an excellent job at setting him up . . . his studies in art history, the clothes from Degas's *At the Beach* that were stolen from someone inside RHD and found on Killroy's body, Lautrec's *Cha-U-Kao* wardrobe that Sean had personally passed on to Cowboy, and finally what appeared to be his botched attempt at killing the detective. Circumstantial evidence, all of it. But enough to keep him tied up for a long time—well after Rachel's murder and Dr. Fields's likely departure. No wonder she knew so much about sociopaths and their games. The woman had played him brilliantly.

Now as he moved through the crowd wearing a pair of aviator sunglasses and a UCLA Bruins stocking cap, Sean searched for any young male with a shaved head and pronounced limp. Despite the heat from the Santa Anas, which had kicked up again, he was shivering. The infection from the gun wound had set in. But he could still move and think. And as long as he had the strength, he'd keep looking. Earlier he'd put a call in to Traci, asking her to shield his son from the news reports. He'd even tried calling the boy half a dozen times. But, as usual, Elliot had not bothered to pick up.

He spotted a pair of cops approaching and abruptly changed direction. It was surprising how many uniforms were present. And undercovers as well. His little education with the detective in the Santa Monica pizzeria made their identification easier. He even saw a parked van belonging to what he guessed to be a SWAT unit. Why so many police? Could Fields have suggested to them he'd be showing up tonight? Maybe. Maybe she'd even said he intended to be the shooter. He wouldn't put it past her. It certainly would enhance the game. But if she was so intent upon her patient taking Rachel out tonight, why would she warn the police?

"He wants to take her out with a bang, a real blaze of glory." Her words slowed him in his tracks. Was it possible? Was she planning on something greater than a single shooting? And if she could pull it off right in front of the police . . . wouldn't that make winning all the sweeter?

He spotted McDoogle and his partner from RHD approaching. Once again he turned and slunk deeper into the crowd. They were all there. Each no doubt anxious to help bring about a little justice, to do a little inner-departmental housecleaning.

He approached the main entrance to The Arena. He'd already ditched the Glock, knowing he'd have to pass through a metal detector. But he'd not planned on seeing uniforms guarding the doors, eyeballing each person as they entered. He veered off and looked for another way in. To his right, he spotted the wheelchair squad, the same fresh-faced kids he'd seen at Rachel's other events. It was risky, but he saw no other alternative. He lowered his head and hobbled toward them, developing a believable limp by the time he arrived.

"Sir?" a pimply-faced young man called out.

Sean continued to pass, pretending he hadn't heard.

"Sir, would you like some help?"

He turned to the youth, who was offering one of the wheelchairs. "I'm okay," he answered gruffly.

"It's a service we offer to all our guests."

Sean shook his head and continued.

"Please," the usher urged, "it would be my privilege. And I can wheel you right up to the front."

Sean pretended to hesitate. "Up front, you say?"

The kid smiled. "Where all the action is."

"Well . . . all right, then." Sean limped to the chair and sat down.

The young man turned and wheeled him up a handicap ramp toward a door that was unmanned by any officer. "Isn't this a lot easier?"

Sean couldn't agree more as an usher from inside pushed open the door and welcomed them.

————

"IT'S LATE," HE whined.

"*Don't worry.*"

"If it doesn't show, everything will be ruined!"

Their host was growing upset and frightened, which meant he could make mistakes. And tonight was not the time for mistakes.

"*It will be here,*" they assured him.

"I don't know." He tapped the dashboard nervously. "I don't know."

Of course he had every right to be concerned. They'd been parked alongside the Chevron station for nearly forty-five minutes, and the tanker still had not arrived. The doctor had assured them her information on the delivery time was correct—information secured from another one of her trysts. And they'd done their part. They'd even driven the route from the gas station to The Arena, carefully planning which approach would be best for crashing through its circular glass walls and destroying as much of the structure as possible.

If the tanker arrived.

The kid turned on the ignition and dropped the car into gear.

"What are you doing?"

"I'm going to find it."

"There is no possible way for you to locate it. Just stay here until—"

"I have to find it!" He was definitely worked up. "Or another one! I'll look till I find another one and—"

"Silence!"

Reluctantly, the boy came to a stop. The years of conditioning had made him so manageable.

"And turn off the ignition."

He complied.

"Patience and obedience; they are the keys."

Three more minutes passed before they heard the deep rumble of an approaching tanker and he turned to see the big rig pulling into the station.

"See?" they reassured him. *"Now you may begin."*

He opened the car door and started toward the tanker. They said nothing more. He knew what to do, had discussed it thoroughly with the doctor. It was important they not distract him.

The driver had pulled the rig to the underground storage tanks, its air brakes hissing sharply as he set them. The kid walked along the back of the truck and approached the driver's side. The man had just opened his door and was crawling out when their host pulled the 9mm from his back waistband, shoved the muzzle into the base of his skull, and fired two rounds, the pops barely noticeable over the sound of the idling tanker.

The driver fell forward against the rig's corrugated steps. The kid pulled his body away and let it tumble to the asphalt. Then he hauled himself up into the cab and shut the door. Over the weeks he'd been carefully studying the big-rig manuals and watching YouTube videos. First, he pressed the yellow button, releasing the air brakes for the tractor. Next, the red button for the trailer's brakes. Then, grabbing the wheel, gripping and regripping it in anticipation, he pushed in the clutch, found first gear, and started forward.

The power steering made it easier to handle than he'd thought, though he did scrape against a parked Lexus, creasing its door and snapping off a mirror. If the owner was nearby and shouting, he didn't hear. Instead, he pulled onto the street, forcing more than one vehicle to squeal to a stop and a horn to blast. But it made little difference. Nothing would stop them.

SEAN WAS HALFWAY through the lobby when he spotted him— young, shaved head, and riding in a wheelchair. No wonder he hadn't seen the limp. And on his lap was a green nylon back- pack—the perfect size for a bomb. Sean leaped from his wheel- chair and raced toward him, shoving his way through the crowd, "Police!" he shouted. "Stop right there! Police!"

The usher escorting the kid looked over his shoulder and slowed to a stop. Sean pushed the people aside, hoping to reach the backpack before it could be detonated. He arrived and snatched it off the kid's lap. Holding it in one hand, he used his other to yank the boy out and throw him to the floor. His arm screamed in pain and he felt part of the duct tape rip away, but the adrenaline pulled him through. Slamming the kid's face into the cement, he jerked the boy's arm behind him. "Don't move!" he shouted. The youth tried resisting, and Sean shoved his knee hard into his back. "Stay down!"

The kid squirmed and turned enough for Sean to see his face. Only then did he realize he hadn't collared a young man, but a young woman. She had no eyebrows, no eyelashes, and though her head was bald, it was not shaved. The dark rings and hollow eyes were his final clue: chemotherapy. She was undergoing chemotherapy . . . with the same effects he'd seen upon his wife.

"There!" a voice shouted.

He looked up and saw two uniforms running toward him. He staggered to his feet and bolted through the crowd.

RACHEL STOOD OFF in the wings, nervously adjusting her clothes—a backless Ralph Lauren with a rented diamond choker— as the stage manager checked her wireless mic one final time.

Mr. Miller was out onstage, doing his usual warm-up for the audience. "So tell me, are you happy you're here tonight?"

"Yes," the crowd roared back.

"I mean *really* happy?"

"Yes!"

"And are you expecting God's best?"

"Yes!"

"Good. Because that's what Rachel is all about. . . ."

Iris, her drama coach, stood beside her. Seeing how nervous she was, the woman took her hands. "You'll do just fine, honey," she said. "It's like all the other venues. Everything's exactly the same."

Rachel nodded and took a breath. It was true. Everything was identical to their smaller rallies—same band, same church choir, same warm-up routine—everything carefully honed to create an excited audience full of anticipation. There would be only two differences: the speech Rachel had been practicing for the past hour; and, of course, her murder.

Iris squeezed her hands. "You'll do great."

Once again Rachel nodded and tried to smile.

Earlier, during the tech rehearsal, she'd gotten the feel of the stage—the lights, the cues, the equipment. She counted nine, maybe ten cameras, plus one on a track hanging from the ceiling. And she had to glance only once at the JumboTron screen behind her to make sure she never looked that way again. Seeing a twenty-foot close-up of your face was more than a little unnerving.

"Just concentrate on the people," Mr. Miller had reminded her during the rehearsal. "Concentrate on the people and you'll be terrific."

"And don't worry about time," the director added. "We have a prerecorded outro should you go longer. Just follow the Spirit's leading." The last phrase didn't quite fit his gutter vocabulary, but she appreciated the effort. "God can do whatever He wants," he assured her, "just as long as He doesn't go into overtime and have to deal with the unions."

Rachel had agreed . . . though she doubted there would be any problem of people wanting to stay longer, given what she would say.

Back onstage, the band began a quiet *thump-thump-thump* that quickly grew in volume as Mr. Miller wound up his introduction. "Why are you here again?" he shouted. "To expect God's—"

"Best!" the audience called back.

"To expect what?"

"God's best!" they shouted.

"That's right," he agreed. "To expect God's best. And so, without any further ado, ladies and gentlemen, it is my great pleasure—no, it is my great *honor*—to introduce to you the young lady who will make sure we receive His best."

That was her cue.

"Ladies and gentlemen . . ."

"Go get 'em, kid," Iris said.

Rachel nodded, taking another deep breath.

"Miss Rachel Delacroix!"

With a prayer on her lips, she stepped out into the light. The audience was on its feet, cheering. She smiled, waving as she took the long walk to center stage. This was the easy part, rehearsed over so many weeks she could do it in her sleep.

"Hello," she called out to the lights. "How is everyone?"

The crowd clapped and cheered.

"Good," she said with a grin, "good." Out of the blue she was hit by a wave of uncertainty. Things had made so much sense back in her father's hospital room. But here, in front of all these people, the lights, the cameras. . . . She took another breath to calm herself. And another. She looked down at her hands. They were as cool as ever. Her heart pounded so loud, she wondered why the microphone didn't pick it up. Well, it was now or never. If she didn't start, she never would. She swallowed and began.

"I'm afraid . . ." Her voice caught and she swallowed again. A stagehand suddenly appeared from below, offering her a bottle of water. She shook her head and pressed on. "I'm afraid if you've come to be healed tonight"—she took another breath—"I'm afraid if that's why you've come, you're going to be disappointed."

The audience chuckled as if she'd made a joke.

She looked up, surprised. "No, I'm serious." She raised her hands, showing them her palms. "See? Whenever God's about to move, He makes my hands real hot, like they're on fire. But not tonight." She looked back at her palms. "Tonight there's nothing. They're completely normal."

She heard people shifting and realized they were still standing. "Please, please take your seats. This shouldn't take too long. Please sit." She paused, waiting as they settled.

"We love you, Rachel!" someone shouted.

"Praise God!" another yelled.

Applause swept through The Arena.

She nodded a thank-you and waited as the clapping faded and the auditorium slowly fell into silence. She took another breath. "And if that's what you came for, to be healed, if that's why you gave your money tonight, then maybe you should get a refund. I mean God, of all people, ought to have a money-back guarantee, right?" She looked into the lights, smiling at her little joke.

There were polite chuckles. She felt her face growing hot, her ears starting to burn.

"But that would be okay, wouldn't it? I mean, if God doesn't deliver?" She talked faster, falling into the speech she'd carefully rehearsed. "I mean if all we did tonight was just worship and tell God how much we loved Him, that should be enough, shouldn't it?"

There was mild agreement, a spattering of amens, but not what she'd hoped. The old fears continued to rise, trying to take hold. But she fought them back. Resisting the temptation to look down at the stage floor, she shaded her eyes from the lights and tried to see their faces. "But we don't have to, do that," she said. "I mean, we can get all worked up and believe something's going to happen, right?" She turned to the choir. "We know how to do that, don't we? I mean we're pros at getting people all worked up, right?"

Most of the choir members continued to smile, though a few began trading looks.

She turned back to the audience. "But when you go home tonight, or tomorrow or the next day, you're going to find"—she tried to swallow, but her mouth had become desert-dry—"you're going to find that we were just another form of entertainment, just another distraction to make you feel good." She tried swallowing again and looked for the stagehand. "I could go for that water, if you still have it."

A bottle suddenly appeared and was handed to her. "Thank you." She unscrewed the cap and took a sip. As she did, she noticed how violently her hands trembled.

"Expect God's best!" someone shouted. It wasn't angry, more of an encouragement. Others applauded and picked up the phrase. "Expect God's best! Expect God's best!"

Rachel's head began growing light.

"Expect God's best! Expect God's best!"

She took a breath and tried shouting over them, "You're right! You're—" But it was futile.

"Expect God's best! Expect God's best!"

She waited for what seemed like forever until the cries faded.

"You're right," she repeated. "God wants us to expect His best. But—"

The auditorium broke into cheers and applause.

Again she waited until they quieted. "But the question is: What *is* God's best?" Remembering her training, she began to focus on their faces—the little Latino woman in the third row, the bald white man behind her, his grinning wife in the sunflower dress. She pushed on. "What if God's best is *not* for you to be healed? What if God's best is not to give us whatever we want?"

She paused, letting the words sink in as she dropped her gaze to the front row, looking at the big mama in the wheelchair, the daughter or granddaughter staring up in awe and a little confusion. "What if Jesus loves us so much that His best is to give us what we need instead of what we want?" Her voice was growing high and thin and she paused to take another drink. "What if, as my daddy says, He knows what will really make us whole and complete? What if He really knows what we need so we won't lack in anything?"

The auditorium grew absolutely silent. Any minute, she expected Mr. Miller to come charging back onstage. But until then she would continue. "Or what if this whole meeting here isn't even about us?"

There was some quiet murmuring, and she felt her body begin to tighten. "Does somebody . . . does somebody have a Bible?"

Hands lifted throughout the auditorium.

She turned to a person in the wheelchair row—a skinny, white-haired gentleman. "Could I"—she moved to the edge of the stage—"could I borrow that?"

Under the watchful eye of a security guard, the old man struggled to his feet and handed it to her. She stooped down and took it. "Thank you." When she rose, she felt light-headed and paused, waiting for the dizziness to pass. She began flipping through the pages, her hands clumsy and shaking. Finally she found the verse and began to read: "'For by Him all things were created: things in Heaven and on Earth, visible and invisible . . . all things were created by Him and for Him.'"

She looked back at the audience. "What if that were true? What if everything really was created by God and for Him?" Her voice was trembling, growing tight and airy. She knew the symptoms—she was shutting down. "What if we were created for Him, not Him for us? What if"—her throat constricted, making each word an effort—"what . . . if instead of . . . God serving us"—she choked out the words, faint and breathy—"what if God's best . . . is us . . . serving . . . Him?"

HIS HEART BEAT in anticipation as he downshifted and turned the tanker onto the dirt service road. Just ahead rose a small knoll. Beyond that, on the other side, lay The Arena. He pressed the accelerator to the floor, and the big rig began building up speed.

His cell phone rang and he pulled it from his jeans. "Hello?"

"I see you, babe." The doctor's voice was calm and in control. As always, it gave him a sense of peace. He looked through the windshield and saw a pair of emergency lights on top of the knoll, less than sixty yards ahead. They flashed on and off, on and off.

"I see you, too!" he cried. He placed the phone between his ear and shoulder and gripped the wheel tighter. "It's gonna be big, isn't it?"

"The biggest."

He continued up the hill. Her BMW was in silhouette, parked so she could look down upon The Arena. She was now forty yards away.

"Everybody's gonna see it, aren't they?"

"From coast to coast." She opened her door and stepped out to face him. "You're all they'll be talking about." His lights had picked her up, and he could see her smiling.

"Everyone will know."

"Everyone. This is your moment of glory, babe. All yours. Enjoy it."

She was fifteen yards away. He raised his hand to the windshield and gave a thumbs-up so she would see it as he passed. That's when they made their move. Focusing all of their energy into his arms and hands, they yanked the wheel hard to the right, directly toward the car.

"What are you doing!" He fought them, trying to stay on the road, but they had the advantage of surprise. "Stop!"

The truck veered off the road, bouncing toward the BMW. The doctor's eyes widened in horror. She turned but had no time to move. Her mouth opened to scream as the truck's right bumper slammed into her, pinning her against the car, pushing them both several feet before the car tipped and rolled off into the weeds.

"What did you do?" he screamed.

They centered the rig back onto the road. The Arena had just crested into sight, three hundred yards away.

"What did you do? What did you do?"

They did not bother to answer.

MILLER STOOD INSIDE the television production trailer. Both he and the director stared at the monitors in disbelief. Rachel had gone completely off-script and frozen.

"What's she up to?" Miller demanded.

The director shook his head. "It ain't good TV, I'll tell you that." He spoke into his headset. "Two, go wide. Cameras five and eight, give me close-ups."

Two of the monitors zoomed in.

"Closer. I want to see that sweat on her upper lip."

Her eyes darted around the auditorium, terrified.

"Punch up eight," the director ordered.

The assistant director pressed a lit button on the control panel, and an extreme close-up of Rachel filled the program monitor.

"Throw it up on the JumboTron."

He hit another button, and the close-up appeared on the giant screen behind her.

Miller had seen enough. He ripped off his headset and crossed toward the trailer door.

"Where you going?" the director called. "This could get interesting."

He flung open the door and headed down the steps. He rounded the trailer and practically ran into Cowboy.

"There you are," the detective said. "I've got news."

Miller didn't stop. "I saw the reports. Your boy wonder's the killer."

"There's more."

"I can hardly wait."

"He's here."

Miller slowed. "You're kidding."

"Wish I was. And according to Dr. Fields, your girl is his next victim."

Miller's stomach dropped. He picked up his pace and ran toward the stage.

———————

"WHAT DID YOU do?" the kid screamed. He searched the side mirror, looking for the doctor.

"Pay attention."

"But—"

"Pay attention!"

The Arena lay 120 yards ahead. Cars filled the lot on both sides, but the road to the service entrance was clear and unimpaired.

"Lock the throttle."

He continued searching for her body. "That's not what we planned! That's not what—"

The stronger ones shouted, *"Turn the throttle lock now!"*

They'd rehearsed every move dozens of times. This was the next step.

"Now!"

And the practice paid off. Despite his panic and confusion, he grabbed the black handle below the ignition and pulled. Once it was out, he twisted it into the lock position. There was one final step.

"Open the door!"

But the kid had lost it. He was still looking in the mirror, searching for the doctor. "Why did you do that? Why did—"

They were sixty yards from The Arena and closing fast.

"Now!"

"Why did you—"

With no time to explain, they attacked his stomach. They cramped his gut with such force the pain threw him forward, nearly hitting his head on the wheel. He still had free will. They always had free will. But it could be controlled. If not with intimidation, then pain.

"Open the door!"

He was crying, sobbing. "Why did you do that to her? Why—" They gripped his stomach again, the cramp so sharp that he shrieked.

"Now!"

He raised his arm, his hand fumbling for the handle until he found it.

Thirty yards.

"Open it!

He opened the door, sounding an alarm in the cab.

"Jump!"

"Why did—"

They hit again, this time on the left side—so powerful his shoulder slammed against the door, opening it farther.

Twenty yards.

"Jump!"

A final cramp threw him off the seat and out of the truck. He hit the steel steps and bounced off them, landing on the asphalt, tumbling like a rag doll, dislocating his shoulder and cracking ribs. If he lost consciousness, it was only for a moment. The explosion of seventy-two hundred gallons of gasoline quickly brought him around. The blast was so intense it sucked the air from his lungs. The heat singed the hair on his face and on his arms.

But he was alive. And they would continue. The mayhem and the ancillary deaths, all planned by the doctor, were nice diversions, as rewarding to them as the doctor's own death. But now, finally, they would be able to destroy the girl.

CHAPTER TWENTY-TWO

T HE EXPLOSION had been on the left side of the complex. Miller could smell smoke the moment he entered the backstage door. Cold water from overhead sprinklers rained down on him, soaking his clothes as he ran past the exiting stagehands. "Rachel!" He grabbed a burly man by the arm. "Where's Rachel?"

The man jabbed his thumb toward the stage. "Still out there!" He yanked his arm free and continued toward the door.

Miller worked his way to the stage, smoke already burning his eyes. "Rachel!" He doubted she could hear him over the hiss of sprinklers and the panic from inside the auditorium. He passed a final panel of curtains and saw her leaning against a light tower. She was drenched. Her hand was over her mouth as she stared out at the pandemonium before her—people shouting and screaming, running toward the exits as thick smoke seeped in from the left side of the auditorium.

He joined her. "We have to get you out of here!"

She continued staring into the auditorium.

"Rachel!"

When she spoke, it was as much to herself as to him. "I don't understand."

"What? What do you mean?"

"It's happening . . . all over again."

"What are you talking about?"

She turned to him. "The smoke, the fire, what happened to Momma and Rebecca."

"We have to get you out of here!" he repeated.

Suddenly the banks of overhead lights starting going off, one after another. Only the JumboTron screen behind them remained working.

"Rachel!"

She looked at him as if he were a stranger, then turned back to the auditorium. An orange glow was coming from the left exits.

"Let's go!" He grabbed her arm, but she resisted. "Rachel!"

"My hands." She held them out to him.

He glanced at them and took them into his own. They were burning up.

"God's here," she said quietly. "He's going to do something. I have to stay."

"Are you crazy?" He motioned toward the smoke-filled auditorium, the people screaming and panicking. "This whole place is going up!"

"I . . . have to stay." She turned to him. "This is where I belong."

"No." He took her arm again. "Absolutely not!" He began pulling her toward the exit, but she fought him.

"Let go!" She twisted, trying to break free. "Let me go, this is where I belong! This is what He wants!"

The last phrase brought him to a stop. Memories of another argument with another prophet on a suicide mission came to mind. He shook his head. "No, you're wrong! There's no reason for you to die! Why would He want you to die?"

She said nothing but quietly searched his face.

He continued, "If you leave now, you can come back even bigger. Don't you see that? This isn't the end. It's the beginning.

If we play it right, everyone will pay attention! You'll be bigger than ever!"

She remained staring. A look of pity began to fill her face. Pity mixed with compassion.

"No." He shook his head. "NO!"

"You go ahead," she softly said.

"Not until you come with me! Not until you see reason!"

A smile flickered across her lips. "There's reason here—greater than you and I can ever understand."

He searched her eyes. He could see it, she had made up her mind . . . with the same misguided logic he'd heard so many centuries before.

"Go." Her voice grew even softer. "Do what you have to do."

He looked down at his grip on her arms, then slowly released it. He turned back to the auditorium. The smoke grew thicker by the second.

"Go," she whispered.

He turned to her a final time.

She gave a nod of understanding.

He took a tentative step backward, hesitated. Then he turned and raced toward the exit, where he would disappear into the night.

———

IT WAS GLORIOUS, just as she'd promised, red and yellow flames filling the night sky. Any minute the reporters would be there. Helicopters, too. But his job was not over. Nor theirs. He'd barely staggered to his feet before they ordered, *"Run! To the other side of the building! Run!"*

He obeyed, every step jarring his ribs, every breath an effort. The parking lot swarmed with people pouring from the exits—shouting, screaming, crying from shock, confusion, terror.

"You did well," they told him. *"Very well."*

He took a painful breath. "Is she still alive?"

"Yes. Hurry!"

He moved against the crowd, each bump causing him to wince in pain. He arrived at a door on the other side of the building and fought against the stream of people as he entered. There was no fire here. Not yet. The lobby was dark save for the harsh glare of emergency lights above the exits.

"Son!"

He looked back to see one of the cops near the door directing the crowd.

"You can't go in!"

He reached for the gun in his back waistband.

"No."

"But—"

"No! The girl!"

He turned from the cop and hid the gun as he continued to shove his way through.

"You!" Another voice shouted, this time from above.

He looked up into the light and shadows of the landing above him and saw the cop, the one who had attacked him on the escalator, who had stopped him from killing the older detective in the apartment. Again he reached for his gun and again he was ordered, *"No!"*

But this time he would not stop. Before they hit him with another cramp, he pulled the 9mm from his pants and fired. The round sparked off a hand railing three feet from the cop. People screamed as he squeezed off two more rounds.

COWBOY HEARD THE shots echo through the lobby. He spun around, spotted action on the second-story landing. A man in a UCLA stocking cap was ducking and running. The light caught his face for the briefest instant. Picasso!

Pulling the gun from his holster, Cowboy started for the stairs. "Police!" he shouted as he pushed through the crowd. "Step aside! Police!" Those who didn't move obeyed when they saw the gun over his head. Arriving at the stairs, he scrambled up them as fast as he could. He noticed further commotion below, in the main lobby, but did not stop. He had seen the murderer of his partner, and that was his only focus.

THE PATTERN WAS coming together. Like an exploding jigsaw puzzle, but in reverse, the pieces joined faster and faster. The smoke, the fire, the unshakable feelings of guilt, Daddy's and Mr. Miller's arguments, the father with his daughter in the wheelchair, the young man who kept appearing in her dreams . . . and the heat in her palms. Everything was locking together. Seamlessly. Now she knew. And with that knowing came a rising confidence, a confidence enabling her to turn and walk back to center stage. The auditorium was dark now, save for the bright lights over the emergency exits and the glow of the JumboTron behind her. Black smoke continued coming in as the last of the audience exited, stragglers being helped by others.

This is what she'd been called to do. God was not interested in big-budget productions—or the lack of them. He was not concerned with people exploiting Him—as long as people weren't exploited. His only interest was in the individual. And that's what He was asking of her now. To reach out to an individual. To be His arms and hands. To embrace one of His children.

Because that child was here.

She spotted a glowing red dot beyond the stage—the light of a TV camera, its operator long gone. She stepped closer to it and glanced over her shoulder at the JumboTron. There was a fleeting glimpse of her arm. She shifted until more of her body came onto the screen. Then she continued forward, looking over her shoulder, careful to stay in frame, until she stood at the edge of the stage, her face filling the screen.

She took a breath, the smoke burning the back of her throat, and called, "Hello?" Her voice blasted through the speakers, ending in earsplitting feedback. She tried again, softer. "Are you there?" She scanned the auditorium, peering into the darkness. "I know"—she coughed—"I know you're here. And I'm sorry for ignoring you . . . all those times. . . . I'm sorry."

———————

HER VOICE STARTLED them.

"But you really are important."

"It's her!" they shouted.

"You wouldn't know it by how I've acted." She coughed again. "But you are very, very important. You mean more to God than you can possibly imagine."

"Where is she?" the host asked as he searched the lobby.

"There!" They directed his gaze to one of the television monitors. Her face was in close-up. He turned back to the landing where the young cop had been, then to the stairs where the older one had raced after him.

"Forget them. It's her."

"He loves you. I'm sorry if that sounds trite, and I wish I had better words for you. But the Creator of the whole universe loves you. He . . . adores you."

The kid frowned, confused. "What—what do I do?"

"You still have the gun."

"He cherishes you more than you can possibly imagine."

Her words had started burning them like acid. *"Kill her!"* they shouted.

He searched the lobby, unsure what to do.

"Inside! She's on the stage! Kill her!"

He nodded and bolted toward what he hoped was the nearest entrance.

SEAN SPRINTED ALONG the second-story hallway that surrounded the auditorium. His shivering had grown worse, and he was starting to become light-headed. He could hear Rachel's soft voice coming from inside. Knew the killer could, too. He also knew Cowboy had spotted him and was close behind, though he hoped the smoke and darkness would provide cover. He turned sharply to one of the doors leading to the auditorium, yanked it open, and entered.

Through the smoke and the rain of the sprinklers he saw her image up on the JumboTron above the stage. Her face and hair were dripping wet as she peered out into the darkness of the auditorium.

"Please, I know you're here," she was saying. "Please let me talk to you."

Sean cupped his hands and shouted over the hiss of the sprinklers, "Rachel, don't! Rachel—"

Gunfire echoed through the auditorium, and the stuffing from the back of a nearby chair exploded. Sean spun around and spotted Cowboy one aisle over, taking aim for a second shot. He leaped to the concrete stairs as another round fired, the bullet glinting off the metal seat bottom just above his head. The impact of the floor against his arm was so intense he feared he would black out. He could feel warm liquid flowing from the opened wound. Keeping low, he crawled on his belly back up the steps. He arrived at the door, pushed it open, and reentered the hallway. He scrambled to his feet, waited for the floor and walls to stop spinning, then started to run. He knew Cowboy would be right behind. He also knew there would be no calling out his name, no demand for his surrender. If the detective did that, he wouldn't have an excuse to kill him.

"I'll stay right here." Rachel's voice echoed faintly through the corridor. "Please, just let me talk with you."

He had to get to her, warn her. But how? No matter what entrance he took back into the auditorium, as soon as he opened the door, Cowboy would hear her voice increase in volume and easily cut him off again. "Always be aware of your surroundings," the detective had told him. "Use them to your advantage." And that's exactly what Cowboy was doing.

Sean continued to run, the edges of his vision beginning to blur. The smoke was so thick he constantly coughed, barely able to catch his breath. Another shot fired. Wild. An obvious attempt to intimidate him. And it did the trick. He dug in, trying to put as much distance as possible between himself and Cowboy, using the hall's curved wall to block the man's vision.

And then he spotted it. Up ahead, a bar.

Lungs burning, head spinning, he pushed himself until he arrived at the counter and darted behind it. He dropped down and scooted underneath, next to a small, galvanized trash can. With luck Cowboy would run past, giving Sean time to double back and lose him. Not far, but enough to duck into the auditorium and help. A flimsy plan, but the best he had.

Fighting not to cough, he pressed flat against the back of the bar and strained to listen. He was shivering hard. He took a breath and held it, forcing himself to stop. He heard Cowboy's coughing as the man approached, then passed. Sean closed his eyes, took another breath and held it, waiting, waiting.

Suddenly his cell phone rang the *Star Wars* theme. He dug into his pants and fumbled to shut it off. Unable to find the right button, he hit *Answer*.

Elliot's voice asked, "Hello? Dad, are you there?"

As much as he wanted to speak, he couldn't, not yet. Not until he was sure Cowboy had gone.

"Dad?"

With effort, he crawled up onto his knees and rose slowly to peek over the counter.

"Can you hear me?" Elliot asked.

The smoke and darkness made it impossible to know for certain, but Sean took the chance. He dropped back down and pressed against the bar, whispering as softly as he could. "Son?"

"I can barely hear you."

He gripped the phone, fighting back a cough. "I can't talk right now, but—"

"Okay, fine," Elliot said.

"No, no," Sean whispered, "I want to, but—"

"Whatever."

"Elliot—"

The line went dead. Or his son was sulking. Either way, there was no response . . . except for Cowboy's sudden appearance around the bar.

"Get up." The detective coughed as he shoved the gun into Sean's face. "Now."

CHAPTER TWENTY-THREE

THEIR HOST finally arrived in the raining auditorium. All he could see through the smoke, darkness, and water was the giant image of the girl hovering above the stage. "God cherishes you," she was saying. "You have no idea how much He cares for you."

"Stop her!" they shouted.

"Please," she said, "you've got to believe me."

"Stop the lies!"

He raised his gun and fired at the screen. A portion exploded in light and sparks, leaving a giant gap of darkness where her forehead had been. He fired two more times. More flashes and sparks as her left cheek disappeared, then her entire jaw.

"Please . . ."

He fired a fourth round, and the image froze with only the mouth and right eye remaining.

"Listen to"—her voice was trembling, but she wouldn't stop—"listen to what I'm saying."

"Where are you?" he shouted at the stage. "I don't see you!"

"I'm here, over to the right."

Gun still raised, he spun to his right but saw nothing.

"No." Suddenly her voice was faint, no longer coming through the speakers. "*My* right."

He turned and spotted her, standing on the opposite side of the stage.

"I'm sorry we haven't talked before." She coughed from nerves or smoke or both. "In my dreams, I always saw you, I just didn't"—more coughing—"I didn't understand."

He continued toward her. "Understand what?"

"*Don't!*" the voices shouted.

"That God wanted to speak to you."

They were eighty feet apart.

"*Don't talk! Shoot!*"

He ignored them. "Yeah?" he sneered. "And what exactly does God want to say?"

"*Kill her!*"

She stepped to the very edge of the stage. "He wants to tell you that He aches to hold you. That"—she coughed—"that every day His heart breaks because He wants to be your Father."

The kid's anger flared as he continued toward her. He knew all about fathers and their love for sons.

"No," she said. "He's not like that."

He blinked, surprised, as if she'd read his mind.

"*Don't listen!*"

"He loves you so much that He gave up His greatest joy for you."

"*Stop her! Kill her!*"

They were twenty feet apart.

"Love me?" he taunted. "You have no idea what I've done."

"Yes"—she kneeled down to his level, her voice shaking—"I do. And in some ways, we're equally guilty." They were so close he could see the moisture in her eyes. "But He still loves me. And He still loves you."

"*Stop her! Stop the lies!*" Their screams grew deafening. "*Kill her!*"

But those eyes—he'd never seen such compassion. They were less than ten feet apart now, and all that emotion, all that love . . . directed solely at him.

"*Kill her!*" They gripped his gut in an impossible cramp and he doubled over.

"Are you all right?" she asked in concern.

He forced himself to rise, refusing to answer.

She hesitated, then continued, "He has so much love for you, He adores you so much that He killed His son for you."

"*Shoot her now!*"

Another cramp, so intense he cried out.

"What's wrong?" She reached toward him. "Are you okay?" But he backed away. "Do you understand what I'm saying? Do you understand that He thought your own life was more important than His own child's?"

SEAN ROSE UNSTEADILY to his feet.

His son called through the phone, "Dad? You there?"

Cowboy reached out, and Sean gave him the phone. Keeping a careful eye on him, Cowboy spoke into it, "Who's this?"

As Cowboy spoke, Sean fought to clear his vision, searching the hallway for some escape.

"Yeah," Cowboy answered, "well, he's a little indisposed right now." Without waiting for a reply, he snapped shut the phone and tossed it to Sean . . . inadvertently giving the rookie a chance to practice what the detective himself had taught him. "*Use every situation to your advantage.*"

Sean pretended to fumble the phone and dropped it on the floor. "Sorry."

Cowboy snorted in disgust at the obvious fear until Sean came up like a rocket with the trash bin in his hand. He slammed it into the man's chest with such force that the detective staggered backward, firing his gun into the ceiling. Before he had a chance to re-cover, Sean hit him again. This time in the face. And again.

Cowboy crumpled to the floor, and Sean nearly followed until he lunged toward the bar and caught himself. He leaned there, coughing, shaking, waiting for his strength to return. But it didn't return. There was none left.

Gritting his teeth against the pain, he somehow rose and stumbled around the bar. He no longer heard Rachel's voice, and that concerned him. After more steps than he could count, he finally reached a door. He leaned against it, fighting for breath, then opened it and staggered back into the auditorium. Up on the screen, through the smoke and rain, he saw her . . . an eerie, broken mosaic of a face, frozen in time.

"Rachel!" He stumbled down the aisle, coughing, head spin-ning. "Rachel!" He saw movement on the stage and headed toward it, his legs on autopilot.

"Sean, no! Stay back!"

But he wouldn't stay back. She had no idea the danger she was in.

"Sean!"

He saw movement below the stage in front of her—feet spread, arms braced, and taking aim. Before he could duck, the muzzle flashed, and for the second time that day he was hit with a sledge-hammer, this time to his chest. And still he continued, legs mov-ing, refusing to stop.

"Sean!"

Another shot flashed, another blow delivered—just below the first. He lurched forward and fell to the concrete, tumbling, roll-ing. The pain was intense but lasted only a moment before it began to fade. Along with his vision. He was becoming a detached viewer, someone watching from far away.

"Sean . . ." Rachel's voice also was fading. "Sean . . ."

Until he saw and heard nothing at all.

RACHEL LEAPED OFF the stage and ran toward him. She didn't know if the young man with the gun would shoot her or not. She didn't care. "Sean!"

His legs were unnaturally twisted. He was faceup, eyes unblinking. She arrived and dropped to her knees. "Didn't I warn you?" Tears streamed down her face. "Didn't I tell you?" She stared at his chest, at the wet darkness spreading across his shirt. "Didn't I?" She lowered her head and began to sob.

"So what do you think now?" The young man stood above her, his voice low and taunting. "You think your God loves me now?"

She tried to answer but only choked on her tears.

"Does He?" He shoved the barrel of the gun under her chin and forced up her head. "Does He love me now?"

She looked into his eyes. Any anger she felt evaporated. The grief was still there but how could she be angry? He was so lost, so frightened. His face began to waver. At first she thought it was from her tears, until it rippled and the frog creature she'd seen in her dreams appeared. She gasped but did not look away. It rippled again, this time becoming the reptile with the bulging eyes. Another ripple. Now a glistening, mucus-covered gargoyle, and another ripple, and another, each face morphing into another—some laughing, others snarling—until the young man's face returned, helpless, confused.

At last she managed an answer; her voice croaking, barely audible. "Yes."

"What?"

"He still loves you." She swallowed. "No matter what you do . . . He wants to be your Father. He wants you to be His son."

The young man stared at her, speechless.

And then she felt it. The heat in her palms. Hotter than before, hotter than she ever remembered. She looked down at them and then back to the young man. "Please"—she stretched her hands to him—"let Him love you. Let Him take the punishment for everything you've ever done. Everything."

The young man leaned forward, scowling as if trying to hear her words. Suddenly he shuddered and doubled over, screaming in pain.

She rose to her feet. "He can help you. He loves you. He'll—"

"No!" He staggered backward out of her reach. "I don't believe you! It's . . . not true!"

"Yes." She reached for him again but was stopped as he pointed the gun at her.

"It's not true!" He was shaking as he lifted the barrel, aiming it at her face. "You're a liar!" Even in the rain, she could see his sweat. But it did not matter. It was in his eyes. As much as she wanted to help, as much as God wanted to help, the young man would not allow it. He had made up his mind. Despite his pain, despite the fear, he'd made his decision and there would be no changing it.

"Down!" he growled. "Get back down!"

Disappointed and confused, she dropped back to her knees beside Sean's body. He'd made his decision, but it made no sense. She'd been called back into the auditorium, her palms on fire. If the Lord didn't intend to work through her, then why were they burning? Why were . . .

She looked back at Sean and understanding quickly took shape. Of course. She hesitated, then carefully reached down and placed her hands on him—one in the pool of his blood-soaked chest, the other on his mutilated upper arm. A wave of nausea rose up inside her, but she pushed it away.

"What are you doing?" the young man demanded.

She said nothing but began to quietly pray. This time there was no begging, no pleading. Just a quiet knowing. "Yes," she whispered, "yes." A fresh set of tears ran down her face. "Yes." She began to smile. "Thank You, yes, thank You," as the understanding grew and the last of the pattern came together. "Thank You." She felt movement. Sean's body twitched. And then again. "Yes . . ." He violently convulsed, then rolled his head to the side and vomited blood.

"Yes . . ." She raised her head toward Heaven, grinning. "Yes . . . yes . . ."

He vomited again, then began to cough, clearing the blood from his lungs.

The young man moved closer, looking over her shoulder. "What did—"

She turned to him.

"What did you do?"

She looked back at Sean, who was blinking, then she answered in a half whisper, "It wasn't me."

The young man inched closer.

She turned to him. "There's nothing He can't do. You just have to let—" Suddenly she saw the red dot of her dreams. It was dancing across the boy's face, into his eyes. He looked up, squinting into it.

"No!" She leaped up, shoving him aside, but she was too late.

The boy's head snapped back as a bullet cleanly entered the center of his forehead. Two more rounds followed in rapid succession, and all three would have struck him if Rachel had not pushed him aside, her momentum replacing his body with her own. For the briefest moment she saw the red firefly on the back of her raised hand before it exploded. Then the light flared into her own eyes. She tried turning away, but the final round entered her neck below the jaw.

———————

THE MOMENT THEY left his body they felt the tug—the whirlpool, the eternal current, always swirling, always pulling toward the Abyss.

"*What do we do?*" the weaker ones cried. "*Where do we go?*"
"*Silence!*" a strong one shouted.

But of course there was no silencing them. Not now. Now when they were vulnerable. Now as they clung together, fighting to hang on to the cluster as it rose and hovered above the auditorium. They'd all heard stories of the Abyss—its terrible burning and utter isolation. The paradox of unspeakable torment when they were finally separated from the Enemy, and yet the unbearable agony that came from that separation.

Their victory over the girl had been sweet, but there was no time to savor it. They streaked across the auditorium, through its wall, and slowed over the parking lot, surveying the thousands of terrified Inferiors.

"*How about her?*" a weaker one shouted, referring to a young woman about the kid's age.

"*Or him?*" another cried.

"*Hurry! I can't hang on!*"

But the experienced ones would not be rushed. It was important they choose correctly. It had to be someone addicted to the flesh so they could be manipulated through its hungers and pleasures. Someone strong enough to destroy others, yet vulnerable enough to, of their own free will, allow the cluster to enter.

They circled to the other side of the building, which was engulfed in flames. Below, paramedics were treating the injured as firemen raced back and forth, uncoiling hoses, shouting instructions, scampering like roaches—while two of their leaders debated fiercely.

"We need the one-and-three-quarter-inch hoses!" the first shouted.

"The two-and-a-half!" the second argued. "We've got to put it down first."

"No, we need to maneuver the lobby and hallways!"

"You're not listening! We have to put it down!"

It was so typical of the Inferiors. Their world was burning up and they were arguing over which hose to use.

"*Help me!*" a weaker member of the cluster cried.

"*Let go of me!*" another shouted.

"*I can't hang on. Help me! I can't—*" They kicked it away, and the current immediately sucked it from sight, leaving behind a chilling scream.

"*Over there!*" A strong one spotted commotion up on the knoll where they had destroyed the doctor. Well, not quite destroyed. As they approached they saw a small handful of Inferiors gathered around the overturned car, trying to help. Because there, trapped underneath the vehicle, was the doctor. She was still alive. Not conscious, but alive.

They dropped quickly to her. Forbidden to enter her soul without permission, they could at least speak to her. "*Doctor?*"

"*Who's . . . who's there?*" Her thoughts were frightened, desperate. A good sign.

"*Things do not look very good,*" they said.

"*Please . . . whoever you are, help me.*"

"*You may find our presence unpleasant, at least at the beginning.*"

"*I don't understand. Please, just help.*"

"*To help you, we must enter as we did the boy.*"

The doctor hesitated, a spark of clarity in her panic.

They chuckled. "*You still don't believe in our existence, do you? You certainly didn't when we occupied him.*"

A group of Inferiors were trying to help by rocking the car. The movement shot pain through her legs.

"*Please, whoever you are, whatever you want—I don't want to die.*"

"*Are you certain?*"

"*Yes, please! Whatever you want. Please—*"

She had not even finished the phrase before they rushed into her open mouth and down her throat. Her body contracted once, twice, the way bodies often do when resisting. But it did not last long.

"We've got movement!" a voice cried. "I saw her move!"

"Get a paramedic!" another shouted. "Hurry!"

The doctor coughed.

"Open your eyes."

"I can't," she protested. *"I—"*

"Open them!"

She complied. It was a small act of obedience, but a beginning.

"She's awake!" the first voice yelled.

She tried moving her mouth, to speak.

"What's that?" A young man came into her vision. He lowered his ear to her lips.

She tried again, the faintest of whispers. "Help . . . me."

"Help's on the way, ma'am. We're getting a paramedic right now."

"No . . ." She gasped, trying to shake her head. "I don't mean—"

"Silence!" They hit her with a blow so powerful that she momentarily lost consciousness. Of course she would try again; a thousand times she would try regaining control. But she was theirs now. It would take time to train her, there would be setbacks . . . but she was theirs.

Once again Rachel is surrounded by the smoke and fog of her dreams. But this is no dream. It is more real than anything she has ever experienced. The mist is not only real, but alive. It gently enfolds her, filling her with awe and peace. She waves her hand through it, and the silvery glow swirls about her fingers. She's seen it before—two, maybe three times, when she had sneaked into her father's church—the glowing fog that surrounded him when he worshiped all alone in the sanctuary, praying over the chairs. She had asked him about it, but he claimed never to have seen it. Maybe he hadn't.

Within the mist, she sees movement, a woman and little girl materialize, walking toward her. Momma and Rebecca! But not the dream version. Like the fog, they are much more real. And they are happy. Their faces radiate the same peace and joy that surround her.

"Momma . . ." She races to her mother and throws her arms around her, holding her for all she was worth, holding and holding, before reaching down and including Rebecca in the embrace. There is no shame here, no guilt. How long they hold one another, she doesn't know, but eventually she hears a voice. Male and familiar:

"God . . . I don't know if you're there . . ."

She lifts her head, peering through the fog but can see no one.

"Please don't let her die . . ."

"Sean?" She turns to Momma. "Is that Sean?"

Her mother continues to smile.

"If you can hear me . . . please, God, don't let her die."

"Is he praying?"

"She's a good person . . . I . . ." His voice breaks and he quietly begins to cry. She feels her own heart rise into her throat.

"I need her, God . . . don't take her."

"He wants me to come back?" Rachel asks. "He's praying for me to come back?"

"Please God . . ."

"Can I do that?" She turns to Momma.

"Please God . . . if You can hear me."

"Can I?"

Her mother doesn't answer, but there is no missing the twinkle in her eyes.

"Oh, Momma." Once again Rachel throws her arms around her until suddenly she is filled with indecision. How can she leave?

How can she turn her back on the two most important women of her life? How can she leave her family, the love that surrounds her, this peace, this joy?

And yet . . .

"God, can you hear me?"

She pulls away from her mother, searching her face. "What should I do?"

Momma gives no answer but reaches out and gently brushes the hair from her eyes, as she has a thousand times before. Rachel's throat tightens, aching beyond belief. Tears spill onto her cheeks. She reaches for her mother's hand, presses it to her face. "Momma." She closes her eyes and kisses it. "Oh, Momma."

Sean's voice continues, "I don't know how to do this . . . what to say . . ."

She opens her eyes, looking back into her mother's face. "He needs me," she whispers. She looks around, then adds, "And Daddy, he needs me too, doesn't he?" She searches her mother's eyes, waiting for some sign, some direction.

"Please God . . ."

And then, ever so tenderly, her mother gives the slightest of nods.

Once again, Rachel throws her arms around her neck, bursting into a fresh set of tears. But Momma only lets her cling a moment before reaching up and pulling Rachel's hands down, holding them in her own. She leans forward and gently kisses Rachel on the forehead . . . and Rachel feels as if her chest will burst.

She looks down and sees her smiling sister. "I'll miss you, peanut," she says, her own voice catching. Rebecca grins up at her, and Rachel tousles her hair as she always has.

"God . . . if you're there . . ."

And then, before she can protest, before she can change her mind, her mother and little sister step back.

"No!" Rachel suddenly panics. "Don't go! Don't—"
They dissolve into the fog.
"Momma, don't go! Not yet! I need—"
Suddenly she is unable to speak. Her eyes become impossibly heavy and she must close them.

She heard the rattle of wheels. Tried to move but felt the confinement of straps around her chest and arms.

"Please God . . ."

With all of her strength, she managed to pry open one eye. There was no smoke now, no fog. Only the night sky with its thousand stars. She blinked, trying to focus.

"There you are."

Sean came into view, staring down at her as he walked beside her. He looked tired, very much the worst for wear, but very much alive.

"Whaa—" She tried to speak but could not.

"Shh." He smiled. "Don't talk."

The rattling wheels stopped and she heard doors open.

Another voice spoke. A woman's. "Sir, you'll have to ride in a separate vehicle."

"I'm LAPD," Sean said. "I'm riding with her."

"But you're hurt."

"I'm fine."

Rachel was jostled, lifted. The ceiling of an ambulance slid into view.

The woman repeated more firmly, "We'll meet you at the hospital."

"I'm riding with her." Sean reappeared inside, smiling back down at her.

"I'll have to report this," the woman said.

"Report all you want," he said.

The woman muttered something as the doors closed, and Sean eased down beside Rachel, grinning at her. "You almost got away from me once." He took her hand and gently held it. "I'm not going to let you do it again."

Rachel smiled. She closed her eyes. And as she drifted off, she thought that would be just fine with her. Just fine, indeed.

EPILOGUE

I T WAS the first cool day of autumn—if you can still call mid-December *autumn*. The Santa Anas were long gone, and a morning chill clung to the city. Sean and Elliot had climbed out of the Taurus and were heading down a cracked and uneven sidewalk. Of course, getting his son up early on a Sunday morning was like pushing the proverbial boulder up the hill, a very steep hill. But all the recent media coverage had given Sean some equity, at least in his son's eyes, at least for the moment.

Elliot remained his usual noncommunicative self. But as they approached the church and he heard the singing—mostly women's voices and mostly in the same key—he said, "Kind of a weird place for a church."

Sean remained quiet as he scanned the street, checking for any lurking trouble. As a couple of white males walking the streets of South Central, it didn't hurt to be careful, even though he suspected "lurking trouble" wouldn't be getting out of bed till noon.

They arrived at the heavy metal door, and Sean pulled it open. The singing was louder, but no better. Still, from past experience, he knew it wasn't about the music. It was about the joy. There were fifteen or so members raising their arms and clapping their hands,

293

one or two coming dangerously close to dancing. Sean threw a nervous look at his son but couldn't read his expression.

The light spilling in from the open door drew the attention of several members including Sarah, Rachel's friend. She waved and motioned for them to join her in the front row.

Sean nodded, and they started forward. "You okay with this?" he called to Elliot.

"Sure," his son replied. And by the look of fascination on his face, he seemed to mean it.

They moved past the worshipers and joined Sarah and Rachel's father, who sat between them in a wheelchair. The stroke had left him unable to talk, much less sing, but it didn't prevent his face from registering pleasure as he listened to the music. He spotted Sean and gave a nod, which Sean returned. Because Sean didn't know the song or exactly how to join in, he was once again feeling just a little too self-conscious and a little too white. Sweet-faced Elliot, on the other hand, seemed drawn into the festivities almost effortlessly.

Up on the platform, Rachel stood by herself. She was also singing—certainly not as animated as the others, but definitely enjoying herself. She wore the same summer dress he'd seen her in that first day at the restaurant. And just as then, he was struck by her open and honest beauty. Her right hand was in a cast, and there was still a bandage under her jaw where they had performed the surgery. But even at that, there was no hiding her elegant nobility.

For Sean the healings at The Arena had been total and complete. X-rays and MRIs showed absolutely no signs of trauma—no bullets, no damaged muscle or bone, not even scar tissue. In fact, if it weren't for the holes in his shirt and the bloodstains, he'd be hard-pressed to prove he'd been shot.

Unfortunately, those were not his only issues. He'd lost track of how many grillings he'd undergone by Internal Affairs—definitely not one of his favorite pastimes. Nor did he appreciate their final recommendation—though, truth be told, he'd been thinking of resigning anyway. With all the media attention insinuating he was guilty until proven guilty (after all, he was a cop), and the morale problem of beating one's coworker unconscious with a trash can (though the reconstructive surgery promised to make Cowboy's face almost as good as new), Sean had to agree he simply was not cut out for the job. Maybe the guys at RHD were right. Maybe he didn't have the testosterone for it. Or maybe, unlike his old man, he was simply wired to see things differently.

"You don't have cop eyes," Cowboy had told him. And he was right. Some saw the worst in humanity—*"Rule number one: everybody lies"*—but Sean was either unwilling or unable to. Not only did he see the glass as half-full, but he kept marveling at its beauty. No, he was definitely not cop material. He could play the game, learn the rules, but when push came to shove he was better suited at seeing the beauty of life rather than searching out its ugliness.

Maybe that's why he'd broken out the paints and canvases again. He certainly wasn't planning on making a living at it. But as Rachel had said on more than one occasion, maybe he shouldn't hide his light under a bushel. He glanced about the church. Even here, as stiff and out of place as he felt, he couldn't help but savor the beauty—the ebony faces, creased and worn, the blue walls with their cracked plaster, the water-stained acoustic ceiling. To him, it all could have been in a photo art exhibit.

Above the door, he spotted the Van Gogh painting—the *Starry Night* Stephie-Ann had given Rachel up in Seattle. It was still in the gaudy gold frame. But even that could not detract from its beauty or Van Gogh's theme of divine light dwelling in every structure except the church. Why Rachel insisted on hanging that indictment there in plain sight, especially after he'd carefully explained its meaning, was beyond him.

Unless she meant for it to serve as a reminder.

She'd been right about Dr. Fields's involvement with the killings. The woman was currently undergoing psychiatric evaluation at Century Regional Detention Facility. Many believed the multiple voices she claimed to be hearing, as well as her own rantings and physical outbursts, were clear signs of a psychotic break. Maybe. Or maybe it was just another one of her games. No one was certain. Either way it would be a long time before she saw the light of day.

The song in the church came to an end with the expected clapping and shouts of "Glory to God! Praise Jesus!"

As they took their seats, Rachel walked the five or six steps across the platform to the makeshift podium. Once she arrived, she looked down at the Bible before her. She closed her eyes, took a deep breath, and raised her head to speak. "In John fourteen . . ." She coughed slightly and tried again. "In John fourteen, verse six, Jesus says, 'I am the way and the truth, and the life. No one comes to the Father except through Me.'"

"Amen," Sarah called out, an obvious attempt to encourage her.

"Preach it, sister," another agreed.

Rachel smiled. Her eyes were drawn to Sean's and he gave her a quiet nod of encouragement. She continued, "Notice Jesus doesn't say, 'No group will come to the Father' or 'No club will come to the Father.' He doesn't even single out a particular religion. What does He say? He says, 'No . . .'" She waited for the congregation to reply, but there was no response. She tried again. "No . . ."

"One," a few called back.

"That's right. 'No one.' You see, our loving Father is not interested in groups or clubs. He really isn't even interested in religion. He's only interested in you."

Sean continued to listen. Did he buy all she was saying? Of course not. But Rachel did. And that was important to him. Afterward, when they would have lunch together, and another one of their long discussions, he'd listen—partially out of interest and partially because it was an excuse to spend time with her.

"In fact, if you turn over to Luke fifteen, you'll read where Jesus talked about leaving the whole flock of ninety-nine sheep behind in the wilderness and risking His life to save just one."

Sean glanced at Rachel's father. He was struggling to move his Bible toward Elliot. His son helped, and soon the old man and the young boy were sharing it. Sean fought back a smile, then stole another glance around the room at the faces—all listening intently.

"And down in verse seven, Jesus says, 'There will be more joy in Heaven over one sinner who repents than over ninety-nine just persons who need no repentance.'"

Sean did not see Jude Miller. In fact, no one had seen him since he'd spoken to Rachel and had fled The Arena. Odd that he would desert her like that. Odder still was that he had not communicated with any of them since. It was as if he had completely vanished. Maybe he was too embarrassed by his cowardice. Or maybe it was the simple fact that he could no longer use and exploit Rachel. Because, after the fire, the dreams and miracles had come to an end. "They accomplished what the Lord wanted," Rachel had explained to him one afternoon. "They're not needed anymore." And then with a smile she had added, "At least for now."

He focused back on her talk.

"And the same is true with the parable of the woman and the lost coin. Even though she had plenty of others, she turned her house upside down until she found that one single coin. When she did, she called her friends to have a party. And according to Jesus"—Rachel looked down at the Bible, found her place, and read—"'In the same way, I tell you, there is rejoicing in the presence of the angels of God over one sinner who repents.'"

Were the healings and all the other hoopla finally over? Sean hoped so. But once again, he didn't know. There was so much about this mysterious young woman that he did not understand. But every time they were together, every meal they shared, every long walk they took, he was sure of one thing: the more he got to know her, the more of her he wanted to know.

Soli Deo gloria

Reading Group Questions for
The Judas Gospel

---

1.   Bill Myers says he likes to explore and stir up thinking as he writes. Did this book do that for you? In what areas?

2.   Do you agree or disagree with the opening quote by Richard Halverson, former chaplain of the U.S. Senate?

3.   In what areas do you agree with Rev. Delacroix? In what areas do you disagree?

4.   Where did Jude Miller's ends stop justifying his means? Is there a balance? What is it?

5.   Myers says that much of the televangelist sections of the novel are based on interviews and personal, behind-the-scenes observation. Does he come down too hard on them? What good do ministers do? What harm? What does he say are the temptations?

6.   Where does he say the *real* error in big ministry lies?

7. Gifts of the Spirit (such as healings) are a controversy within the church. Some say they no longer apply today and are emotional manipulation or the works of the devil. What is Myers's position? What is yours? What does Scripture say?

8. To what extent does God expect to wait upon us? To what extent does He expect us to serve Him? What is the balance, and how do we find it?

9. How does this novel fit in with Myers's body of work? For instance, how does it build upon *Eli* (a retelling of the gospel as if it happened today in America) or *The God Hater* (a view of the gospel from God's perspective)?

10. Would you recommend this book to others? Who and why?

If you have a reader's group of six or more people and would like Bill to chat with you by speakerphone for thirty minutes, please contact him at his website www.BillMyers.com.

A Conversation
with Bill Myers

––––––

1. *What was the inspiration behind* The Judas Gospel?
I write to explore. In *The Judas Gospel* I wanted to explore the balance and dividing lines between the first-century Gospel and the big business Gospel of today. We know God, in His great grace, can and does use anything. But in our own walk, how much is too much? How much is too little? When are we limiting ministry with too small a vision? When does ministry become a machine, seeing people as cogs, gears, and prizes?

2. *You're known for your tales of supernatural suspense. When plotting a story, do you come up with these elements first, or do you work them in after you've come up with a basic plot?*
I usually mull over a theme for years, taking notes, reading, and praying. My office is filled with notebooks on subjects. When I think it's time, I look for entertaining elements that candy coat the medicine so it doesn't taste too bad going down. I think Jesus did much the same thing with His parables—clothing truths in entertainment. Wrapping flesh-and-blood characters around facts and figures.

3. How was Rachel Delacroix's character formed? Did you have a general idea in mind, or did you know immediately who she was and what she believed in?

I spend time thinking of a character that will engage the reader but will also allow me to pursue the story's themes. Still, as they show up on the page, it's important that I give them room to breathe and do what they want. Otherwise they become cardboard cutouts, just puppets whose strings are pulled and manipulated. If that happens I have to stop and go back to find where they stopped being real. If they cease being real to me, they cease being real to the audience and then I'm simply writing an elaborate tract. Critics once asked the famous film director Frank Capra (*It's a Wonderful Life, Mr. Smith Goes to Washington*) how he got away with being so corny. He said something like, "Once I get you to care about my characters, I can do whatever I want."

4. Do you do a lot of research for your books? Did you have to do much research for the detective scenes in The Judas Gospel?

I read from twenty to eighty nonfiction books per novel, making marks, jotting down ideas in those notebooks that are all over my office. Visiting locations is great, too. Actually, research is my favorite part of writing. Who else gets paid to visit serial killers, genetic scientists, UFO abductees, CIA agents, sociopaths, the deeply devout? And yes, I did the same sort of research regarding the detective scenes.

5. Is it ever difficult for you to find sympathy for some of the characters in your books?

No. For some reason I even care for my bad guys. I suspect most of that comes from my time in Scripture and prayer. It seems the more time I spend with Christ, the more I see others through His lens. Even my most villainous villains come off more as crippled than just bad, more in need of His love than simply being evil. I hate what they do, but ache over their refusal to be healed.

6. *In the book you comment, "With so many other messages competing for attention, how could the average person even hope to hear God?" (p. 109). How do you tackle this problem in your own life?*
I have to be very intentional. I try to spend an hour or so in worship and Scripture each morning before the day begins. For twenty-three hours a day the world screams into my ears that black is white, that wrong is right, that I should be angry, discontent, that God doesn't care, that He's forgotten the details, that I must buy this or that to find peace and joy. If I'm not proactive in spending time seeing truth every day, then my internal compass starts going askew and I forget where north lies.

7. *Paintings and fine art play a large role in* The Judas Gospel. *As someone who works in both the film and book industry, how does art expand your knowledge and appreciation for the world?*
I believe the great artists, whether they know it or not, strive to touch the Infinite. They struggle to capture some universal element that's Eternal. And when they do, it's breathtaking. I don't pretend to understand art, but there have been times that a work is so powerful in capturing the spirit of humanity or of God that I'm nearly overwhelmed. I remember one of the very first Van Goghs I saw in person. It was so powerful I had to sit down.

8. *In addition to being a writer, you are an award-winning filmmaker. How is writing a novel different from making a film?*
Filmmaking is a collaborative effort. As a producer or director, I love to create an environment where my fellow artists can flourish and contribute to making the project greater than what one person imagines. Writing a novel is far more solitary and much slower as

you test and retest the ideas on your own. I love the solitude where it's just God and me poking at a scene, but I also love the community where I get to play with others.

9.   *You have said that you were not much of a reader growing up, but now you read all the time. Do you have any favorite books, or books that you've found particularly inspiring as an adult?*
I love reading the older Christian writers—the Tozers, the Spurgeons, even some of the ancient Christian mystics. Men and women who have spent a lifetime discovering truths and whose shoulders I can stand upon. I also love poetry. George Herbert takes my breath away. That said, nothing, absolutely nothing beats the Scriptures. I'm not speaking just as a follower of Christ but as an artist. There are insights into the Eternal and the human heart that no one has come close to capturing.

10.   *What do you hope to accomplish through your books? What would you like readers to gain from reading them?*
That's easy. No matter where we're at spiritually—whether scoffer, seeker, or believer—I want to draw us closer into the heart of Christ.

11.   *What projects are you working on now?*
I've always got something going on. From films (www.amaris media.com) to my adult novels and kid's books (www.billmyers .com). Friends tease me for being so prolific. But these arenas are so different that I'm constantly refreshed as I jump back and forth from one to another . . . hopefully without doing too much damage to their art form.

Also available from
BILL MYERS

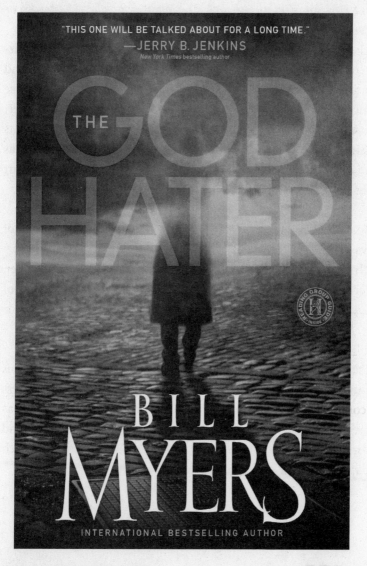

"THIS ONE WILL BE TALKED ABOUT FOR A LONG TIME."
—JERRY B. JENKINS
New York Times bestselling author

THE GOD HATER

BILL MYERS

INTERNATIONAL BESTSELLING AUTHOR